The Whack Club

Susan Bennett

Prologue

"That cat is so totally no shits," said Irish.

On the television screen, Don Corleone, holding forth on respect, stopped patting the cat to wave his hand. The cat reached up and batted his fingers insistently.

"Hey paisano," said Teresa. I no care if you're the Godfather. You're done patting me when I say you're done."

"The Godfather," said Isabella, "He has a soft spot for pussy cats."

"Pity the same couldn't be said of horses," returned Irish.

In the wee small hours, when Irish lay awake wondering how the hell she landed herself in this mess, sometimes she tried to pinpoint the exact moment such conversations became normal in her home. But in the days that followed, when blood flowed and life as she knew it went to hell in a handbasket, Irish looked back and wondered how she had ever lived without them.

Part One

THE BIG HOUSE

Chapter One

Fresh from the Manhattan train, Isabella Albrici and her best friend Teresa Benedetti shivered against the sudden cold and manoeuvred fashionably outsized buttons through their cashmere coats. They crested the hill laughing, striding on steady ankles hardened by years of walking in heels as big as their hair.

Glossy paper bags, overflowing with trophies bagged from a serious day's Fifth Avenue hunting, dangled from their fingers. Isabella linked arms with Teresa and gave her forearm a little squeeze.

Like an eclipse blocking the sun, darkness seeped over Teresa's features, as it always did, the closer they drew to the car. Now that the day's shopping was behind them, Teresa's thoughts had turned to home and the son who would not be there waiting for her.

Eight years had passed since Gabriel's sudden, violent death at the hands of a drug dealer. The passage of time had done little to alleviate his grieving mother's pain. Isabella knew what came next. Eyes swimming, Teresa would delve into the past and return with a memory.

She would begin, *Did I ever tell you about the time Gabriel…*

and Isabella would say *No* even though Teresa had told her a thousand times already.

Isabella settled her face into a portrait of interest and prepared to listen attentively, while a few miles away, the F.B.I. gazed attentively at her house and prepared their battering ram.

"Son of a bitch."

Isabella accelerated past the F.B.I. van in the driveway. The Mercedes rocked to a halt outside the front door, their unbuckled seat belts snapping back on the inertia reels before the engine had died.

Isabella adopted her standard F.B.I. gait: fast enough to let them know she was pissed off, not so fast they would think her scared. She strode into the marble foyer with Teresa hard on her heels.

The chief son of a bitch was in her kitchen, riffling through the wad of take out menus and miscellaneous notes he had excised from the junk drawer.

"You won't find any evidence there," she told him by way of greeting.

"No, Missus Albrici?" he said breezily, without raising his gaze. "You sure about that?"

"Absolutely. You'd have to be able to read, Agent Jameson."

Propped against the kitchen bench, Dominic laughed quietly.

Jameson tossed the wad of papers to the bench. Isabella

peeled off her gloves and flipped them to land beside the papers. She faced him like a gunslinger, thrusting closed fists to her hips.

"What pissy excuse do you have for persecuting my husband this time, Agent Jameson?"

Jameson eyed her steadily.

"Actually, Missus Albrici, we're here for you."

Isabella raised her eyebrows high as they would go, her gaze unwavering even as the *F.B.I.* writ large and fluorescent on his vest grew larger and brighter. She resisted the temptation to glance at Domenic.

"I can hardly wait to hear whatever delusional fantasy your fucked up little mind has dreamed up this time."

"Missus Albrici, language, please."

"Certainly. Fuck you."

Jameson smiled tightly then fanned the wad of papers. Isabella and Teresa watched impassively, with the carefully trained countenance of the mob wife.

Jameson slid forth a piece of paper. "That your signature, Missus Albrici?"

Isabella gave it a cursory glance. "So now literacy is a crime?"

He excised another FedEx slip. "Did you address this article?"

"I know all the letters of the alphabet. I can count all my fingers and toes too."

A few FedEx receipts fluttered to the floor, spiralling down with carbon sheets trailing.

"Is that your signature also, Missus Albrici?"

"Our house is rich with pens. Call the I.R.S. and demand an immediate audit."

"I'll take that as a *yes*."

An agent shouldered his way into the kitchen carrying a slit courier satchel. He handed it to Jameson. His gaze trained on Isabella's face, Jameson spilled its contents over her kitchen bench.

"I hope you're planning on cleaning that shit up," she said, even as her heart took off at a gallop and her mind cried *diamonds*.

"Isabella Albrici, you are under arrest."

Her face was stone. Those were the rules of engagement: no running, no reaction. But there were rules for both sides, and one of them was no handcuffs.

Isabella stole a glance at Domenic, expecting him to begin the customary spousal feeb taunting: *Our lawyer'll have her out in an hour!* but Domenic was silent.

"The other one too," said Jameson.

"What, my husband now?"

Jameson ignored her. The agent walked past Domenic to Teresa.

"Teresa Benedetti, you are under arrest."

"What the hell for?" demanded Teresa.

"We found stones at your house too."

It was no mean feat with her hands cuffed behind her, but Isabella squared her shoulders, lifted her chin and held her head high, even as an agent marched her out her own front door, reading her rights as he went. When she and Teresa were thrown in a holding cell along with hookers, drunks, junkies and indigents, still, she held her head high, when a lawyer didn't materialise to get her out, and when her twisting gut told her she would be spending the night there. After every other woman in the tank had fallen asleep, dozing on the benches where they sat, only then did Isabella let her shoulders drop and her face fall into her hands, where she quietly sobbed her heart out and wondered just what the hell was happening.

Chapter Two

She was still awake when the first grey light filtered into the holding cell around four a.m. – the traditional hour, as she was about to learn, for the drunks and junkies to start drying out, the hookers to start pacing and every tortured soul in between to cry out for their lost mothers, lovers and dealers.

Teresa dozed against Isabella's shoulder until a uniform appeared in front of the bars and jangled his keys.

"Albrici, Benedetti, on your feet ladies, you have an appointment with destiny."

Isabella gently shook Teresa awake and made a point of keeping the uniform waiting for a full ten heartbeats before standing up.

"We can't go to court like this. We need a shower and a change of clothes."

"It's a good thing you're not headed for court then, Albrici. Where you're going, you'll look fine just as you are."

"What do you mean?"

"You're going to the big house, ladies. Your limousine awaits."

Isabella lowered her chin and set her eyes to terminal. "The hell we are. We're entitled to a hearing!"

"You've had your hearing. Yours was the first case of the day, as a matter of fact."

"How is that possible?" Teresa demanded, taking a step toward him. "We weren't even there."

"Because your lawyer was there. Bail was opposed, you've been remanded in custody, which means, *ladies*, you're headed for the big house, and the only thing I have left to say to either one of you is, get a move on, toots."

As one they squared their shoulders and lifted their chins. Isabella swept out of the cell and through the police station holding her head high. She maintained her regal composure when they stepped into the alley and the waiting pack of press exploded, as screws slapped leg irons on her in the back of the prison van and the other prisoners wept pitifully around her. She held her head high when the doors of Edna Mahan prison opened to swallow them – she, sweeping into the joint like she owned it – through the strip search when the screws made sport of the mob wife, when her clothes and jewellery were taken from her and she, shivering and naked stepped into prison overalls. She held it high when she walked the longest walk of her life, past endless rows and layers of prison cells, with every occupant giving their full attention to her passing. Then, after the lights went out and the whimpers and sobs from the other cells choked into silence, Isabella rose from her bunk, lowered her head into the toilet and retched up every ounce of her terror and violation.

Isabella climbed back into the top bunk, with the careful stealth peculiar to mothers trying not to wake their children. She had just turned her face to the wall when Teresa spoke.

"Bella?"

"Yes, baby?"

"What do you suppose is going on?"

"I don't know," she whispered. "I wish to God I did."

Isabella tossed to her other side to inhale the meagre breath of moonlight afforded by the narrow window, then lay on her back staring at the ceiling of her prison cell, wondering what Domenic had done and why he had done it.

Chapter Three

Truth was, Isabella hadn't known he was a made man when they had met. Truth also was, the knowledge excited her.

He was so handsome, and now, so darkly dangerous, and he wanted *her*.

They noticed each other one summer at the Jersey Shore. Domenic's appraisal turned to appreciation, then to undisguised hunger.

For three weeks, the young man watched Isabella on the beach, then, one day, no more. She returned every day for two weeks but he didn't come.

Then he showed up at her door.

Isabella opened it to him herself, her breath catching at the sight of Domenic standing on the step in his finely tailored suit.

When he asked for her father, she stood back to let him pass into the kitchen. A half hour later, her father introduced them. Dominic bowed formally.

"Isabella." He said her name once, then stepped out into the summer's night.

Within a year of their honeymoon, her new husband had taken his first mistress.

Chapter Four

In the morning, the first chink showed in Teresa's armour. A posse of female screws came to take stock of the new arrivals. Teresa bowed her head under their scrutiny. Isabella stepped in front of her.

"May I help you?" she enquired.

The screws guffawed. "You're quite the lady, aren't you, Albrici?" the runt of the litter said. "Let's see how your ladyship fairs after ten hours of laundry detail."

Isabella beamed a bright smile at her. "I'll be there right after my manicure, girls."

The screws stopped laughing.

"The Don can't help you in here, Albrici."

Isabella smiled a thousand watt, knock the paint off the walls smile, that said, *You wanna count on that, bitch?*

In the mess, they took their trays and stood in line, shuffling forward in the queue, not making eye contact.

They found a table with no one on it and sat down.

Isabella pushed her spoon through the mound of grey slush that an inmate slopped onto her tray. "What do you suppose this is?" she asked Teresa.

Teresa eased her spoon into the middle of it and flipped some over, as if expecting to uncover something. "Could be…

maybe oatmeal that got put through the wash along with dirty overalls?" Teresa shook her head at the travesty before her. Isabella leaned in and lowered her voice.

"Listen, how bad can it be?" she whispered. "We know how to do laundry, right? We already do it every damned day. At least we won't be finding souvenirs from their whores."

"Eh, Madonn', you never know."

Isabella grinned.

Nothing could have prepared them for the next ten hours. The laundry was like a factory; the noise was brutal. The incessant thump, hum and drone from the machines penetrated their skulls so that within ten minutes Isabella had a thumping headache, within fifteen, a blinding migraine. Every hiss of steam was a screaming train whistle, every opened or closed door a pickaxe into her skull, every flash of light or movement a screwdriver through her brain, the rhythmic lift and fall of the steam presses a tortured dirge. She didn't let it show.

Here, there were no union regulated weight limits; no one to care for the welfare of these lost women, forced to shoulder weights beyond their capability. Teresa staggered under her burden of laundry bags.

The constant vibration beat the very oxygen from the air; the furnace heat robbed their mouths and skin of moisture. Sweat exploded from their scalps and dripped acidly into their eyes.

Dermatitis strafed Isabella's hands. Her blood smeared the washed laundry and she had to wash it all over again. Vision swimming, she stared at her bleeding hands, wondering what to do.

"Put a rubber on it, Albrici." Someone tossed a box at her, the corner hit her in the jaw. It was a box of latex gloves. Swaying on her feet, Isabella managed to fit the gloves over her hands.

The latex only made things worse. She swayed some more and kept washing.

Most of the women didn't even raise a sweat. When the ten-hour shift was over, the prisoners from the other work details swarmed in to join the throng filing to the prisoners' mess. Isabella realised there were thousands of them.

The same posse of screws from this morning stood on the side of the thoroughfare, arms crossed against their chests, watching she and Teresa pass. It took everything she had and then some, but Isabella straightened her back. Beside her, Teresa did the same.

An inmate serving food slopped a heavy serving of something grey onto Teresa's tray. The tray dived; her knees gave way. Isabella pressed her flank to Teresa's and she straightened up.

They had a table to themselves again.

Isabella and Teresa sat silently, staring at the mess of food on the trays before them. Everything was grey. The potatoes were grey. The meat was grey. The gravy was grey. Even the goddamned peas were grey.

"What do you suppose this is?" whispered Isabella through parched lips.

Teresa shook her head. "Maybe once it said, *moo,* maybe *baa,* or maybe even *oink.* God only knows what's been done to it since then."

Isabella managed a weak smile. Such food would never see the inside of their mouths. Besides, neither of them could muster an appetite knowing what came next.

In silence, they walked to the shower block. They stripped, Isabella willing her face not to betray her by blushing, then wrapped towels around their nudity and joined the queue. Behind her, Teresa inspected the walls and fittings like she was appraising real estate.

Nobody acknowledged them and they acknowledged no one else, moving forward space by space in the queue as the stalls emptied. Isabella's migraine had returned with a vengeance; her vision swam in and out of focus. She willed herself not to sway, not to fall.

Isabella stepped into a stall. On the edge of her blurry vision she perceived a small dark-haired woman move forward, as though to beat Isabella to the shower. Isabella turned the tap resolutely, the hot water nearly collapsing her already jelly knees.

She gave her back to the stream, turning to face the front of the open stall, showing anyone who cared to notice that she was perfectly at her ease.

Truth was, she couldn't wait for it to be over.

They walked back to their cell in silence.

Isabella hadn't known it was possible to be so comprehensively exhausted and yet be unable to sleep. She lay on her bunk, stared at the ceiling and slept not a wink.

Chapter Five

Isabella had remonstrated with Domenic over that first mistress. Actually, she had entreated, beseeched and begged.

She was walking home from grocery shopping, carrying the paper bags from which she would prepare her new husband's dinner, when Domenic and his mistress walked straight past her, climbed into his car and drove away.

What stung the most – and it stung like acid – was that Domenic hadn't noticed her standing there. If the situation were reversed, she could be blindfolded – or blind – and still every fibre of her being would know Domenic was near. But Domenic hadn't even known she was there.

The cruellest cut: she was Isabella's complete opposite. With breasts pushed out of a low-cut dress that left nothing to the imagination, her less than subtle make-up, dangly earrings and strappy high heeled sandals didn't so much say *come fuck me* as *come fuck me senseless*. She was everything Isabella was raised not to be, and yet her husband wanted this whore more than he wanted his Isabella, she who worshipped the ground he walked on.

Chapter Six

Had she not already been awake, Isabella's fears for Teresa would have kept her up at night.

A little older than Isabella, Teresa too had known the travails of La Casa Nostra's wife. Her husband survived a mob war only to be taken by heart attack; her only son – her only child – was murdered by a drug dealer. Now she had landed in the pen by way of some diamonds she had never seen before but from which she could not distance herself, much less ask how they came to be found at her home, thank you very much, Don Albrici.

The morning after their first hellish ten-hour shift on laundry row, Teresa started aging at a rate of knots.

Isabella's hands were a nightmare, but they could not be compared to the crushing weight her friend was forced to hump.

Teresa's practised stoicism struck Isabella as a tragedy in itself, but what nearly brought Teresa undone was the sacrilege the sons of bitches committed against food.

Their second night in the prison mess, when they had taken their places at their exclusive table, Isabella asked of Teresa, "What do you suppose this is?"

Tonight's slops – presumably vegetables – were still grey,

the meat, if indeed it was meat, was by contrast, red. Well, one side of it was red, the other, grey.

Staring at the grey side, Teresa replied, "I don't know, but it deserves a decent burial." She flipped it to the raw side. "If it starts crawling, I swear to God, Bella, I'm outta here."

On their eighth night in the mess, Isabella, regarding the mound of grey meat and vaguely coloured bits in the gelatinous hill on her tray, asked again, "What do you suppose this is?"

Teresa licked her lips as though tasting the meal she could have cooked with her own hands. "Madonn'! Maybe meat harvested from an animal that died of anaemia in a nuclear holocaust?"

By now, they had no choice but to eat. Isabella's worried gaze locked on her friend's face as she excised a piece of the inedible from a mound of the indelible and put it in her mouth. Teresa didn't chew, she swallowed. Her eyes brimmed with tears.

Dominic had better get them the hell out of here, and soon.

Chapter Seven

When pleading didn't work, Isabella had turned to prayer. She prayed for the strength to endure, for loyalty and devotion.

Most of all she prayed for Domenic's steady succession of whores to be struck down dead.

His laundry bore the evidence of his liaisons with such monotonous regularity, Isabella wondered if he didn't leave things for her to find purposely: condoms, lipstick stains, acrylic nails, and always, always, the stench of expensive perfume too heavily applied.

In the early years of their marriage, when she thought she could take no more, Isabella turned to her priest, who counselled subjugation of the self, devotion to her husband and duty to her family.

As the years wore on and Domenic moved up through the family, she prayed less often for his fidelity and more often for his life. Through wars, hits, M.I.A's, F.B.I. raids and an escalating number of acquaintances who ate at her table one day and disappeared into the witness protection program the next – and others who suddenly lacked the requisite number of fingers to grasp the cannoli trays or the teeth to eat them – Isabella fell to her knees and prayed only for her husband to return home, reeking of perfume or no.

She prayed for Domenic to abstain from violence, and she prayed for him to be more violent than those trying to kill him. She tried to hate the sin but love the sinner, but she was no longer sure who the sinner or what the sin was. She prayed she would stop loving him then prayed to love him more. At last she prayed for forgiveness for the man she couldn't stop loving for treating her so cruelly and for herself for loving him anyway. On her fortieth birthday, Isabella drew a breath, blew out her candles, and wished for the death of the mother who had raised him this way.

Isabella knew only too well, sometimes what feeds the heart, starves the soul. To hope is to hunger, and one can only be hungry for so long before the appetite fails. For twenty years of marriage Isabella hungered for a meal that never came. Then one day she found a reason to pray again. His name was Dante Alessandri, he was one of her husband's soldiers, and when Isabella wasn't praying for delivery from temptation, she was hoping like hell to find her way into Dante's bed.

Chapter Eight

Isabella knew through firsthand experience that Domenic would not be able to visit until he had been placed on the offender's list of approved visitors. But two weeks had passed since he had been approved and still, no Domenic, or his lawyer.

The inmates seemed to be asking the same question: *Why hadn't Domenic Albrici, Don of New Jersey's most powerful family sprung his wife from the joint?*

While Isabella and Teresa continued to enjoy the privilege of their own table in the prisoners' mess, the other women, who until now had wisely left well enough alone, grew curious about the mob wives in their midst. They were beginning to look at them less like untouchable chattels of the family Albrici and more like new meat to be slapped to the bottom of the prison pecking order.

In the laundry, a young African American woman stared at them, Teresa in particular. Then in the shower block that evening, after their usual exchange in the prisoners' mess when Isabella asked, "What do you suppose this is?" and Teresa slowly replied, "Incredible. It looks a bit like chicken, but it doesn't taste a bit like chicken. How come snake tastes a bit like chicken, ostrich tastes a bit like chicken and even kangaroo tastes a bit like chicken, but this is chicken, and it doesn't taste a bit like chicken?" a woman tried to push in front of Isabella in the showers. Isabella stopped her dead in her tracks with an imperious, "Excuse me," stepped around her and took her rightful place. She was certain it was same small dark-haired woman from before. Isabella turned on the hot water and thought no more of it.

Friday seemed to make it into the laundry. In this place where no weekend existed, from where there would be no trips to restaurants or dinner parties to attend, somehow the spirit of Friday had survived. There was an air of anticipation, a remembered excitement.

Teresa staggered a fraction less under her laundry loads. Isabella's skin seemed sting less viciously. By the time they sat down to dinner, their spirits had lifted as much as it is possible for a spirit to lift when you've gone from being a Fifth Avenue customer to a guest of the government on the same day. Dinner put paid to that.

Isabella uttered her customary question, "What do you suppose this is?" and attempted to penetrate the mound on her tray with her fork.

Teresa glowered at her tray.

"Madonn!" Teresa all but shouted. "What insult to the sons of Italy is this shit?"

"Teresa," Isabella whispered, glancing at the curious inmates around them. "Keep your voice down, honey. I'm sure it's al dente."

Teresa spat the pasta from her mouth like she had been

spitting all her life. It hit the tray with a *pttttwang!* "Al dente?" she roared. "Al dente for cadmium fucking steel!"

A murmured laugh rippled through the nearest tables as the young African American woman who had stared at them in the laundry plonked her tray at their table and sat down.

"Did *you* cook that?" Teresa asked the girl suspiciously.

"Uh-uh. And lady, bad pasta is the least of your problems."

Isabella's smile was powered by adrenalin. "Oh really?" she asked evenly, casually scooping another forkful of glug from her tray and holding the fork aloft in her best table manner. "And what would you know about that?"

"What I know about that is you're dissin' the wrong bitch in the shower."

"You're going to have to enlighten me. I don't believe I have disrespected anyone."

"You keep stopping Bobby Hernandez from taking her shower."

"That small dark-haired girl that keeps trying to push in on me? I'm afraid she's just going to have to wait her turn like anyone else."

"Lady, her turn is whenever she wants it to be."

"That so? Well from now on it's going to have to be when it is her turn."

"You prepared to fight her for that?"

Isabella held her gaze, fixed her smile and said nothing.

"You think you up to it–" began the girl. Teresa cut her off.

"Excuse me, young lady? What are you in here for?"

She swivelled to face Teresa and looked her square in the eye. "Junk," she said.

Teresa's lip curled distastefully. "Then I am sorry, but I'm going to have to ask you to leave our table."

The young woman's jaw tightened. She pushed herself away from the table, lifted her chin in the air and sauntered away.

Wondering whether she had just been threatened or whether she had just been warned, Isabella uncrossed the legs she had pressed together in the hope she wouldn't pee herself.

In the exercise yard, the women split into groups. The African Americans joined with other African Americans, the Hispanics came together, as did the Caucasians.

Keeping to themselves, Isabella and Teresa leaned against the wall, the frosty air pluming the air in front of their faces, their eyes turned hungrily to the pale New Jersey sun. It was a sight Isabella knew she would never take for granted again.

The African Americans were playing around with a soccer ball, which someone kicked into the Hispanic group. One of the girls, a tall and splendidly handsome young woman with cornrows ran to retrieve it. The wiry, dark-haired woman Isabella now knew as Bobby Hernandez snatched it from the ground and held it from the other girl. A scuffle broke out, followed almost immediately by whistles and intervention from the screws.

Beside her, Teresa, regarded the scuffling women with hard eyes, spat on the ground and said, "Junkies," under her breath.

Isabella stared at her. It was the second time in as many days that Teresa had spat.

Later, they were in the rec room when the news came: Isabella had a visitor.

At last, Domenic had come.

Despite everything, despite herself, the mere sight of him was enough to drive the breath from her lungs. Suddenly self-conscious in her prison overalls before this brown-eyed, olive-skinned man in his finely cut Italian suit, Isabella smoothed a lock of hair behind her ear, smiled at him shyly and approached the dividing partition with her eyes lowered.

"Isabella."

"How's things at home?"

He tilted his face, seesawed his hand to say, *eh, so so.*

"You eating okay?"

He spread his hands "I come all the way out here now you're going to bust my chops?"

"No. Domenic–"

She knew better than to ask about the diamonds, but she had to know why she and Teresa were still in the pen.

"Shouldn't I at least talk to a lawyer, Domenic?" she whispered.

"You trust me, don't you?"

"Of course."

"I have to go." Domenic stepped away from the partition,

then turned to face her again. "So, now you're a real stand-up guy," he said, suddenly careless of the screws.

He left without a backward glance.

That night, when she climbed to her bunk, she slept soundly for having laid eyes on her husband.

But while she slept soundly, Isabella dreamed of Dante Alessandri.

Chapter Nine

Where Domenic was handsome, Dante was... beautiful. Domenic's face was chiselled, all high planes and hard jaw, while Dante's face was full-lipped and sensual. While many of her husband's soldiers had let themselves go, Domenic had kept his physique, but Dante didn't just maintain his physique, he built it – at least she guessed he did by the way his muscles worked beneath his shirt whenever she stole a glance, which was often.

Best of all were his eyes.

Domenic's eyes were darkly startling, chocolate brown pools without pupils that swallowed her whole. Dante's eyes were pale blue, soft as a kiss and light as a cloud. His hair curled in tousled waves around his collar, complimenting his fair skin and blue eyes all the more.

While his voice spoke to Missus Albrici, his eyes spoke to Bella.

Isabella dreamed about the creases in his cheeks, the ones that reached right down into his chin whenever he smiled. She dreamed of touching her fingers to the lines of his smile, then to his lips. How she longed to hear the breath catch in Dante's throat.

Dante brought her cakes, Italian pastries, from Cicero's across town – cannoli oozing sweet custard, stacked napoleons, pasticciotti and delicately layered sfogliatelle, barchette di mandorla, lemon torta della nonna, and her favourites: nut horns rolled in walnuts, cinnamon and sugar.

One morning she looked up and caught Dante watching her eat. When their eyes met, he didn't look away.

Domenic came into the kitchen. Isabella turned around and dropped the coffee pot into the sink, terrified that one look at her would reveal her feelings.

Isabella watched him them leave, willing Dante to turn for a last glance: if he did, she would know that he shared her feelings.

But Dante had left without turning around, and thereafter when he came to the door, he refused her invitation to come in. Isabella's cheeks burned with shame. Dante had seen past her made up face and into the loneliness within her. He had taken pity on her and she had embarrassed him.

Isabella stopped answering the doorbell when he came, leaving Domenic to open the door himself.

Isabella knew it was for the best. If Domenic had even suspected her feelings for Dante, he would kill them both.

This morning's dream ended as it usually did, just at the point Dante was about to cover her. Isabella's dream gaze had fallen to his abdomen when a woman's fearful cry tore her from sleep. It was her own.

Her eyes flew open. She lay on the top bunk with a pounding heart, the sweat pouring from her, straining her ears to listen for Teresa. There was a moment's silence, then Teresa's soft, rhythmic breathing resumed.

As quietly as she could, Isabella eased herself over and turned her face to the meagre light through the narrow window.

As dawn broke properly, Isabella lay on her back listening to Teresa's sleeping whimpers for her lost son, then she listened to Teresa's angrily growled instructions on the proper cooking of pasta – *al dente, you googoots!* – which, before she woke, would turn into some apparently very satisfying dream concerning buffalo mozzarella.

The sun was up. Now it was officially Sunday.

They swallowed their morning grey and walked across the exercise yard on their way to the prison chapel. Somebody kicked a soccer ball at them. Without thinking, Isabella caught it and tossed it back. The handsome girl with the cornrows held up her hands to catch it and beamed a smile at her. Beside her stood the girl who had come to their table. Isabella let her guard down for a minute and smiled back.

In the chapel, Isabella knelt and prayed for the safety of her husband and for the safety of the man she loved. She prayed for her own soul, sinful in loving him, and she prayed for her sinful soul in not loving her husband enough.

Isabella and Teresa knelt together, turning their hearts and prayers to a Madonna who already knew every beat of their hearts and all their prayers by rote.

Chapter Ten

Teresa seemed to be dying by degrees. Her jaw clenched as they approached the laundry; the black circles beneath her eyes seemed to bore into her skull. Just as Isabella feared Teresa was about to succumb, her prayers were answered: their work detail was reassigned to grounds maintenance.

Out in the fresh air, Teresa thrived. Her stooped back straightened. If her face was still deathly pale, at least the dark circles had lessened. A tiny spark ventured into her eyes.

Teresa worked with plants while Isabella had to do most of the humping and hefting. For once, Teresa had got it easier than Isabella and Isabella did everything she could to make it easier still. When Teresa transplanted seedlings, it was a sight that twisted Isabella's heart into knots. Teresa was so gentle with the tiny living things, cupping each in her palm tenderly as an infant.

They were barely on garden detail a week, just long enough to start enjoying it, when they were reassigned. That Friday evening, the usual screws glee club lined the thoroughfare where the prisoners filed through to the mess. The runt watched them come with a triumphant glare.

"Albrici, Benedetti, as of Monday, you're back on laundry detail." They kept walking, Isabella trying for a devil-may-care rise of her eyebrows, but knowing she hadn't succeeded. Teresa managed a full three steps before she staggered. Isabella drew Teresa against her and helped her to keep walking. From behind them a chorus of laughter rang out, echoing off the walls.

If the screws and inmates were forgetting she was a mafia wife, Isabella knew it because her mafia husband wasn't putting in an appearance to remind them.

Domenic had visited her only once more and that was over four weeks ago. On his first visit he had looked strained. The next, he regarded Isabella with a new softness. She dared hope he missed her, that maybe when she got out, theirs could be a proper marriage, unsullied by mistresses. Now she wondered how much longer Teresa could last.

Teresa didn't even try for their now traditional joke, *What do you suppose this is?* Her dinner was untouched.

"Come on, Teresa," Isabella urged, "Let's go try for the shower." Teresa stood up and allowed herself to be led.

Tonight of all nights had to be the night Bobby Hernandez renewed her efforts to usurp their place in the queue. The mistake she made was trying to push in front of Teresa instead of Isabella. Teresa stumbled as the little bitch shouldered her in the back. Isabella dropped her shower bag to the floor and whirled around like lightning strike looking for a body of water.

Naked as the day she was born Isabella marched *one two three* strides, turned Hernandez out of Teresa's stall and held her at arm's length.

"You, miss, will learn to wait your fucking turn. Don't make me tell you again."

The other women erupted in howls and catcalls. Bobby Hernandez's eyes caught fire.

Isabella held the girl long enough to let the message sink in, then turned around, scooped up her bag and had a shower.

Afterwards, when they had dressed, ignoring the acid bath that was Bobby Hernandez's eyes, Isabella slipped her arm around Teresa's waist and guided her through the prison corridors, not caring who saw them or how vulnerable it made them look.

When Isabella and Teresa got back to their cell, they got word: tomorrow, they were due in court.

Isabella knew they were entitled to appear before the court properly attired. Yet here they were bouncing along in the back of a prison van, still in their prison overalls.

She and Teresa exchanged a glance as the van swung around a corner and the swaying mass of humanity in its back fell against each other, grimacing. Their handcuffed wrists made balancing difficult; the hard benches bruised their backsides with every bounce.

In an alley behind the court, the driver's and passenger's doors creaked open then slammed shut. The first flash erupted as the back door opened, setting off a flurry of others. Isabella shot Teresa a look as the growing chorus of *whoompf whoompf whoompf* fed upon itself, swelling in number until it sounded like mortar fire at dawn.

The doors swung open. "Albrici."

She would be brought out first. Isabella wondered how much money had changed hands to make that happen.

Isabella rose and shuffled forward in a crouch. At the open doors she waited in vain for the leg irons to be removed so she could step down safely. The guard's face twisted into an evil smile.

Isabella realised she would be made to tumble from the van in front of the press.

A much sharper cut: Teresa would be made to jump down the same way.

Hovering on the precipice, Isabella took a deep breath, told herself she was taking the first step toward home, and jumped. She came down heavily, hands cuffed behind her, head bowed.

It was like a lightning storm in the black of night, flash after flash, searing and blinding. Isabella couldn't raise her head high, she could only shuffle forward.

Move, she told herself. *Every step is a step toward Domenic and home.*

Home.

Shouts rained upon her like falling bricks. "Designer clothes!!!!! Designer clothes!!!!! DIAMONDS ISABELLA WHAT ABOUT THE DIAMONDS ISABELLA WHAT ABOUT THE DIAMONDS–"

Her mouth was a desert. Three steps had taken a lifetime. Isabella twisted to look over her shoulder, knowing she had given the photographers a clear shot, but caring only for the precious cargo that would follow her down.

Oh sweet Jesus.

Teresa Benedetti was a glory – an oil painting – of defiance. She catapulted from the prison van and stood up straight, her shoulders pressing back the rim of the van's roof and her toes pointed down.

Slowly, magnificently, Teresa turned her face to the photographers, the reporter and screws, staring them down as though not one of them would recognise well-cooked pasta or a properly ripened tomato if it bit them on the ass.

Isabella sent up a prayer for Teresa's painless landing.

Oof. Soft as it was among the shouting, when the sound of air being driven from Teresa's lungs reached Isabella's ears, she knew her prayer had missed its mark.

More flashes erupted as she and Teresa were led into court. Hungry for the faces of family and friends, Isabella looked to the public gallery, but saw only photographers and reporters salivating to record every moment of her ignominy. To be in prison overalls in prison was a bad enough thing, but to be in prison overalls in public... Isabella could not have been more ashamed had she been naked.

At the bar table, Isabella and Teresa were placed either side of a man Isabella presumed to be their lawyer. Isabella licked her lips and whispered, "Why are we still shackled?" He stared forward, not acknowledging that she had spoken.

She wanted to stamp her feet and shout, *Come on come on come on come on get it the fuck over with.* She wanted to shout at the lawyer to look Teresa's pain etched face and get the cuffs and leg irons off so at least she could sit straight.

The judge entered; the court fell silent. Isabella tried to listen to what was being said, but now they were nearly free, concentration was near impossible. When she heard Domenic called as a witness, her heart clamoured. *Home. Come on,*

Domenic, get us out of here. But something was wrong. Domenic had been called as a witness for the prosecution.

When Isabella offered a confused frown to the lawyer, he rose.

"Objection, your honour. Disclosure," he said.

No. That's wrong.

"Counsel for the defence has not been notified of the district attorney's intention to call this witness."

That wasn't the objection... the objection was that Domenic had been called by the wrong side. The side not on her side.

"I'm going to allow it."

The world turned white and swam before Isabella's eyes. Domenic passed the bar table. Here was her husband. Here was her husband to make everything right. She needed water.

Domenic took his seat in the witness box and was sworn in.

"Mister Albrici, please tell the court how often your wife, Isabella Albrici, received courier deliveries to your home."

"Very regularly."

"Were you aware what these parcels contained?"

"Yes. Supplies to make costume jewellery."

Oh thank God. Oh sweet merciful Jesus.

"My wife and her friend Teresa Benedetti made jewellery for our neighbourhood church to sell from a stall at the Saturday markets. It was very popular."

Isabella's eyes fell closed as relief quaked through her. She desperately needed water.

"And you sometimes signed for these packages?"

"That's correct."

"Did you ever open them?"

"Absolutely not. They were addressed to my wife and were her personal business."

"But on the last occasion – on the day of your wife's arrest – you opened a FedEx satchel addressed to Missus Albrici."

"In error, yes. I was expecting my own delivery. When the satchel arrived for my wife, I thought it was mine and opened it."

"And what did you find in your wife's satchel, Mister Albrici?"

"Diamonds."

Isabella's vision swam.

"And what did you do upon making that discovery?"

Domenic's lips brushed against the microphone when he spoke. "I immediately notified the authorities of my wife's criminal enterprise."

In the public gallery, the reporters roared. Teresa made a sound like she had been punched in the stomach.

Isabella's chair overturned and crashed to the floor. She was on her feet and shouting. The judge made a racket with his gavel as Teresa sobbed.

As the judge ordered her to be returned to prison, Domenic met Isabella's gaze with melting eyes.

Some part of her mind dully noted the prison van was minus some of its passengers on the way back. Isabella was vaguely aware that her mouth was open, and her head was hitting the side of the van.

A woman's sobs penetrated her numbness. Teresa's pleas for her to lift herself from the floor eventually sank in.

Isabella crawled onto the bench, her back striking the side with a clang. The screw in the passenger seat turned his head briefly, studied her without interest, then turned forward again.

Before she walked through the prison gates, Isabella Albrici had once thought her journey down the aisle to be the longest of her life. Then, Isabella feared she would perish beneath the stares of so many family and friends.

Now thousands watched her. None of them family. None of them friends. None of them well-wishers. All of them knowing she enjoyed the protection of Don Albrici no more.

Dazed, Isabella lay on her back on the hard bunk until her battered body's protests forced her to roll over. She faced the narrow window as the lights went out and the first sobs started up from the other cells. With no face left to keep, Isabella joined in.

When Teresa spoke, her voice was hard.

"Bella. You can do this," she said.

"No, I can't, Teresa. For my family I could do this. For my husband I could do this. But not for myself. I don't know how."

"Then you will learn. You will learn how to be a woman who cares only for herself, is cared for only by herself. We will both learn to be such women."

"Why, Teresa? Why did he do this thing to me, to us?"

"Who knows, Bella?" Teresa whispered. "Who knows why our men do anything."

Chapter Eleven

She knew he would come, and in that she was not mistaken.

Isabella faced Domenic across the visiting area. Apart from a guard, they were alone.

She walked toward the partition. Domenic did not rise.

Isabella took her time, wanting to take in every last detail of the man to whom she had given her youth, her heart and her soul – along with her pride and self-respect – this man who had for twenty years enjoyed the unwavering loyalty and devotion of his wife, and for most of it, also her love.

He watched her come, meeting her gaze squarely. The amber light softened the sharp planes of his face.

Isabella took her seat opposite him.

"Why?" she asked simply.

Domenic glanced over his shoulder. When the guard departed without a word, Isabella smiled bitterly.

"It couldn't be helped."

"You're going to have to explain that to me, Domenic."

"There was no other way."

"When a man betrays his wife, there is always another way."

"By the time I was warned the Feds were coming, they were practically on our doorstep."

Warned – by Agent Lance fucking Jameson, no doubt. No

wonder the son of a bitch made such a show of questioning her at the house. Isabella said nothing, waited.

"I had to think quickly."

"You mean to tell me that you were smuggling diamonds into our home via Fed fucking Ex?"

"You know better than to ask that."

"You could have said nothing."

"I told you. I had to think quickly. I thought we could make a connection with your jewellery supplies, claim some mix up and get you off that way, but it couldn't be done."

"What about Teresa? Why did she have to land in here along with me?"

"Teresa was… unfortunate." Domenic spread his hands. "Maybe it was for the best. I'd hate to think of you in here alone."

"What about, *omerta,* Domenic? They'll kill you."

He shook his head. "They think you were already talking to the Feds."

She stared at him. "Dear God, Domenic you've killed me."

"I got you a pass."

"A pass? There is no pass for that."

"I swear, Bella. I got you a pass."

"If I get out of here alive, I'm as good as dead – you know it, Domenic."

Isabella left in a daze. On the way back to the cell she passed the recreation room. The television news blared into the corridor.

Teresa's house had been firebombed.

The next time Isabella and Teresa went to the prisoners' mess, their exclusive table was no more. It was occupied by the women they had seen playing with the soccer ball in the exercise yard.

Isabella and Teresa paused without looking at each other, then carried their trays to the table. There were two empty seats. They waited. The handsome girl with the cornrows smiled.

"Looks like you'll need to learn how to get along in here after all," she said.

Isabella thought they had been usurped. It would be some time before she understood they were being protected.

Chapter Twelve

When exhaustion overtook her and she fell asleep in the forsaken grey hours just before dawn, Isabella dreamed that Dante Alessandri held her in his arms as though he would never let her go.

Isabella and Teresa seldom talked. Some things didn't need to be spoken. Others were better left unsaid.

The days blurred. Where one day ended and another began didn't matter.

To hope is to hunger, and one can only be hungry for so long before the appetite fails. Hope lived no longer in the breast of Isabella Albrici.

The letting go was easy. It was the hanging on that had nearly killed her.

Isabella felt as though she were treading water in a tepid pool. If nothing soothed, then at least nothing hurt. She felt neither excitement nor pain, pleasure, nor fear. Just the easiness of her small lukewarm pool, untouched by any ray of sun, its high sides keeping the wider ocean from view.

Along with acceptance came self-knowledge: she had no-one to blame but herself.

Now that Isabella was the Don's wife in name only, her relationship with Teresa changed. Teresa neither looked to be led, nor allowed herself to be. Their friendship was the friendship of their girlhood again; they were equals.

And because they were no longer to be feared – thanks to Domenic's betrayal – Teresa and Isabella were jostled and pressed along with the rest of the prison population, but they were also accepted.

Teresa and Isabella were adopted into the guardianship of the black soccer playing group. They came to know that the statuesque girl with the cornrows was called Desiree and the girl who had first come to their table was Eve. When they were in the shower queue, or the exercise yard, the prisoners' mess or the laundry, Desiree and Eve or some other member of the group would come to be standing alongside them.

Teresa's loads in the prison laundry became lighter and fewer, shared by hands which passed them along with a choreographic ease born from years of experience. Isabella's tortured hands were granted a reprieve when one morning she arrived in the laundry, her skin still bloodied and split from the previous day, to find Desiree at her station. With a nod, Desiree directed Isabella away from the wash and to one of the industrial steam presses. Teresa and Isabella simply fell in with the other women and the guards let it happen without interference.

A rhythm was established. Maybe not a rhythm to dance to, but a rhythm to breathe by. They worked, went to sleep by the weeping of less able souls, went to chapel every Sunday, prayed, but not for much.

They were not called back to court. Their case was buried in a recurring avalanche of technicalities which were argued, dismissed and revived.

One night, after the weepers had cried themselves to sleep, Isabella spoke quietly to Teresa, lying awake in the bunk beneath her

"The original sin wasn't sex," she said. "It was marriage."

Chapter Thirteen

Maybe she had seen too many movies.

Isabella had imagined the sort of women who landed in prison to be big butch types – knuckle cracking, deep-voiced, tattooed behemoths with tags like *Big Bertha*. But there weren't many women like that here, and they weren't the ones you had to watch for.

In the pen, big didn't necessarily mean scary, nor could the capacity for mean necessarily be measured by size.

Isabella and Teresa were women for whom small packages had always meant good things. That was before Bobby Hernandez, a woman whose capacity for viciousness so exceeded her wiry body that it beggared belief.

Whenever a scuffle broke out, she was there. Whenever a tray of food was overturned in the mess or a drink landed on a game in the rec room, she was there. Whenever a smoke detector was triggered, Bobby Hernandez was the fire. Whenever prison life began to sail along a little too smoothly, something would happen to trigger a lock down and the revocation of privileges for all prisoners and that something was inevitably Bobby Hernandez. When there was an accident on a work detail, she could always be seen walking away from its epicentre. She threw the first punch in every brawl. Whenever a woman slipped in the shower, Bobby Hernandez could be found standing over that woman, her eyes blazing with hatred.

While Isabella's sanity fed on indifference, Bobby Hernandez's insanity fed on the pain of others, and her appetite was insatiable.

After the last incident in the shower, when Isabella had evicted her from Teresa's stall with the warning to back off, Bobby Hernandez had left Isabella and Teresa alone. Isabella assumed she had lost interest. It never occurred to Isabella that she was enjoying the protection of Desiree and her group, or that such protection may come at a price.

She of all people – who time and again had witnessed the tangible evidence of power struggles, or more accurately what was no longer tangible i.e. fingers, teeth and sometimes whole people – really should have known better, should have known that power struggles never end, they just fall dormant, only to erupt more fiercely than ever before.

Bobby Hernandez was the sort of whack job who grew all the more psychotic for biding her time. Bobby Hernandez was the lava flow that overruns the village while it sleeps.

When the time came, it was all the more shocking for the calm preceding it.

By then, Isabella understood that the prison version of friendship didn't follow the usual rules.

The same questions considered solicitous on the outside weren't asked. You didn't ask what someone did – for a living or otherwise – or how their kids were doing. You didn't ask how a woman was. Here respect was measured by space – how much of it you gave someone when they needed it or by closing the space when they need that. Friendship was marked by standing next to someone in a queue, by creating a space next to you for them in the rec room, by returning to the same corner in the exercise yard you shared the day before, by coming back to your cell to find a phone card on your mattress, or by an extra serve of grey being slopped onto your dinner tray.

Prison friendships were almost silent. Hours might pass just being together, without a word spoken.

Isabella would only understand how deep Desiree's near silent friendship ran after it was too late.

Perhaps because the day had been unseasonably warm, a welcome break in the New Jersey winter, the collective mood ran a little higher after their turn in the exercise yard. Perhaps for the same reason, their unpalatable dinner of grey hit home in a way all of them had thought themselves to be past feeling. Isabella looked up to see Desiree regarding her tray as though seeing the food for the first time. Staring at it, she gave her head a tiny shake. Isabella struck out from the centre of her tepid pool and was trying to scale the side too high to be climbed. Every instinct in Isabella wanted to feed this young woman in the way that all human beings deserved to be fed: with good fresh food that gave pleasure and meaning to everyday life.

Teresa must have felt it too, because her eyes were moist.

"Whaddya suppose this is?" Isabella revived the old joke.

Teresa didn't miss a beat. "Eh, Bella. Obviously, it's Sunday roast."

"Sunday roast. You sure about that?"

Teresa spread her hands expansively. "Sure. Sunday roast

cooked by Hannibal Lecter with the parts he wouldn't eat himself."

A fork clattered to a tray.

"And given that it's Thursday, a very well-aged Sunday roast at that." Teresa gave an exaggerated shrug.

"You mean *aged* in the way of well-hung meat?"

"No. I mean *aged* in the way of a long dead corpse."

The girls writhed.

"As a matter of fact, Bella, I'd say the corpse this meat came from died of cirrhosis of the liver, then was left out in the sun for a month before it ended up in this–" Teresa lifted a forkful into the air, turned the fork over and let the contents drop back to the tray. The tray spun ninety degrees on the table. "...casserole, this very fine spezzatina of dead alcoholic with suntan."

Eve and Desiree locked eyes across the table, willing themselves and each other to keep the food in their mouths. Tears streamed down their cheeks.

"But surely the seasonings..." Isabella turned her hands eloquently.

"Ah yes, the seasonings. I'd say sage–"

"Ah, sage..."

"Sage grown on the graves of rotting lepers–"

Desiree's hand slammed on the table. She turned her face to the ceiling. Her throat worked convulsively. Eve doubled over at the end of the bench.

"...and if I'm not mistaken, this very sage we're eating now was once applied as a poultice to the wounds of the rotten corpses while they still lived–"

Desiree shot to her feet. Eve fell off the bench.

"Madonn'!" cried Teresa. "What's your problem girl? You don't like your casseroled corpse?"

Desiree swallowed and gasped. "Oh you evil bitches."

"You no like a da casserole recipe, girl? Then you're not gonna like hearing what went into the dessert cannoli."

Bowed by laughter, Desiree curled forward – and Isabella looked straight into the malevolent eye of Bobby Hernandez.

The out of season sunshine persisted through to the next day, as did the lightness of mood.

Friday that wasn't really Friday made it into the laundry once again. An unfamiliar noise trilled intermittently between the ceaseless thump, drone and hiss of machines. Isabella glanced up, her eyes lighting automatically on the window.

The chirping noise stopped. Thinking she had imagined it, Isabella returned her attention to the steam press.

There it was again. She looked up just in time to see Desiree, lips pursed, avert her face.

Isabella suppressed a smile and lowered her face. *What sort of world do we live in that girls still young enough to play games go to prison?*

Desiree turned around and let loose a startling whistle that was answered from a far corner of the laundry. Desiree and Eve began to whistle an intricately tuneful duet of *Mockingbird*.

The laundry grew as quiet as it was possible for it to be. Bags that had been dragged along the floor were picked up and carried. Lids and doors that had been left to fall under their own weight were guided down gently. Sunshine poured in the window, casting warm gold over the beautiful black girl whistling prettily enough to incite jealousy in the birds of God's own garden.

Just for a moment, Isabella's eyes fell closed.

Whoops. Desiree made a mistake. Isabella opened her eyes. Blinded by the sudden sunshine and blocked by a shadow, Isabella couldn't see her. The shadow moved away as Isabella's eyes adjusted to the light.

Slowly, Desiree turned around. She had spilled some blue laundry liquid on the front of her overalls.

"Well come on, kiddo," Isabella said. "Intermission's over."

Eve sounded another one of those questioning high-pitched whistles that said, *You there?*

Desiree didn't answer. She stared down at the blue laundry liquid then looked back up at Isabella, and at last Isabella looked properly at her face. Sixty seconds ago, Desiree's expression had shyly asked, *Like me?* Now it begged, *Help me.*

Isabella let go of the steam press as Desiree staggered a half circle on buckling knees. The blue was three dimensional and it stuck out of Desiree's body, glinting in the sun: *shank.*

Around it, a red pool bloomed.

Isabella roared. A steam press crashed to the floor.

"Oh sweet Jesus." Isabella caught Desiree and cradled her in her arms. "Oh sweet Jesus." She stroked her face. Women circled around. "For the love of God, get an ambulance!"

A cry rent the air. Teresa stepped smoothly into Eve's path and caught her, pressing Eve's head into her shoulder so she couldn't see Desiree. Eve struggled to free herself. She didn't stand a chance.

Desiree's mouth worked soundlessly. "Sssh, baby, it's okay, it's okay, baby, it's okay," Isabella sobbed, staring at the hateful blue shank sticking out of Desiree. *Better or worse to take it out?*

The dark red pool around the blue shank stopped spreading and started gushing. "Oh, no, baby, don't do that." Isabella pleaded, rocking Desiree in her arms. Desiree raised her head, stared at the shank and tried to grasp it. Isabella brushed her fingers aside, grasped the end of the shank and wrenched it from her body with a hand that did not waver for being cut to shreds.

Desiree sighed heavily.

Isabella dropped the shank to the floor and pressed the heel of her hand to the pulsing wound. "Ambulance here soon, baby. All better then."

The blood stopped pulsing beneath the heel of Isabella's hand.

"Where the fuck is that ambulance?" roared Isabella.

"Bella." It was Teresa.

"She is with her God now. Let her be."

A ray of sun fell upon Desiree, and she was smiling. Isabella stroked Desiree's face. The skin beneath her fingers was soft and unlined.

Behind Eve, a screw looked into Isabella's blurry eyes and smiled.

Isabella's hand throbbed painfully from the stitches hastily sewn by the prison doctor, sans local anaesthetic. Standing before the Governor, week kneed, her head thudding, she fought to stay upright and conscious.

"Okay, Albrici," he began wearily. "Let's have it. What did you see?"

"It was Bobby Hernandez."

Phillips took his feet down from the desk and leaned forward in his chair.

"You saw Hernandez do it?"

"I saw…"

"Albrici, did you see Hernandez do it?"

"I saw…" She had seen a shadow, that much was certain. A shadow she had been certain contained Hernandez.

"I know it was her."

"Albrici, did you or did you not see Hernandez shank Baker?"

She wanted to scream, *Her name was Desiree. She was twenty-four years old and she was beautiful.*

Isabella swayed on her feet and licked her parched lips.

"Look," she said, "there was that incident in the mess the night before."

"Incident, Albrici? If you call one prisoner giving another prisoner–" he consulted the report on his desk, "…*a nasty look* an incident, then you haven't been in here long enough."

"Why don't you ask the other women? They must have seen her do it too."

"Oh, Albrici, you really are green. The other women? You mean the other inmates. And they didn't see a thing."

So that's how that felt. That's how it felt when someone dear passed from this earth unavenged because nobody saw a thing.

As if he had read her thoughts, Phillips turned the screw. "You'd know all about that, wouldn't you, Albrici?"

The room started spinning. She was going to throw up.

"Get out, Albrici."

The runt screw, Evans, was in the corner of the room. She grabbed a fistful of Isabella's overalls and made to escort her back to the block. Isabella shrugged her off none too gently and strode away.

Isabella found Eve in the cell she shared with Desiree, her head bowed beneath the edge of the top bunk. Dry-eyed, Eve stared at a ragged hole in the linoleum floor. Teresa was beside her, her arm around her shoulders. Isabella took the other side.

"Eve, I'm so sorry."

Eve lifted her gaze from the floor. "You should be. It's your fault she's dead."

"You don't mean that!" cried Teresa.

"I mean every damned word. As soon as your man ditched you, you were dead meat. Everybody in this place knows better than to fuck with that psycho. But not you."

"Eve, if I could, I'd trade my life for Desiree's in a heartbeat–"

"You got Desiree shanked just as surely as if you did it yourself."

Teresa stood up. "Don't you talk, you young missy about people who get other people killed. My son, my beautiful Gabriel, without a stain on his soul, died because of people like you with your filthy habit."

"Teresa–"

"Shut up, Isabella. Let's hear it, you stupid bitch. Let's hear all about your son who died because of people like me."

The colour drained from Teresa's face. "My boy, who never touched a drop of your filthy junk in his life, was murdered by a drug dealer you keep in business with your disgusting habit."

Eve smiled. "Weren't no drug dealer killed your boy. Your old man did him."

Isabella struggled to keep hold of Teresa. "Why do you say this to me?"

"Because it's true."

"You can't know this!"

"Yes I can."

"How?"

"Because I was there. Your boy was staying with me and my daddy when he got shot."

"You lie."

"He had a freckle above his right eye–"

"You saw his picture on the news!"

"He liked pepperoni and bell pepper on his pizza. Fresh tomato too. He couldn't have shrimp 'cause he was allergic."

Teresa leaned on Isabella for support.

Eve pushed herself off the bunk. "He had trouble with your people, and my daddy took him in, gave him a place to hide. They found him."

Eve took a step toward them.

"Your old man, now him I recognised from the news. He went down for kneecapping that man because an off-duty cop saw him do it and testified. You went with him to court."

Holding Teresa's horrified gaze, Eve took another step.

"He gunned your boy down and he shot my daddy dead for protecting him."

Isabella gasped, "How did you survive?"

"How do you think I survived, lady?"

It wasn't the question that Isabella had meant to ask, but what Eve said next banished all temptation to clarify it.

"And just for the record, I didn't do junk until after the first time a john raped me."

Eve took a last look at Teresa, gave them her back and swayed leisurely from the cell.

Chapter Fourteen

As in life, Desiree's death was honoured by space – a space left in the dinner queue, an empty seat at the table, a gap in the line for the shower, a corner within their corner of the exercise yard.

Isabella and Teresa still took their meals at the same table. Eve neither repelled nor welcomed them.

They barely spoke, all of them mourning in their own quiet way, while the malevolent eye of Bobby Hernandez hunted Isabella with naked hunger.

Inside or out, Isabella Albrici was a woman living on borrowed time.

The stitches came out on the tenth day. Inspecting the damage, Isabella walked to the laundry, knowing the scars were hers for life.

Eve looked up when Isabella walked in then looked down again. Isabella took her place at the steam press.

Eve was due before the parole board next week. Isabella wondered what her chances were if she did get out. What life awaited her on the outside, with no family to support or protect her?

A flurry of Spanish accented by anger erupted outside. The lone screw in the room – Stewart – sighed and went out to investigate, calling, "Break it up" as she walked through the door.

At the steam press, Isabella was so lost in her thoughts about Eve that she could have been forgiven for not noticing when Bobby Hernandez crept up behind her, shank in hand.

In the corridor, Stewart took her time sauntering over to the scuffling women, pausing to exchange a word with another guard.

"Why is it always, *always*, Hernandez's gang?" she sighed.

"It's that hot Latino blood. It's supposed to make them wonderful lovers."

Stewart eyed off the pair. "Maybe that's what their problem is too."

The other guard snickered.

The morbidly obese Stewart sighed again. Someone was going to pay the price for making her walk forty feet. "Break it up and get to your work details right now."

Engaged in a tug of war, the women ignored her.

"Right, ladies, what seems to be the problem?

"Is my towel."

"No! Is my towel."

Stewart reached between them and wrested the towel away. "No. Is mine," she puffed.

From the laundry room a heavy thump sounded. Stewart's

eyes opened wide. Twenty-five years in the prison service had taught her to recognise the sound of a body hitting the floor when she heard it.

Breathlessly, she took off for the laundry.

It was the look on Eve's face – the same stricken expression that Desiree had worn – that warned her. Isabella whirled around, her fist already flying. She dealt Bobby Hernandez an almighty blow that sent her flying with a sickening crack. Her head smashed against a machine on the way down to the floor where she sprawled, regarding Isabella balefully through the vee of her knees.

"Get up you little bitch." Isabella's voice was low and completely calm. She didn't have a quaver, a quiver, a tear left in her. "I said, get up."

Isabella launched herself at her just as Bobby Hernandez sprang from the floor. Hernandez connected with Isabella's fist, the impetus of her own forward movement adding to her injury. She fell to the floor, her nose pushed halfway across her face.

"That didn't do anything to improve your looks."

Screaming maniacally in Spanish, Hernandez leapt up and charged Isabella, her arm held high. Isabella saw the flash of yellow but kept her eyes glued to the psycho's face as she grew close enough for Isabella to smell her breath and sweaty armpit, and that arm came down in slow motion, the anticipation of victory in her eyes – and only then did Isabella, who until this day had never thrown a punch in her life, draw her fist back and ram it forward with enough force to send the psycho bitch flying in a volcanic burst of blood. Hernandez fell through the air, the blood from her smashed nose arcing a bright red rainbow as she went down.

The women formed a circle and were chanting. Isabella only had eyes for Hernandez.

The shank, fashioned from a plastic milk bottle, was bright yellow. "Yellow this time, Bobby? Bad news, bitch: yellow is not my fucking colour."

Isabella leapt up and jumped on the hand clutching the shank until it couldn't be seen for blood. Panting, she leaned over and yanked Hernandez from the floor by her hair. Hernandez tried to pull away but she was no match for Isabella's anger. Isabella propelled her to the steam press and pushed the lid open with such force that it bounced on its hinges.

Isabella frantically scanned the crowd for Eve's face then seized Bobby Hernandez's squirming hand, thrust it in the steam press and crashed the lid down.

Bobby grimaced so awfully that Isabella's chest filled with pity but then she remembered Desiree's lovely face and leaned on the lid with all her might.

Hernandez's mouth opened in a silent scream.

"One sound, bitch. Make one fucking sound and today is the day you die."

By the time Prison Officer Stewart made it back to the laundry room, Bobby Hernandez was lying in a smashed and bloodied heap at her own station, and Isabella's steam press had been thoroughly scrubbed with cleaning fluid administered by many quick hands.

Marched before the governor, Isabella looked Phillips straight in the eye and said, "I didn't see a thing."

She walked directly from the governor's office to the prisoners' mess, looking straight ahead, never turning left or right to gaze at the faces that raised as she passed.

Isabella dropped her tray to the table. Eve leaned on Teresa's shoulder crying her heart out like the twenty-year-old girl she really was.

From that day, whenever a woman fell in the shower, or anywhere else, it was always Bobby Hernandez. Whenever there was an accident on work detail, it was always she who was injured. Whenever a tray was overturned in the mess, it was always spilled on her person.

And that day, when Isabella got back to her cell, she hung her head over the toilet and vomited in a way she would not have thought possible. With every heave, she cursed the husband who had turned her into this animal and then cursed herself for letting him do it to her. She prayed for a soul surely lost to God before she remembered she didn't pray any more. Isabella retched until she thought she had expelled her internal organs and was amazed to find they weren't in the bowl along with the rest of her stomach contents.

Chapter Fifteen

Legit. Most of their business was legit. It was a claim oft repeated by Domenic and much believed by Isabella. If a small part of their business occasionally strolled through some grey legal areas, or went fishing in murky waters, well, the important thing was that most of their business was legitimate.

And if every acquaintance who suddenly disappeared was said to have gone into the witness protection program, while others were innocent victims of drug dealers – and if their clan suffered a disproportionate number of deaths at the hands of drug dealers when compared with the general population – well, it was better to believe all that too.

Following Eve's revelation, Teresa and Isabella faced the truth, and it wasn't only that Teresa's son had been the slain by the very same man who had broken bread at their table, drank their wine and toasted their health. That was a great horror, but for Teresa there were two greater: that man had shared her bed, and she had raised her own son to this way of life.

Teresa and Isabella – the other women they knew – had married into the mob. They had a choice. Not so their children.

Now two young women, twenty years their junior, who should have had their whole lives ahead of them, had come to their aid and one lay dead, the other, friendless and fatherless, with a life of sorrow behind her and no life to speak of ahead of her.

At night in their bunks, Teresa and Isabella were treated to an insider's view of hell. Neither of them doubted a special place had been reserved for them within it.

Late one night, Teresa whispered in the voice of a little girl, "It wasn't meant to be like this."

"What wasn't, honey?"

"Life."

Hearing Teresa turn over, Isabella wondered if she had been talking in her sleep.

Overnight, Teresa seemed to shrink. She barely spoke. Sometimes she didn't seem to know where she was. Stopping dead in her tracks, Teresa dropped whatever she was carrying and looked around in a panic. Isabella or Eve captured her hands within their own and tried to reorient her, reminding Teresa where she was and who she was with. "Your old friend, Isabella, and your new friend, Eve."

One evening, when they were trying to convince her to eat, Teresa whispered, "I have lived off the flesh of my son."

Isabella approached Evans. "She needs help," Isabella said. The screws had watched the latest incident with interest. Isabella wouldn't be surprised if they were placing wagers on the exact time Teresa lost it.

"This isn't a spa, Albrici. Maybe a slap from Johnny Nightstick might revive her."

In the morning, Isabella found Teresa staring at the top bunk. She didn't appear to have slept or moved from the position they had left her in last night.

Isabella tried to help her to get dressed, but Teresa fought her, taking off for the laundry before Isabella was finished.

"Where are your shoes, Benedetti?" demanded Officer Stewart.

"I'll go get them," Isabella said.

"You'll get to work," then, to Teresa, "Benedetti. Snap out of it. Go get your damned shoes."

After five minutes, when Teresa hadn't returned, Stewart hailed Isabella.

"Albrici. Go get Benedetti. I swear to you if she comes back here without shoes on, or if you're gone longer than three minutes, I'll see you two are rehoused in separate cells."

It was a three-minute walk from the laundry. When their cell came into view, Isabella would make it in forty-five seconds, but every second would last a lifetime.

The finest minds in the New Jersey Department of Corrections, ably assisted by engineers and institutional experts, had designed these cells to eradicate possible hanging points.

They were no match for a mother consumed by guilt.

The bunk was not as high as Teresa was tall, so she had tied her legs to her chest with one end of the bedsheet.

Isabella screamed.

Twenty seconds into Isabella's run, Eve ran by her side. Twenty-five seconds and Eve edged past her. At thirty seconds Eve outstripped her; by thirty-five seconds she had left Isabella behind. For the last ten seconds of Isabella's run, she watched Eve on the floor, Teresa on her young shoulders, straining to keep the bigger woman held up.

"Isabella," she gasped. "Quick, untie her!"

Together they eased Teresa's body to the floor.

"I think she's alive," cried Eve.

Isabella sobbed, looking into Teresa's staring eyes. "No, she's dead."

Eve slipped her fingers beneath the noose. "Her heart's beating!"

Still, Isabella didn't believe it. Then Teresa blinked and her heart soared.

A crowd gathered around them. Someone tried to push Isabella aside and she pushed them back without looking, unwilling to move from Teresa's side.

"ALBRICI." A nightstick crashed into her face.

Isabella had the sense of being too close to the floor. *Teresa's bunk.* She was on Teresa's bunk. Someone was on the bunk above her.

Eve dropped lightly to the floor. "She's alive. They've taken her to the prison hospital."

Isabella shoved a shaking fist to her mouth and whispered a prayer of thanks before she remembered she didn't pray any more.

"How'd I get up here?"

"You ladies want me to keep lifting you, you're gonna hafta maybe lose some Italian off those bones."

Isabella rolled way from the wall and reached out her hand. The lip of Eve, tough stuff extraordinaire, trembled. She kept her distance. "This is all my fault."

"No, honey. This is the fault of many people, mine included. But if there is one person whose fault this is not, it's yours." Isabella wiggled her fingers.

Eve dropped to her knees and lay her head in Isabella's lap. As Isabella stroked her hair, Eve held up a letter. "I got parole."

Isabella Albrici had never been more alone in her life.

Chapter Sixteen

How Isabella wished she had something to offer the young woman about to be tossed back into a world which had already found it did not care for her. How she wished to have at her disposal just some of her jewels or other fine things.

Isabella was tormented by a dream in which she handed Eve the same diamonds that had been used to send them to prison.

Eve was set free four days after her parole was approved.

They sat on the edge of Teresa's bunk, Eve in the street clothes she had been wearing when she was brought in. Isabella couldn't bear to look at them. She kept her gaze on Eve's face.

"Where will you go?"

Eve shrugged. "Halfway house. They put me there. No choice."

"I'm sure it will be lovely," Isabella said.

The whites of Eve's eyes grew large in her ebony face. They started to laugh.

Then there was nothing left to say. Isabella put on her best face and stood up.

"Well, goodbye Eve."

"I'd come see you but you know they won't let me."

"I know."

A phone card and a scrap of folded paper lay on Teresa's

bunk. Isabella smiled and swiped at her tears with the back of her hand.

"Maybe they'll let you see her soon," Eve said.

"Maybe they will, honey."

Eve gave her one last long look then stepped outside the cell.

Isabella was consumed by a sudden need to know. "Eve, what did Desiree do? I mean to wind up in here?"

Grief stole the youth from Eve's face. "She didn't really do anything. It was more she was done, you know?"

God help her, Isabella thought she did know. If only she could say the same for herself.

They didn't let Isabella see Teresa in the prison hospital.

Without Teresa to look after, without Eve's company and without the once homicidal, now broken, Bobby Hernandez to keep her on her toes, Isabella fell into unwelcome introspection.

She was lying on her bunk staring at the ceiling when one of Eve's friends came to her cell.

"Isabella, you'd better come to the rec room."

Isabella dropped to the floor and followed. In the rec room, every face turned. When a newsflash came on, someone turned the television volume up. Way up.

"… in breaking news… the diamonds allegedly smuggled by Isabella Albrici – wife of infamous mob boss, Domenic Albrici – and her associate, Teresa Benedetti, have gone missing from State's evidence."

"You know what this means, don't you Isabella? No evidence, no case. You're as good as free."

For Isabella, that meant good as dead.

"Well, Albrici," said Governor Phillips. "You already know the news. So, unless you're going to tell me how you arranged for those diamonds to disappear from evidence, I'm sure I don't need to tell you that we can't hold you."

Isabella tried hard not to shake. She was the last person in the world who wanted those diamonds to go missing. With no husband to speak of, no money of her own, no job and certainly no friends on the outside, she had no place to stay and no way of securing one.

"Why are you still here, Albrici?"

"I believe it's customary for inmates to be given a place in a halfway house."

He smiled. "Only ex-cons, of whose number you are not, never having been convicted. You're on your own.

She planted her feet apart to stop them shaking. "I'm not going anywhere until I've seen Teresa."

"Benedetti was discharged yesterday into the care of Saint Jude's."

Isabella didn't need to be told to get out a second time.

Taken to the same room on the way out they had been taken to on the way in, Isabella was handed their personal effects in two outsized brown paper bags with their last names stencilled across them.

She let her prison overalls drop to the floor and stepped into tailored cashmere trousers that once fit like a glove but now were too baggy. Isabella threw on her silk blouse, buttoning the wrists and smoothing it into the waistband. Unsteady in her now unaccustomed high-heeled boots, she buttoned her cashmere coat and wobbled down the corridor, out the door and toward the prison gates.

She was about to become a free woman.

She was about to die.

She wondered how many steps they would let her take before the bullet came.

Isabella stepped through the narrow prison gate, her vision swimming.

Where once she held her head high, now she held her breath.

When she lasted all of five seconds without being shot to hell, she figured that with God's grace she just might make it to Saint Jude's alive.

Chapter Seventeen

Distance was disorienting. Objects were too close to her, or so far away that it seemed she walked forever getting any closer to the next street.

Not long ago, Isabella thought there could be no noise worse than the prison laundry, but now the street noises seemed unbearably loud and chaotic. An accelerating motorbike zoomed past, startling her so that she whirled around then fell off the kerb. Tyres squealed and a cab driver stood on his horn.

Flinching, Isabella stepped around the car onto the opposite kerb and hurried away as best she could in her wobbly boots.

In prison, humanity moved en masse and one way – to work detail, from work detail, to the prisoner's mess, to the shower block – and no one was in a hurry to get anywhere. Out here, the movement was unpredictable, people darted and dived and everyone was in a hurry.

At the hospital entrance, Isabella waited for a screw to open the gate.

"Excuse me?" A voice from behind her. "Are you planning on going in?"

She muttered an apology and pushed through the door, expecting at any moment to hear sirens and the order for lockdown.

It was a relief to be inside the hospital, with its finite space. She found a water cooler in the foyer and drew some into a little plastic cup. Isabella glanced nervously over the rim, expecting a guard to reprimand her for being out of bounds.

The receptionist must have recognized her. When Isabella asked her for directions, her smile fell. Isabella accepted her curt instructions and scurried away, head bowed, stopping once more at a door on the way to Teresa's room to wait for a screw to open it before another *excuse me* from behind her prompted her to move forward.

Teresa lay in bed, her back to the door.

Isabella walked soundlessly to the bed, then smoothed Teresa's lank hair away from her face and whispered, "Hi, honey, how ya doing?"

Silence. Teresa's eyes were open, her face turned toward the window. Her eyes were dead. The bruises on her neck were brutal.

"Oh honey."

Isabella swiped at her face with the back of her hand, wishing she had brought the little plastic cup of water with her. She rested the paper bag holding Teresa's things on the bed; it sagged and crinkled as she put it down.

"I love you, Teresa," she whispered. "Isn't it funny how we women never say that to each other?"

Behind her, a rustling and a quiet *ahem*. Isabella turned to face a nun.

"Thank you for taking care of my friend, sister," Isabella said.

The nun's lip curled. "Perhaps you might leave her to rest," she said.

Isabella heard the message loud and clear: *Get out, mob bitch.*

Isabella made her way blindly through the diving and darting pedestrians, remembering Teresa as she was thirty years ago, vibrant and full of life.

Before her blurring eyes, two solid figures materialised from the chaos, stepping from a restaurant door into her path.

Domenic, a woman, a baby swaddled in blue: laughing! laughing! laughing!

Domenic's heel slid over the toe of Isabella's boot, trailing a pale scar through the leather. He raised his arm distractedly as if to fend off the intruder trespassing on their circle.

Just like the first time, Domenic had no idea Isabella was there.

The woman was at least fifteen years her junior. And she had given Domenic the one thing Isabella couldn't: a son.

Chapter Eighteen

For the one thing she could not give him, Domenic had sentenced her death.

Isabella found herself sitting in a park without quite knowing how she got there. Her toes were cold, her backside numb. The wind riffled leaves and chilled her ears.

No doubt about it: she and Teresa were finished.

Teresa was as good as dead. Hers was a heart that could find no reason to keep beating.

Isabella didn't want to be on this earth to face that grief. Which was just as well, given she was likely to have grown cold in her own grave by then.

There would be no sudden disappearance into the witness protection program for Isabella Albrici. Her death would come with a message – a nice loud and clear message, sans the fucking *nice*.

When the diamonds disappeared, some part of her hoped that Domenic had made good, but the truth was likely to be far more sinister.

Someone else had made the evidence go away so they could get at her.

Isabella was not long for this life. And then, what awaited her in the next?

She had lived off the wages of sin. She was beyond grace, but perhaps not beyond redemption.

In her foggy mind flickered the tiniest light.

Turning her eyes to the heavens, Isabella grieved for the way her life would be ending, so soon – today – then she wiped her face and stood up.

Her credit cards would have been stopped, but there was a little money in her purse. Just a little. Enough.

On her way to the railway station, she bought a knife.

Part Two

THE WHACK CLUB

Chapter Nineteen

It has been said that some people eat to live while others live to eat.

Irish was a woman who lived to exercise, because the more she exercised, the more she could eat.

The woman was all breasts, hips and curves. Her waist made a giggling concession to the notion of small, if only to make her other curves appear curvier, but it didn't take itself too seriously.

She exercised six days a week and chose her routes so that her six mile run would take in the meanest hills and end outside one of her favourite cake shops or delicatessens.

Today was no exception. And today's dilemma was nothing new, either.

Strictly speaking, Irish could stand to lose a little weight. With a B.M.I. that hung lustily on the healthy maximum, it wouldn't kill her to shed a few pounds and go for one click beneath.

But while Irish was a woman perfectly content to run, stair-train, walk or swim almost any distance to lose weight, she was not a woman prepared to diet for a single day.

Hence her dilemma. The end of her run had seen her land outside both her favourite cake shop and her favourite deli. They were side by side, and both were Italian.

Now, these Italians were people after her own heart – people who lived to eat, and oh did they know a thing or two about tormenting a well-rounded woman with food.

Cicero's cake shop had those damnable cannoli – something that she hadn't tasted before coming to America and something she had trouble not tasting ever since. More than anything she wanted to crack Cicero's recipe. Was it orange blossom water in the filling? Probably not. Italians wouldn't lean on a middle Eastern ingredient. So, it had to be orange peel. But there was no peel in it. Once, she scooped out the filling and spread it over a plate, but it was perfectly smooth, no peel, no zest, zip, nada. So, how'd they do it then? How did they make the orange taste?

One more cannoli might reveal the secret.

But then.

Alfonso's delicatessen next door had the finest Italian fennel pork sausages on the planet – or at least those parts of the planet she had travelled (which excluded Italy, and in fact most other parts of the planet as well) – and with those fine Italian fennel pork sausages she could cook *that* pasta – her eyes closed and her mouth watered – fettuccine with fennel sausage, lemon cream and nutmeg.

She paced between the windows, money burning a hole in her pocket.

Irish resolved to have the cannoli. Then reconsidered the sausage. But it wasn't just a matter of the sausage. Alfonso's also did the finest homemade pasta she had ever tasted. The stuff was silk. *Lemon cream sausage pasta it is then.* Just to make sure, so that she would have no regrets, she paced back to the window of

Cicero's bakery. The cannoli had lost a tiny measure of its appeal. *Pasta it is.* But then a nut horn rolled in walnuts and orange called to her from the back of the window. *Take me! Take me, Irish! Or I'll die in here like a puppy in a pet shop window in the middle of summer.* Or worse – it could go stale and have to be thrown out before it could be eaten.

Her eyes glued to the window, Irish took off for Alfonso's next door and paced *smack* side-on into a woman coming the other way.

"Oh shit, sorry!"

"It's okay," muttered the other woman.

Irish was a woman's woman. The only thing that could tear her eyes away from a cake shop window was the sound of tears in another woman's voice, and they were even louder than the nut horn crying, *Take me! Take me, PLEASE, Irish!*

"Hey, you okay?"

"Fine. Thanks for asking." The woman stared straight ahead, like she was looking at something that wasn't there. To Irish, she looked like a woman in serious need of a croissant. Or perhaps something richer.

Irish stared after her for a second or two then tried to return her attention to the window, but there was something about the woman that wouldn't let go. Irish had seen her somewhere. *Where? Why is this more important than cake? It just is, Irish.*

The news… missing diamonds.

It was *her* – the gangster's wife! Irish spun around and stared after her. *Jesus. If that's the haircut they give you in prison, then they're putting the wrong people behind bars.* It looked like a blind and drunk samurai had taken to it with a blunt sword.

Her writer's curiosity kicked in; there was a story here, for sure. On impulse, Irish followed her.

Irish rounded the corner, caught up with Isabella almost immediately and dropped back. She didn't know what she would say if Albrici turned around and asked her what she was doing. Isabella did glance over her shoulder once while crossing the road, and her eyes lit on Irish, but she didn't seem to notice her.

When Isabella disappeared into the railway station, Irish closed the gap until she had her in sight again. The train came in almost immediately. Irish got into the same carriage but at the other end. At first, she peered at Isabella Albrici discreetly, but after a couple of stops her observation grew bolder. Isabella wouldn't have noticed Irish if she had bright yellow skin and hair made from flashing lights.

Her hair worried Irish. The more she thought about it, only one person ever gave a woman a haircut like that – herself. There was something deeply worrying about that hair.

When Isabella changed trains at Hoboken, so did Irish.

Isabella alighted at Ridgewood. Irish hung back on the platform, waiting for her to clear the gate, then sprinted to catch up.

Isabella kept a steady pace, turning left, right, left again. The wide streets, almost devoid of fences, afforded Irish a clear view, so she dropped back a little to give Isabella some space.

Irish whistled under her breath. If money had an address, then it was Ridgewood, New Jersey. The houses were tall and broad, set back on deep blocks of land, with rolling green lawns out the front and lush, tall old trees all around. Irish was fascinated by affluent American suburbs without fences. Where she came from, the more money you had, the higher the fence.

Isabella turned a corner and Irish jogged to catch up, glancing up at the street sign as she went. *Spring Avenue.*

The House of Albrici – Irish had seen it on the news. It was the only house in the street with a fence; a high wrought iron fence, beautifully ornate and spiky enough to impale anyone tempted to climb over – and iron gates too, even if they did stand open.

Isabella slipped through the gates and climbed the steep winding driveway toward the house.

Irish watched her go, inexplicably compelled to see Isabella to her front door.

Isabella reached into her coat, *for her house keys,* thought Irish. *Okay, then.* The sweat from her run had cooled on her skin and now she was growing cold. Just then the sun broke through the clouds, warming Irish and glinting off the knife in Isabella's hand.

Oh Jesus. And I was so close to cracking that cannoli recipe.

Irish hit the driveway at full pelt. *To draw or not to draw?* She jumped onto the lawn to muffle the sound of her flying feet. If Don Albrici was in the house and he saw her running with a weapon, he would probably think 'law.' *Good thing or bad? Probably good.* On the other hand, she was wearing her under shoulder holster, which meant Irish would have to lift up her sweatshirt to get at it, treating the Don to a view of her jiggling breasts. *No way.* But what were Isabella Albrici's chances of survival if she didn't? *Non-existent.* Irish flipped up her top, released the double locking mechanism and drew her gun, levelling it clear over Isabella's shoulder at the house.

At the garage, Isabella wailed. "He's not home!"

Irish pulled up beside her, chest heaving. "Thank Christ. Let's move. Pronto."

Isabella eyed off Irish's gun. She held out her hands in front of her.

"Oh, I'm not… please excuse me." Irish turned around – away from the house, just in case – lifted her top again and holstered her weapon. "I'm not law. Let's get the hell out of here, before he gets home."

"No. I came here to whack my husband, and I'm not leaving until I have."

"You can't do that, Isabella."

"You're not a cop. Why should you care if I whack him?"

"It's not him I'm worried about – it's you."

"Then let me kill him."

"You can't."

"I can and I will."

Irish cast a nervous glance at the gate. "Isabella, do me a favour and look at the knife in your hand."

Isabella did. "I didn't have much money. It was the longest knife I could find for the price."

"And it's a very fine knife."

"Nice and long."

"That it is," agreed Irish. "But it's a serrated bread knife."

Isabella held the offending article in front of her face with a kind of distant wonder. "Oh. Fuck it."

"No good for whacking husbands."

Isabella tilted her head. "Maybe I could…"

"What? Slice him to death?"

"Hey, yeah…"

"He's not really likely to lie still and let you do that, now is he?"

Irish cast another frantic gaze at the gate. Every instinct in her said that Domenic Albrici was about to drive through those gates.

"Isabella, please. Let's get the hell out of here."

Isabella didn't move.

"If you won't think about yourself, then won't you please think about me? I'm not leaving you here and if I stay, he'll kill us both."

Irish watched Isabella snap out of it. "Is there a back way out?"

"No. Only through the neighbour's property."

"Well that's no good to us, is it? We'll just have to tough this out." Irish gathered Isabella into her shoulder and turned her toward the gate. "Now how about you put that nice long bread knife into your coat pocket?" Irish wondered how many attempts Isabella would have made at hacking her husband to death before she noticed the knife still wore the clear plastic blade guard it came with.

A car swooshed up the street. Irish held her breath and kept walking. The car kept going. They made it through the gate, Irish keeping Isabella's face carefully turned into her shoulder.

When they made it around the corner without a shot ringing out, Irish dared to breathe.

She guided Isabella into the gap between two hedges and flipped her phone open.

"I think we'll have a cab over the train for the ride home."

"I can't afford a cab."

"Under the circumstances, it's my treat," said Irish. "You've had a pretty big day."

Maybe Isabella had fallen into a stupor, or maybe, after her time in prison, she was just enjoying being in a car again watching the sights go by. One thing was certain: she was a woman with nothing left in her. Isabella was so dead beat it was cruel just watching her keep her eyes open.

Irish would have liked nothing better than to take Isabella back to her apartment, leave her there in a warm bath or tucked into bed while Irish went back out and rustled up the makings for dinner.

But could she trust her?

The block on Irish's kitchen bench overflowed with cleavers and knives – some of them short, some of them long, as Isabella favoured – all of them kept professionally sharpened. Irish asked the driver to let them out in front of Cicero's and Alfonso's.

"Not long, Isabella. You'll come home with me, take a hot bath, be my guest for dinner. Maybe we'll talk."

She left Isabella standing in a corner of Alfonso's while she bought the finnochio sausages, the fettuccine, lemons and cream. *To hell with it – just for today.* After Alfonso's, she ducked next door to Cicero's and picked up some cakes as well.

Night fell as Irish let them into her apartment. "Make yourself at home. I'll just start your bath. Okay?" Irish handed her the small paper bag from the lingerie store. "Here. I brought you some new undies. Help yourself to clean clothes from my wardrobe."

Isabella's eyes glistened.

"After you've bathed and eaten a proper dinner, you'll stay here the night and maybe in the morning we can talk about–"

Isabella glanced sharply at the door.

"I can't stay the night," she said.

"Yes, you can."

"You don't understand."

"Help me to understand then."

Isabella regarded her with impossibly large green eyes. "They think I've talked to the Feds."

"Oh Jesus." Irish ran a hand through her hair. "I'm going to show you something. No kidding now – woman to woman – promise me you'll honour my trust."

Irish led Isabella into her bedroom and switched on the lamp. Apart from the bed and bedside table, there was only a large, two-toned carved camphorwood chest in the room. Irish popped the lock with a slide key.

Isabella had never seen more guns in one place, and coming from whence she came, that was saying something.

Irish held the lid open. "If, in the unlikely even your fr... former friends followed you here, I can help you out. Now will you stay?"

Isabella nodded once, slowly. When she came back from her bath, swaddled in Irish's clothes, they ate dinner. Isabella closed her eyes at the first taste. It was a long time before she swallowed. And when Irish served the nut horns for dessert,

Isabella stared at the plate for a full two minutes before she snatched one up and gulped it down in two bites.

She stared at the remaining nut horn.

"Go ahead," Irish told her softly. "It's yours."

Isabella lifted the nut horn from the plate and cradled it in the palm of her hand as though it were a baby.

Chapter Twenty

In the morning, Irish found Isabella already up and on the telephone. Abruptly Isabella thrust the handset away from her, holding it at arm's length.

The engaged signal beeped from the earpiece. Irish took the handset and replaced it on the cradle. "What's wrong?"

"They're discharging her because she doesn't have insurance," Isabella replied. "I don't have anywhere I can take her."

Irish knew exactly who and what she was talking about. The news reports had made great sport of the mob wife who would rather kill herself than do an honest day's work in prison.

"Bring her here."

"I don't even know your name."

"I'm Irish, and I'm pleased to meet you."

Isabella grasped her outstretched hand. "I'm Italian... no I meant your name?"

Irish grinned, waiting for the usual confusion to resolve itself.

"Oh, you mean... you're called Irish?"

"Yep."

"But that's not your real name?"

"Nope," she agreed cheerfully, "There's a good reason why it's the only one I go by."

Isabella of all people knew better than to ask. "You don't sound very Irish."

"That's because I'm not."

"You're not Irish, but you're called Irish?"

"If I told you, I'd have to kill you." Immediately the words left her mouth, Irish could have cut her tongue out, but Isabella smiled. "It's a story you're better off not knowing. Come on. Let's go get your friend."

The staff at Saint Jude's had tried to dress Teresa in the contents from the stencilled bag and Teresa had become so distressed that she blackened a nun's eye. If she didn't wish Missus Benedetti to be escorted to the street naked, Isabella had been loftily informed, then perhaps she could bring garments to the hospital Missus Benedetti would consider fine enough to clothe herself in.

Teresa lay on her side with her back to the door. Over her broad hand lay another: small, black and with long delicate fingers. A little girl sprang up to embrace Isabella. On second glance, Irish realised she was a malnourished young woman.

No prizes for guessing where they had made their acquaintance then.

Irish drew the curtain around them and waited while they got Teresa into a sweatsuit.

People stared at them on the way out. It was a relief to finally be in the taxi.

Eve and Isabella climbed into the back seat either side of Teresa. In the front, Irish lowered the sun visor and studied them in the mirror. *What a scrawny bunch of women.* Today was a day for Alfonso's and Cicero's for sure.

In her apartment, Irish turned up the heating and fetched a mohair throw to wrap around Teresa. It was hard not to focus on those bruises.

Teresa stared dumbly, but if she had blackened a nun's eye, then there had to be life in there yet.

While Eve and Isabella tried to convince Teresa to eat, Irish left them to it, went into the kitchen to see to the coffee and wondered – for the first time of what would be many – just what the hell she had got herself into.

The cakes had been a mistake. Their stomachs weren't used to being full, and they filled up too quickly – just a couple of sandwiches and a savoury pastry each had done them in – except for Teresa, who ate nothing.

It made Irish feel bad to do it, but the subject of Isabella's suicidal mission had to be raised.

"Isabella, maybe it's time you told your friends where we met yesterday."

"Ridgewood," Isabella said.

"Isn't that where your old man lives?" asked Eve.

Isabella nodded.

"Why'd you go there for?"

"To whack him."

The silence was palpable. *Thank God. Now all that remained was to leave them to dissuade Isabella from trying again.* Irish scooped up the platter of cakes to put them in the refrigerator.

"I want in."

"Me too."

The platter thudded back to the table, the cakes bouncing and tumbling over each other.

Teresa Benedetti had come to life. She stared at Isabella.

"Madonn'! What happened to your hair?"

"I noticed too," said Eve. "You get into a fight with Edward Scissorhands? He got the better of you, girl."

Irish caught her breath. "Excuse me, ladies, you seem to be missing the point. Yesterday, your friend Isabella tried to take out her husband with a knife."

"*He* deserved it – her hair didn't. It's gonna take you forever to grow that out, girl."

"Si, Bella. That's not a bad hair day, it's a bad hair millennium."

Irish's hand raised itself in the air and hovered as though it couldn't quite work out what to do with itself. In the end it settled itself on the side of her head.

"When do we kill the strunz?" This from Teresa Benedetti.

"Excuse me, Missus Benedetti?" Teresa turned to face her. "My name is Irish. Welcome to my home."

"Piacere," Teresa said cordially.

"I don't think I'm making myself clear here. Isabella …."

"Si?"

"… tried to whack …"

"Si?"

"… her husband …" Here Irish nodded emphatically, as if to say, *you know, THE DON.*

"Si?"

"With a *bread knife*, Missus Benedetti."

Teresa shrugged expansively. "So? Next time she knows better. Rome wasn't built in a day, girly."

Isabella gave Teresa an answering shrug that said *obvious, no?*

"Aren't you forgetting something? She hits him, someone's going to hit her."

"I'm as good as dead anyway. But I don't want you having anything to do with this, Eve."

"You saying I'm not entitled, Isabella?"

Irish watched helplessly, her head going back and forward.

"No, I'd never say that. You want in, honey, you're in."

"Isabella, Jesus. You're not really going to let this young woman sign her own death warrant!"

"I respect her decision. Thank you for your hospitality, Miss Irish. It's time we were leaving."

"Wait! Wait – just a minute – hear me out."

Three faces turned. "What if there's a better way? A way that doesn't involve any of you dying?

"That way doesn't exist. If they don't kill me for hitting Domenic, they'll kill me for ratting."

"If they wanted you dead, couldn't they have arranged for it to happen while you were in jail?"

The three others exchanged meaningful glances.

"Nah," said Eve. "Bobby Hernandez was psycho long before you came along."

"The only way I could survive would be if we were to take out the whole crew."

"Hey, great idea," said Teresa.

"Do you even know how to use a gun? I couldn't help but notice you're less than handy with a knife."

"We can learn."

"I'll help you," Irish blurted.

"Why would you do that?"

"I told you yesterday – I don't care what happens to him, but I care what happens to you."

"We would be making you an accessory."

"Not if you don't get caught. Let me help you. I can show you how to use a gun, and maybe you'll all get to walk away after you've… finished."

"Why would you do that? Why would you help us?"

Irish was nothing if not fast. "Frankly, sister, I've yet to meet the man who wouldn't benefit from a bullet through the little grey matter he can own to."

"Can Eve stay too?"

When Irish hesitated, Eve got to her feet. "I got my own place. Don't you worry about me, Isabella."

"You're all welcome to stay. I only hesitated because… if you're visited by a parole officer, isn't there something about not associating… I mean, couldn't you all go back to jail?"

Eve shook her head. "They haven't been convicted. I'm the only con here."

"Okay, but if a parole officer comes here to check on Eve, what are the chances of them making a fast buck reporting your whereabouts to your husband, Isabella?"

"Trust me, he already knows."

Oh good.

Chapter Twenty-One

Her apartment was old and huge which was why she had bought it. Though not as spacious as the master bedroom, the apartment boasted three other bedrooms, one of which Irish used as her study, another which served as a second sitting room cum guest room that she sometimes, just for a change of scene, liked to work in. The room was furnished with two comfortable sofas which folded out into beds.

Irish began to relocate her office into the living room to give them a room each but Isabella insisted on sharing a room with Teresa. Eve took the room with the high antique bed while Isabella and Teresa took a fold out bed each. Irish promised Isabella that she would go out first thing in the morning and buy some proper beds.

Isabella wouldn't hear of it. She said they wouldn't be staying long enough.

Which was why, in the wee small hours, Irish lay in her bed staring at the ceiling.

Damn her rapacious appetite. If she hadn't been flitting between Cicero's and Alfonso's, she would have dodged this bullet. *And then what?* A woman would have gone to her death.

Yesterday Irish would have said anything to keep them

here – including promising to teach them to shoot – but now she questioned whether she was prepared to make good on that promise.

Surely Isabella Albrici was entitled to the means of defending herself against those who would cut her down in a spray of bullets. Or maybe cut her up. Or perhaps cut her down then cut her up. Irish tossed to her side. If only Isabella didn't intend to use the self-defence skills Irish taught her to ice her husband, then there wouldn't be a problem.

Whole other cupcake, Irish. Damn those sausages. Damn that cannoli.

Irish had meant it when she said she was yet to meet the man who wouldn't benefit from a bullet through what little grey matter he could own to.

She just didn't mean a literal bullet.

Well, most of the time, she didn't.

Okay, a lot of the time, she did.

Just the same, it was not within her first-hand experience to have fired said bullet into said grey matter – not even at target practise, where no matter how she tried to keep her gun raised, all her shots seemed to find a happy home in the target's groin.

Did she have the right to do this?

Did she have any right not to do this?

Not helping them would be a certain death sentence but then, so was helping them.

Last night, when she spirited the platter of uneaten cakes away to the refrigerator, the three women had followed their departure with countenances ranging from forlorn (Eve) to devastated (Isabella). In between was Teresa, who emerged from her near catalepsy long enough to look stricken.

Yep, they were natural born killers, all right. Take away their cakes and they looked fit to cry. And she was about to set them loose with guns.

What choice did she – they – really have?

To whack or to be whacked?

Irish tossed to her other side.

Maybe… just maybe… if she could keep them here long enough… Irish could give them a reason to live, to make a new life, just as she had done after leaving her own, not inconsiderable mistakes behind her.

Irish would teach them how to shoot, but she wouldn't be in any hurry to do it.

Starting first thing in the morning, Irish would remind them that life was for living.

She was up early but they were up earlier.

When she shuffled into the kitchen, a vision in pink chenille and Big Bird slippers, they were already huddled around her old kitchen table, dressed in their meagre clothes, trying to warm themselves by the coffee pot. Her stomach turned. How anyone could drink coffee before breakfast, morning tea, then lunch was beyond her.

They murmured *good mornings* at her, regarding her with three sets of wary eyes over three rims of evil java. They had taken the coarsest mugs she had to drink out of. One was a novelty cup she got as a present for her twenty-first birthday. It bore the slogan, *Behind Every Successful Woman There's A Man Who's Surprised.*

Yes, well. If Irish wasn't successful, there was going to be at least one man who was more than surprised. Then dead.

Irish half closed the kitchen door to get to the central heating control. "Here 'tis," she announced cheerfully. "Now you know where it is, please help yourself."

Three slight, shivering bodies grunted.

"Who's for some oatmeal?"

"No thanks."

"No thanks."

"No thanks."

Okay. Oatmeal not big on their happy list. Time to knock their socks off.

Irish swung into action, slapping a sauté pan on the stove and reaching for muesli, cinnamon sticks, vanilla pods and shredded coconut. After she toasted them all together then presented the result smothered with vanilla yoghurt, topped with ripe banana, and that topped with fresh passionfruit pulp, she would defy any of them not to eat, much less still have a death wish.

"Excuse me, but I thought you were going to teach us how to shoot."

Irish froze mid shake of the sauté pan. She twisted at the waist and gave them a breezy smile. "Not before breakfast, ladies, surely?"

There was a general grunt and they went back to huddling over their coffee cups.

Irish turned forward and let the smile fall away. *These jailbirds are uncivilised types, for sure.*

She plated the muesli and dug a long elegant spoon into each bowl by way of encouragement. A couple of tentative *clinks.* Then a little chorus of *clink clink clink.* Then it sounded like a race was on, *clink clink clink CLINK CLINK CLINK!!!!!* the smacking of spoons on bowls got louder and faster until it turned into scraping.

While they polished off the muesli and fruit, Irish set to work on the mains, putting a saucepan of water on to poach organic, free-range eggs and lighting the flame to grill bacon and ripe fit-to-burst tomatoes.

Before they could protest, she whipped the noxious pre-lunch coffee from the table and replaced it with a brewing pot of Irish breakfast tea and glasses of fresh pineapple juice. Then she laid out the good cutlery – forks with deeply curved tines and elegant knives – together with a little glass bowl of imported sea salt flakes and the black pepper mill.

While the eggs simmered, she plated up halved tomatoes, bacon and thick slices of toasted gutsy sourdough bread onto china plates.

There was a tentative lifting of knives and forks while three pairs of eyes flitted from item to item on the plate, looked to their neighbour's plate, then returned to their own.

Oh boy. Something is very wrong with the see-eat reflex in this room.

Irish led by example. Sprinkling a little of the sea salt and cracking plenty of black pepper over her poached egg, Irish sliced off a solider of toasted sourdough, made a show of dropping her cutlery to the table, then used her fingers to dip the toast solider into the egg while nibbling on the bacon she held in her other hand.

Two other knives and forks dropped to their plates. Eve still wasn't sure how to proceed.

"What's that stuff?" she pointed her chin to the little bowl of salt.

"Salt flakes."

"Yeah?" this on a high pitch. "Why are they that colour?"

"Aren't they pretty?"

Teresa held up the bowl and tilted her head. "Pink!"

"That's their natural colour. They come from under the Murray River in Australia."

"You're shitting me, right? You buy salt all the way from Australia?"

Irish nodded.

"Why, girl?"

"Because it tastes better."

And then Eve was gone. Her body was still in the room, but she went somewhere else – somewhere where you buy salt all the way from Australia because it tastes better. She carefully excised a few flakes from the bowl then tipped them on her egg from high in the air, watching them fall. "Pink salt!" she murmured.

Again, the modest amount of food was more than they could manage. They stared at their half-eaten food with hunched shoulders and bowed heads.

"We've insulted your hospitality," murmured Isabella.

"I made too much. After dinner, I'll make sure you have enough room for those cakes we bought yesterday." The cakes were starting to worry her – they might get stale before they could be eaten. The cannoli were already a day old. "Maybe I should toss them and get some fresh ones." She hadn't meant to say it aloud.

Three chairs scraped noisily on the floor.

"No."

"Don't do that."

"Okay, I promise. At ease."

They sank back into their chairs. Irish turned around and gave her attention to the dirty dishes with a grin. *Yep. Natural born killers all right.* She would have them whisked away to some foreign country with clean hands and full stomachs before they knew it.

"You were going to teach us how to shoot," said Isabella.

"After breakfast," added Teresa.

The plate dropped from her hand and rocked on the sink. Irish spun around to face them.

"Let's get a few things straight. You need a plan, and I'm not going to teach you how to shoot until you have one."

"Shoot. Dead. Done," offered Isabella.

"Do you really want this man dead or are you just playing?" Irish held up her hands to forestall argument. "You know your husband. So, you tell me, is he a skilled, cold-blooded killer or no?"

Years of practise were not easily defeated. Isabella stared at her mutely, but there was no mistaking the fire in her eyes.

"So, what do you suppose your chances are of you – you, rank amateur, complete novice – of just waltzing up to this man and capping him without him capping you first? The question is, ladies, are you serious about succeeding here or not?"

Coming from farming stock, Irish knew a thing or two about lead cows. If she could take Isabella down, then the others would follow. She seized on the flicker of uncertainty in Isabella's eyes.

"And let me ask you something else. Would you tolerate me showing contempt for your hospitality the way you're showing contempt for mine?"

Isabella got to her feet, the colour draining from face. "If you mean the food ..."

"No, I mean the worry. I'm responsible for the three of you now–"

"The hell you are," said Eve.

Irish ignored her and kept her gaze trained carefully on Isabella's. "Whether you like it or not, your problem has become my problem. Whatever happens to you now, I'll have to live with. Do me the courtesy of an honest response."

Isabella nodded curtly.

"If the situation were reversed, and I were in your home right now, wouldn't you want me to be comfortable?"

Three answers of unhesitant *yes*, loudest from the Italians. Irish tried hard not to grin.

"If you were in my shoes, wouldn't you make sure I had plenty to eat?"

"Yes."

"As well as clothes to wear?"

"Yes."

"Every comfort I could wish for – shampoos, hand creams, moisturisers ..."

Isabella's Italian hospitality motor was in overdrive. "Yes, of course."

"Good – we're agreed. Ladies, please prepare to go shopping."

None of them moved. "Then, this evening, we'll have dinner, followed by those cakes. Maybe we'll put up the card table, have a drink or two and draw up a whack plan."

Irish returned her attention to the dishes. After they left the room, she allowed herself a wide grin.

Abruptly her vision swam with somersaulting stars.

By the time Irish realised she had just been smacked in the back of the head, the culprit had left the kitchen.

Chapter Twenty-Two

Irish would have whipped her credit cards until they yelped, but two hours in and they weren't even whimpering. Never had she seen women less willing to shop.

They were so jumpy that she led them into the ladies' room for reassurance. Irish folded up her jeans to reveal the .22 in the ankle holster on her right leg.

"Number one," she said.

She flipped up the back of her jacket and turned around to show them the .32 holstered in the small of her back.

"Number two," she said.

Next she shrugged the jacket away from her arm to reveal the .38 snub nose revolver holstered under her shoulder. "Number three."

In vain, Irish waited for relief to seep into their faces.

They all selected the first shampoo, hand cream and moisturiser they picked up. The cashier rang them up, Irish paid then handed them each their own small paper bags of toiletries, and thus encouraged, led them to the upper floors where the clothes racks lived.

To no avail.

Eve confounded her. What twenty-year old girl wasn't interested in clothes? Eve looked at food like she didn't know what it was, and at clothes like they didn't exist in the universe of Eve.

Teresa was even worse. Irish tried to tempt Isabella, whose attempts to appear interested were courteous but no more.

Irish scratched the back of her head and replaced a silk and lace blouse on the rack.

Smiling politely, Isabella reached in and retrieved it – and that's when Irish noticed her right hand.

Whatever happened to that hand had been gruesome, and the means by which it had been put back together, brutal. The scars were livid and coarse; they looked like they had been made by a crude blanket stitch.

Slowly she raised her eyes to Isabella's. Isabella held her gaze for what felt like forever. Irish dared not blink.

"Tell you what," Irish said quietly. "Maybe the shopping wasn't such a hot idea. Just one more stop, then we can head home."

Isabella eyed her warily.

"If you'll accompany me to the bank, we can open bank accounts and I'll deposit–"

"That's very kind of you, Miss Irish, but bank accounts make a person easy to find."

Irish had miscalculated. This lead cow had balls and horns.

"Okay," she agreed slowly. Irish fished her keys out of her bag and slipped the apartment key from the split ring. "How about you all head home and get some rest? I'll pick up a few bits and pieces and meet you at the apartment in a little while."

That was at eleven a.m.

It was nearly dark when Irish returned. She tipped the cab

driver generously to help her carry her parcels up the stairs to the landing. Isabella greeted her at the door.

"We've been thinking." Eve and Teresa came to stand behind her.

Oh good, a deputation.

Irish parked herself at the telephone table and made a show of taking off her shoes.

"We need jobs but we're not qualified to do anything and then there's ... the other difficulties," said Isabella.

"Isabella and I can cook and Eve can learn. If we could use your kitchen, we could make food to sell to the local delis and cake shops."

"That's a great idea! And, Eve? I've been thinking, rather than have your parole officer snooping around here, how about you and I go find an apartment – just for a front – you'll stay here. We'll rent the cheapest and nastiest apartment we can find–"

"The sort of place you'd expect to find a con like me."

"The sort of place you'd expect to find an *ex* con like you. We can get your mail redirected here."

They emptied onto the landing and carted their presents in, inspecting the piles of boxes and bags uncertainly. As they unwrapped parcels, Irish thought they seemed to be more excited for each other than themselves. Teresa discovered a shirt meant for Eve, whose head was bowed over a bag holding a wrap meant for Teresa. Teresa tapped her on the shoulder and handed over the shirt. Eve grinned and handed over the wrap.

Irish kept perfectly still and watched.

The designer shirt was a maelstrom of colour. It was retro, it was fitted, with fluted sleeves that flared at the wrist, and it had cost Irish twice as much as she had ever spent on a good dress blouse for herself. One look at Teresa's face as Eve held it against her chest, and Irish would gladly have paid ten times more.

Eve shook out the wrap – floral embroidered cashmere with matching silk brocade – and draped it over Teresa's shoulder. Teresa's eyes took on that look again – the one that said Elvis had left the building – but she came back just as quickly when Eve fingered the fine material like a little kid discovering something new and wondrous.

Their reaction to their new sweats and runners was polite but indifferent. Little did they know that Irish had big plans for those sweats and runners.

To the strains of swishing tissue paper and glossy bags, Isabella, Teresa and Eve unwrapped shoes – casual, dress and running – blouses, shirts, belts, jeans, pants and skirts, sweats, socks, panties, bras and nighties – some naughty, some nice, some just built for comfort – as well as tee shirts, sweaters and tailored jackets: every practical necessity and then some spiritual ones. Irish had spent as much time selecting beautiful wraps and scarves as she had finding the right running shoes. Eve pushed herself up from the floor where she had been sitting cross-legged, and, all long legs and sylphish grace danced across to Irish, a beautiful abstract silk scarf in hand, which she wrapped around Irish's neck.

She bobbed down and kissed Irish on the cheek.

Startled, Irish watched her dance back to the others as a paper bag crackled.

"Oh now, what has Miss Irish given us here?"

Ah. Irish was dreading this moment.

Isabella held in her hands the three wrapped parcels, each bearing a gift tag inscribed with their names.

One at a time, they peeled the paper apart, let it drift to the floor, then prised their new wallets from the boxes. Eve tipped her box over and let it fall into her other hand. Isabella lifted hers with one finger by a corner. They did what women always do – inspected every nook and cranny – peering into card slots, already imagining what goes where, their minds separating coins into different zipped compartments – a system that would never be adhered to past the first outing. They opened, closed, folded, peered, zipped and unzipped. Three heads bowed. All zips were stilled.

Irish had swung by the bank on the way home. Because the bills were brand new, the neat pile of notes that was twenty thousand dollars took up a surprisingly small space in each wallet, although it did add a pleasing amount of weight.

"We can't accept this–"

"Maybe one day, when you get to where you're going, you can pay me back, if you want to," said Irish. "But you know, I'm never going to miss it, and there's plenty more where that came from."

Irish tried for a matter of fact tone, but her heart was in her throat. Teresa and Eve turned a questioning gaze to Isabella. Isabella's voice betrayed a wealth of emotion.

"Thank you, Irish."

"There's plenty more where that came from, plenty for all of us." As she said it, Irish looked at each of them in turn. Teresa returned her gaze for half a second then blinked. When her eyes opened again, she wasn't in residence.

Okay. Time to knock this on the head.

"You know what, ladies?" Irish began, looking at Teresa. "I'm exhausted. How about I just get a microwave risotto out of the freezer for tonight?"

"Sounds good," said poor clueless Eve.

"Yeah. That's what we'll do. You can't tell the difference anyway. All that nonsense about continuous stirring and fresh stock. I've used long-grain rice instead of carnaroli. A bouillon cube and powdered parmesan too. Tonight, we'll just have one of the store-bought, ready-made risottos from the freezer. I'll just go pop it in the microwave now."

Not only was Elvis back in the building, but it looked like he was none too pleased about what was playing on the tube. Giving Irish her solemn brown eyes, Teresa announced, "I will cook the risotto," before sweeping regally into the kitchen.

Irish poured them all a generous glass of chilled sauvignon blanc. Suddenly, they started laughing. Quietly at first, but then they laughed at each other laughing and it went from a chuckle to a full belly laugh. Irish lifted her wine glass. "Salut."

"Salut," they chorused, clinking glasses.

Irish drank and smiled, remembering that less than forty-eight hours ago, her apartment was silent of noise other than that of her own making. Now, her home was filled with laughter and she would have company other than the television for dinner.

After dinner, they cleared the table, opened another bottle of wine and put music on. Then Irish lit candles while Isabella shuffled a deck of cards.

So began the inaugural meeting of the first chapter of the New Jersey Mob Suffragette Whack Club.

Chapter Twenty-Three

Irish rummaged in the walnut cutler desk until she found a writing pad. She brought it to the table and flipped it open.

"What's first on the agenda?"

Teresa and Isabella stared at her. "We're not so big on writing things down," Isabella said.

Irish coloured and tossed the pad back into the desk, stealing a glance at Eve. Eve had a cannoli in one hand, a piece of soft nougat in the other and was eyeing off the sweet bowl filled with dusted jelly babies.

"I say the first order of business is a fitness plan," said Irish.

Teresa eyed her suspiciously. "You don't have to be fit to shoot a gun."

"No, but you do have to be fit to run like buggery after you have."

Teresa's eyebrows glanced up then fell again. "Good point, maybe."

Isabella finished shuffling then dealt the cards. "Then we'll do both. Exercise in the mornings, learn to shoot after that."

Irish drew a breath. "So, you waltz into the local firing range and start target practise. Isn't your sudden interest in firearms proficiency bound to get back to the good Don? Some two-bit hustler looking for a fast buck–"

Teresa and Isabella exchanged glances loaded with meaning.

"Or a crooked cop–"

"Fucking Jameson," spat Teresa.

Irish knew better than to ask. "And what about Eve, here?" Halfway to the little sweets bowl, Eve looked up at hearing her name, decided whatever it was wasn't as important as a jelly baby then went back to what she was doing. "She's on parole. What's happens to her if she gets caught carrying a gun?"

"You promised to teach us how to shoot."

"And I will. I'm just saying there's a way to go about it." Irish took a swig of sauvignon blanc and gave that a moment to sink in.

"Which is?"

"I'll use my connections to get you some private time at the range after hours, when it's closed to the public."

Teresa and Isabella hesitated, then nodded.

Irish spread her cards. "Now, will someone please tell me what we're playing and pass the cannoli."

Full of risotto, good wine and Italian cakes, Irish would drift contentedly off to sleep smiling at her own cunning, never suspecting that Isabella and Teresa, lying in their foldout beds, were entertaining their own thoughts.

"Eh, Bella. Who is this woman helping us?"

"She said not to ask any questions," Isabella whispered. "I think she's ex I.R.A. Or an arms dealer. Possibly both."

The silence was profound.

"Isabella, do we really want one such as this helping us?"

"What choice do we have?

More silence.

"Besides, she's a good cook."

Rustling in the dark told Isabella that Teresa had rolled over to go to sleep.

Chapter Twenty-Four

When Irish woke to the smell of brewing coffee, she bounced out of bed, flew down the hall and burst into the kitchen. "No coffee before exercise, ladies!"

Coffee pot in hand, Teresa dropped her gaze to Irish's chest. She put her hand on her hip and nudged Isabella, who took a look for herself and put her hand on her hip as well.

"What? It's my *Sopranos* tee shirt. I always sleep in it."

"Eh. No wonder you sleep alone then."

"Hey!" Suddenly self-conscious, Irish shifted from foot to foot. "Put that coffee down!" she blurted.

Isabella and Teresa exchanged a glance. "Or you'll what, Godmother? Whack us with one of your cannoli?"

"Wise guy," returned Irish.

They howled with laughter before Irish even realised what she had said.

"Oh Je–"

Isabella jiggled a wooden spoon from the utensil holder on the bench. "Say hello to my little friend." Teresa fell over laughing before remembering the coffee pot in her hand. Coffee slopped from the top as she slapped it on the bench.

"Very funny, ladies. How about you get some oatmeal on?"

Their laughter dissolved. Irish held up her hands. "Sorry.

I forgot. No oatmeal. How about you start on some cereal while I throw on some sweats? After breakfast we'll start with some long walks then see if we can't build our way up to runs…"

Three faces paled – even Eve's.

"Okay," Irish said patiently. "How about some stair training then? Right here in the building? No need to go outside."

As well as the external fire escape, her building had two sets of stairs. The front stairs were open, carpeted and softly lit by wall lamps, while the back stairs were bare concrete and enclosed. She used them for stair training on the days it was either too wet or too hot to go out and had never encountered another soul.

Irish opened the stairwell door. The cold hit them like an atomic blast. Eve, Teresa and Isabella shivered pitifully. "It's okay," she told them. "You'll warm up soon, believe me."

Irish started them off gently, leading them down seven flights to the bottom floor by way of a warm up before she started them going up. Even so, they struggled.

"It doesn't matter if you can't run up and down at first, or even jog. Walking is just fine. The important thing is not to stop."

Irish realised she was talking to herself. When she turned around, she was alone.

She jogged down and found them on the landing below. Eve and Isabella leaned against the wall while Teresa sat on the step.

"Let's take a sip from our water bottles and try again. This time, try not to stop."

She slowed it right down so that they were barely moving, but by the third floor they were falling behind and complaining loudly.

"My arches hurt."

"I'm cold."

"The stairs are hard."

Jesus. Wasn't prison supposed to toughen one up?

"My ears are cold."

"My water's too cold."

"My ass is sore."

"Your ass is sore? My ass is–"

"For the love of God, I thought hard labour was supposed to make you fit. What did you do in that prison all day, the fucking laundry?"

Irish hadn't turned around, which was just as well, or else the fist that flew toward the back of her head before Isabella lunged and caught Teresa's hand may well have offended her.

"If there was any more bitching behind me, I'd think I was being followed by bloody men."

"Oh, now you're being rude," declared Isabella.

Irish shot her a wicked grin and took on a whiny voice. "I can't climb the nasty stairs all on my own. Why not? Because I'm a man!"

A murmur of agreement rippled through the other three.

"Oh honey, I can't possibly work and cook dinner on the same day. I might get… I might get… oh, honey I might get tired! Why? Because I'm a man!"

The murmured agreement grew louder.

"And baby? I can't possibly be in the room with you while you give birth, because it would hurt me too much to see you in pain!"

The women roared.

"What does that make me, ladies?"

"A man!" they chorused.

"And when you do get home from the hospital?" Turning around, Irish laid her palms flat on her thighs and leaned in.

The others leaned in too. "Uh-huh?"

"You won't mind catching up on the housework, will you honey?"

"Uh-oh."

"I couldn't do it because I was so worried about you!"

"Oh no!"

"What does that make me?

"A man!" they roared.

"Ladies, how do we make a man insane?"

"Well, I don't know Irish," said Isabella. "How do you make a man insane?"

"Why, we simply ask him to do two things at once. And having him made him insane, how do we finish him off? Talk to him while he's walking down the stairs."

"Oh no! Not multi-tasking! The kiss of death, si!"

"And remember, ladies – presuming that we want to – how do we save a man from drowning?" Irish spread her hands. "We take our foot off his head."

She waited for the laughter to subside.

"It's a good thing God only gave us one of their ribs, else we would have wiped the floor with them a couple of centuries ago. Now ladies, get a move on."

They attacked the stairs with such gusto that by the end of the session, Irish was breathless with admiration.

Irish set them the ostensible task of securing up-to-date photos
of the men they meant to hit. Without being able to return home
to select from their own happy snaps, surely, she reasoned, the
task would prove difficult.

Teresa and Isabella could cull images from newspaper
archives, but that would involve a trip to the library, if not several,
and considering their shared reluctance for the outdoors, that
seemed a project unlikely to be embraced with any enthusiasm
any time soon.

Irish didn't know that the F.B.I surveilled mob funerals.
In fact, these *the gang's all here* photo opportunities delighted
the Feds, being, as they were, a veritable black carpet La Casa
Nostra *who's who*. Anyone who was anyone attended family
funerals, as well as anyone who was trying to be someone. And
when recording inductees to the Jersey hall of fame, the Feds
didn't spare the Fuji.

Given the regular opportunities afforded by the high
prevalence of occupational hazards in the mob workplace –
any decent workplace inspector would have shut them down
– the Feds' fervour, combined with the speed and availability
of the internet in Irish's apartment, as operated by skilled and
intelligent persons, conspiring with the best quality printer
money could buy, resulted in Irish being presented with a
crystal clear group A3 portrait printed on photo quality
paper with superior ink almost the minute she walked in the
door.

She and Eve let themselves in, fresh from renting a crummy
front place for Eve, the duplicate keys they had cut for Irish's
apartment on the way home dangling from split rings on their

fingers. As they opened the front door, the smell of chocolate wafted like a sexed-up wraith to greet them. It was all Irish could do not to drool.

They found Isabella and Teresa in the living room.

"Come sta," Irish greeted them, the smell of cocoa inspiring a suddenly deeply held and demonstrative affection for all things Italian.

"Oh, we don't speak Italian," Teresa said.

"No? I thought—"

Isabella held up the glossy family portrait. "We've got the photo you wanted." Irish's tastebuds shut down. "And we were thinking, if we can't go to the shooting range, then maybe we can target practise dry firing right here in the apartment." Isabella held the photo up higher. "We've got this to aim at, if you'll give us some guns."

Irish clenched her jaw. "What a splendid idea. Let's see what you've got there."

She had enjoyed dressing this morning in her *for town* clothes – a floaty blouse, form fitting pants and tailored wool jacket – almost as much as she had enjoyed seeing Eve dressed up in her funky new jeans and exploded paint gun shirt, but now, as Irish strode across the room to view an image she had little wish to see, her fitted clothes felt constricting and she wanted nothing more than to get out of them and shed the various guns holstered beneath.

Irish took the proffered photo and did a double take.

"GOOD GOD!" she roared. "I've never seen so many fat bastards in my life. Look at them. Jesus! Jesus! and more Jesus! We're gonna need elephant guns to bring this herd down—"

Eve fell to the floor, her mouth split in an agonised rictus of silent laughter.

Irish held up the photo. "You want to see this?"

Unable to speak for laughter, Eve nodded, pushed herself from the floor and came closer.

And then the world went to hell in a hand basket.

Eve screamed blue bloody murder. Irish reached for her but Teresa charged in and slapped her hand away.

Teresa ushered Eve to the bedroom she shared with Isabella. The door closed.

Isabella steadied herself against the wall, the hand over her mouth jerking up and down.

"Isabella, what just happened?"

"It's not my story to tell." It was all she would say.

"I'll see you and I'll raise you."

Things had settled down by dinner time. Teresa and Eve emerged from the bedroom, hand in hand. They each took a corner of the photo and tacked it firmly to the wall, which, concluded Irish, was most assuredly not a good sign.

They gathered at the table with a bottle of wine, ready to convene the second Whack Club meeting.

"I'd kill for a cigarette," said Irish.

"I'd kill for some junk," said Eve.

Irish glanced up sharply.

Teresa patted Eve's hand. "You don't do that shit no more. You're a good girl now."

Teresa turned to Irish. "So, you smoke, Miss Irish?"

"Smoked," Irish replied, checking out her hand. "In another life."

"You're quite the international woman of mystery, Godmother." Then to Eve: "See? She's a reformed character too. We're all good girls here."

Irish sipped her wine and glanced at the photo on the living room wall. "Isabella, Teresa, I have to ask: what the hell did you feed those men?"

"Eh. They feed themselves – one thing a man can do."

There was murmured agreement.

"Almost without dribbling," Teresa added as an afterthought.

Irish got up and walked over to the photo. "Okay, let's hear it. Who are these characters?" Some of them were vaguely familiar. Of course, she recognised Dominic Albrici. Loath as she was to admit it, even to herself, Irish didn't have a problem understanding what Isabella saw in her man. "The good Don, I know. Who's this chappie at his left?"

They came over to join her. Irish tapped a finger to the head of tall thin man with slicked back hair.

"Johnny Acerbi. He's a captain," supplied Isabella.

"And these two behind him?" They were young but their pudgy features were already blurred.

"Vincente De Paulis and Paolo Discenza," replied Isabella. "They're in Johnny's crew."

Beside her, Teresa's breathing changed. "And who are these four standing together here?"

"Cino Malatesta, Bruno Merlini, Vittori Pavone and Benito Recchio. Cino is their Capo."

"And a head case," added Teresa.

"The five scattered at the back here?"

"Teodore Saracini, Peter Ventresca..." Isabella fell silent.

"Carlo Scatera." Teresa's voice was hard.

"The others are Sergio Virrini and Dante Alessandri."

Not all of them were overweight and certainly some were easy on the eye. One guy in the picture was really rattling Irish's ovaries. "Who is that fine looking fellow?"

"Dante Alessandri." Isabella lowered her gaze and headed back to the table. The other three followed.

"So that's twelve men, excluding your husband."

Irish sipped her wine, giving that a moment to sink in. *Step one: get them thinking about it. Step two: demonstrate the improbability of success. Step three: help them run away without taking a whack detour.*

Once again, she had miscalculated.

"Better we kill them all in one hit, before they get the chance to kill us back."

The wine in Irish's mouth squelched into her cheeks and trebled in volume.

Eve gathered the cards and shuffled. "I've been thinking, when we start clipping your old men, they're going to think it's the competition. Won't we start a mob war?"

Oh thank God. The voice of reason.

"No bad thing," said Isabella. "Save us the trouble of whacking them all ourselves."

Irish tipped her head back and tried to get the wine to go down her throat.

"Who wants to be saved the trouble?" said Teresa, shrugging.

Irish forced the wine down. "But they won't have a reason to suspect you. While they're busy blaming each other, you could be done with your couple of hits then slip quietly out of town, to some tropical paradise. How about Australia?"

Eve squealed. "Snakes and spiders! I'd be too frightened. No, I think you were right the first time, Irish. It's better that we kill them all in one day, before they've got a chance to react."

"Si, you were right with the first plan, Irish. We're gonna need to be real fit to pop them all in one hit." Teresa raised her glass. "Salut. To Irish's grand plan."

"Salut," they chorused.

"You're smarter than I gave you credit for," Isabella said.

Irish stared at her. "Thanks."

"Tomorrow morning, we work on getting fit. In the afternoon, we'll start target practise right here in the apartment."

Isabella locked eyes with her. Irish dared not blink.

"On the other hand, if you wanted to avoid starting a mob war, you could use less obvious means."

"You mean like a skillet to the back of the head?" Teresa said. "Nah, no good. They'd know a woman had done it, for sure. That's like poison – a woman's murder weapon. Bring half the damned family and all the fucking F.B.I. straight to our door. Bullets are better."

"So tomorrow you'll start showing us how to use guns, like you promised," said Isabella.

Irish's mouth went dry. "I haven't yet decided what type of gun to use. There's no point in starting then changing halfway through. That would only slow you down. I'll need some time to think–"

"It's unfair to make that your responsibility. Why don't we help you choose?"

Okay, Isabella, let's talk about the big nasty, scary reality of guns.

"Your basic choice is revolver versus semi-automatic."

"Go on."

"Revolvers are easier to use and faster to put into action when you need them. Their sights are more accurate. Their ammunition packs more of a punch." Irish nodded in the direction of the photo. "Given the size of some of those bastards, that's a worthy consideration."

Isabella didn't bat an eyelid.

"On the other hand, semi-autos have a greater ammo capacity."

"So we get more tries."

"Exactly. Magazines are easier to operate than the speed loaders revolvers use. They're also lighter."

"Meaning we can carry more of them."

"Right. I venture you're going to need all the magazines you can carry." Irish gave that a moment to sink in. "Semi-autos are quieter. The flash and noise can be suppressed where they can't be with a revolver, an advantage you'll need if you're hoping to pop one of your former friends without one of his current friends popping you."

Across the table, Isabella was cool as a cucumber.

"Semi-autos are lighter to carry and easier to conceal," said Irish. "Most have an external safety switch, meaning it's easy to see and feel when your weapon is safe – however – that makes them more complicated and, therefore, slower to put into use, but their trigger pull is lighter than a revolver's, which makes them faster to shoot once you get going."

Isabella thought on it, but only for a moment. "Semi-automatics it is."

"Not so fast. There's one small problem – reliability. It's virtually impossible for a revolver to malfunction. They rarely hang fire, but if they do, it might not end well for the shooter. Semi-autos, on the other hand, can whoopsie in several ways and when they do, they're a bastard to clear. If a semi-auto malfunctions, no two ways about it, you're on your own. By the time you get it cleared, bang, bang, you're dead, baby. And you're likely to have broken a fingernail too."

Isabella barely hesitated. "Fingernails notwithstanding, I'd still say semi-autos it is."

"Okay," Irish capitulated tightly. "I'll pick them up tomorrow afternoon."

That night, while the rest of the house slept, Isabella crept from her bed and slipped into the darkened living room to gaze upon the moonlit family portrait.

There was only one problem with the grand plan: Dante Alessandri.

Chapter Twenty-Five

However begrudgingly, next day Irish made good on her promise, returning in the afternoon with two cartons of low fat milk, a loaf of multigrain wholemeal bread sliced for toast (and a pane di casa to go with dinner) and three brand spanking new semi-automatic pistols, complete with three equally brand spanking new leather cross draw holsters.

Eve bounded into the hall to greet her. "Teresa! Isabella! Come on! Irish is gonna teach us how to shoot!"

Irish waited until the other two presented themselves. "No," she said slowly, "Irish is going to teach you how to *draw*."

Eve shrugged. "Whatever."

"No, honey, not *whatever*. If you're serious about this, if you really want to learn how to shoot, then you're going to have to take this part seriously, because let me tell you sugar, you ain't going no further until you learn how to draw properly."

In the living room, Irish unpacked her purchases onto the round mahogany table, feeling Isabella's eyes on her all the while.

"Okay, ladies, here we are. Three rather fetching, compact semi-automatic Smith and Wesson CS45 Chief's Specials."

They gathered round. If Irish had hoped that the reality of an actual, tangible gun would bring them to their senses, she would be disappointed, although she entertained a moment of hope when Teresa said, "Wait a minute."

"Yes, Teresa?"

"Don't you need a licence for these things?"

Irish blinked and put her hand on her hip. "Would you prefer to apply for a licence, Teresa?"

"No, it's not that. I'm just wondering how you got them, is all. I wouldn't want you to get in any trouble."

Oh jolly. I'm not in any trouble as it is. No trouble, officer, move along, move along, nothing to see here.

"Let's just say I made use of some connections and leave it at that. Unless you really want to apply for a licence like good responsible citizens?"

"No, it's okay."

"Maybe not."

"Chill."

"I'm glad that's settled. Now, before practising with a weapon, we always make sure it's empty. By empty I mean, no bullets, no rounds, no ammo, no *ah whoopsie, what was that fucking bang* – ergo, no magazine." Irish drew her Chief's Special from its holster and discharged the magazine to show them how. She slipped the magazine into her pocket then held up the gun to demonstrate the empty check.

"See that space? That's where the magazine – a la bangy thing – would normally be. No bangy thing, no *Hell, sister, where did your head go, girl?* Got it?"

Reluctantly, she handed them each a Chief. They set about discharging the magazine as she had done. Isabella's plopped straight to the floor. Teresa almost caught hers, but her co-ordination wasn't up to the task. It pinged off Isabella's, bounced, then disappeared under the table. Eve's magazine was nowhere in sight, and eyes to the floor, she was turning in circles like a hapless puppy chasing its tail.

"Okay ladies, I trust we now see the need for practise. If you will please be so good as to attach your cross-draw holsters to your belts, like so–" she proffered her waist for inspection – "insert your weapons, thus," – she demonstrated – "and follow me to my bedroom, then we may proceed."

In her bedroom, Irish opened the wardrobe doors to expose full length mirrors then backed up. She and Isabella occupied one mirror while Teresa and Eve occupied the other. Irish glanced across both mirrors at waist level. Three out of four cross-draw holsters were on backwards. She stretched her neck, rolling her head from side to side. "Let's try that again." There was a confused murmuring, the unbuckling of belts, the repositioning of holsters. Two were replaced in the same position; one fell to the floor with the weapon still in it.

"Mother–"

Teresa's arm shot out. She clipped Eve in the back of the head. "Nasty word. You be a good girl."

"And again," said Irish.

A few minutes later, four out of four holstered guns were attached – all pointing in the right direction – to four out of four belts.

"Jolly, ladies. Now let's draw."

Before she could instruct them further, they went for their guns, which the holsters' locking mechanisms prevented them from withdrawing. When the holsters refused to give up their booty, they took to yanking. If Irish had been in a better mood, the consequent contortions, gyrations and general turning in circles amid grunts, curses and one case of persistent low growling would have been frankly hilarious.

"In order to draw, we must first release the gun from the holster's locking mechanism."

Eve looked at her indignantly. "Well ain't it a damned shame you didn't tell us that in the first place."

Irish pointed a finger in the air. "Now if we can all turn forward."

Feet apart, arms pushed out and finger twitching, Eve looked like an old west gunslinger trying to outdraw the other guy – herself – in the mirror. Teresa rubbed her own shoulder while Isabella breathed hard enough for Irish to take pity and give her a moment to recover.

"You will observe that your holsters – known as cross draw holsters – are worn on your left side." They murmured. "As we are all right-handed, the left side of your body, in shooting terms, is known as the *support* side, while the right side of your body is known as the *strong* side."

They took turns at putting their left hands in front of them muttering *support*, then putting their right hand forward and murmuring *strong*.

"In order to draw our weapons from these cross draw holsters, we take our right hand–" Irish held hers up, "slide it across our abdomen like so until we reach our left side." So far so good – they knew right from left. "Now grasp your weapon firmly by fitting your hand into the backslide – that's the grooved bit at the back." She waited for them to find it. "Then curl these three fingers around the grip – and this manoeuvre is a right bastard on fingernails, so for the love of God, mind how you go – lay your trigger finger along the side of the frame, push down twice, twist and pull to release your weapons." In one smooth movement, Irish held her liberated weapon up." And there you go – simple."

It was a travesty. Not one of them managed it. Eve tried to persuade her weapon to come out by turning in circles and muttering the word Teresa had stopped her from saying before, while Teresa abandoned her efforts in favour of clipping Eve in the back of the head. Isabella appeared to get a cramp in her shoulder every time she reached across her abdomen.

"Okay, stop. Stop! Take a breath, face forward, relax and try again."

Irish holstered her gun. "Now. Using our right hand, we reach across our middle, fit our hand into the backslide, curl these three fingers around the grip, then push push twist pull."

There was a lot of grunting but not a lot of drawing. Irish holstered her gun and showed them once more. Suddenly, Eve's eyes widened. She looked like a kid who had dedicated days to worrying a loose tooth with her tongue at the moment it finally came free.

"I did it!" Eve used her newly liberated pistol to scratch the back of her head.

"JESUS CHRIST, EVE! Don't let me ever see you do that again!"

Eve lowered the gun. "What? My head was itchy."

Irish stopped breathing. Then suddenly she was laughing. Her prayers had been answered. Isabella and Teresa couldn't even get their guns out of their holsters. They would realise how ill-equipped they were to execute their plan and… she realised the two women were watching her, guns in hand. Suddenly it felt like Irish would never laugh again.

"What next?" Isabella demanded.

"Nothing next," Irish snapped. "You do it again."

"Don't we point it at something once we've taken it out?"

"Absolutely not. You do nothing else until you've mastered the draw. You holster your weapon and you draw it repeatedly until it's second nature. Now, please turn back to the mirror and make like Gary Cooper."

"Who's that?" This, from Eve.

"Harrison Ford's daddy."

Eve looked blank.

"Brad Pitt's granddaddy," said Irish.

"Brad Pitt…" Eve's brow furrowed. Her expression cleared. "That old dude, right?"

Wisely, the three older women holstered their guns.

Isabella had no trouble with the second draw, nor did Teresa. Irish recognised natural ability when she saw it, and God help her, she saw it here. Her heart slid all the way down to her stomach.

"So, as soon as we've got this part down, we can start learning to shoot," said Isabella.

"Not quite," Irish replied tightly. "The holsters need to be broken in so they're soft and pliable, or else you won't be able to access your gun in a hurry and accidents might happen. It takes several hundred draws to break a leather holster in," she lied.

"Don't they come in nylon? The holsters I mean?"

"They do, but the nylon ones don't have locking mechanisms," Irish lied again. "Which means you might lose your weapon if you have to run. I venture you're going to be doing a lot of running," she said pointedly. "Besides, the nylon ones are ugly." Well that much was true.

"Something else?" said Teresa.

"Shoot."

"What's with this cross draw business? I mean, isn't it unusual?"

"It is."

Irish swept her right arm back, elbow in the air, as though to draw from a conventional strong side hip holster.

"You see me do this – what do you think?"

"You're going for a gun," Eve replied. The other two nodded.

"Right."

Irish reached behind her as though she were going for her small-of-the back holster.

"You see me do this – what do you think?

"Gun," Teresa said without hesitation.

"Gun."

"Gun."

"Okay." Irish reached right to left across her abdomen in the cross draw manoeuvre she had just taught them. "You see me do this – what do you think?"

Teresa spread her hands. "Honestly? I'd think you had period cramps."

"Precisely!" cried Irish. "And any man with half a brain faced with that should be running long before you draw."

They fell about laughing, but her words would prove truer than any of them could have imagined.

Chapter Twenty-Six

Teresa and Isabella were not ones to ask how a person made their crust. Therefore, they made no enquiry of Irish as to why she didn't have to go out to work. They did, however, express concern that their presence may be interfering with her earning a living. Irish assured them that was not the case: she had recently completed a project and was currently on hiatus. She was in fact, enjoying both the break and their company very much, which was true, or at least it was when she wasn't lying awake at night worrying her guts out – a fact she omitted from her reassurances.

While their continued reluctance to set foot out of doors was understandable, Irish needed to get them outside as part of her master plan to renew their interest in the big wide wonderful world.

Within two weeks, their stair-training endurance had increased remarkably, and their improving health was evident. Irish hoped it was a result of exercise induced endorphins but suspected it owed more to their practise draw sessions.

The women spent hours cooking, experimenting, adapting long held recipes. They ate their experiments for dinner. Irish wasn't about to complain about that any time soon.

In there right beside them was Eve, who, God love her, had

no discernible palate other than *sweet*, knew next to nothing about cooking, but who was as determined to learn as they were to teach her, and they did it so tenderly and with such patience that it was beautiful to behold.

Irish often left her study in the afternoon to steal into the kitchen for the sheer pleasure of watching them work. Quiet as a mouse, she sat at the kitchen table, her head propped in her hands, listening and watching.

To call Teresa Benedetti an incredible cook would be to do her an injustice.

With renewed interest, Teresa was faring better, but sometimes she just faded away, although rarely while cooking, and seldom, Irish noticed, around Eve. If deprived of Eve's company, Teresa could be found staring into space, surrounded by the pieces of something she had been holding.

Together they wooed Teresa back, doing their best to make the here and now a safe place for her to return to. She often seemed to be on the verge of tears. Irish prayed that the tears would fall, that Teresa would have a great heaving – healing – cry about it all, whatever *it* was.

When Teresa handled the gun, she was a woman transformed. She was a person Irish very much wished never to come across in a dark alley.

If only Irish could get them out of the apartment and interested in the outside world again, she would take Teresa to a farmer's market to see and smell the vibrancy of the earth, the majesty of sunrise and sunset as a riot of colour in the peppers and tomatoes, the crisp night sky in every dewy lettuce leaf, the tenderness of spring in the baby spinach leaves and sweet little carrots, good honest dirt sluiced away to expose the succulent fruit beneath.

Irish dared raise the subject one evening after a superb ragu dinner and more than one glass of wine, when everyone was feeling full and rosy. *Surely it was safe for them to go for a walk in the beautiful sunshine, no? If the goon squad came after them, she was adequately equipped and fully prepared to defend them all. Okay. Okay?*

In a little while she heard dishes being washed then the soft sounds of a house closing down for the night: the swishing of water in a wash hand basin, the methodical clicking of light switches, doors quietly closed by considerate fingers. In the still of the night, while Irish was yet to sleep, the house came back to life. Through her closed door she heard soft, inaudible conversation.

When she rose the next day to be greeted with the news that the women wished to go out for a walk, she couldn't have been happier.

Not knowing that their sudden resolve was owed to their hunger to commence the hunt, Irish was delighted to take the ladies out.

"How come a nice girl like you sleeps alone, eh?"

Teresa sprung the enquiry on her before they rounded the first corner. Irish answered with a vague smile. She put her foot on a low stone fence and stretched her hamstring.

"Damn girl, they are the ugliest shoes I've ever seen."

Irish's runners were a shade of fluorescent green violent

enough to make you puke like a drunk when you were sober, contrasted by an equally fluorescent pink tick that clashed so badly with the green that if you looked at it for more than a second, your brain threatened to eject the eyes from your head to end its pain. On top of the green and pink, they had yellow toe caps that fairly irradiated the exposed eye.

"They do the job."

"Wouldn't be seen dead in that puke fest, myself."

"I'm flat footed. These are about the only runners that suit my feet."

Eve looked far from convinced. Teresa cuffed her on the back of the head. "See? You shouldn't make fun. She's got a disability." Teresa gave Eve another cuff. "And you shouldn't interrupt. Irish was telling us why a nice girl like her sleeps alone."

"I'm a little long in the tooth to be called a girl, Teresa." She set off at a cracking pace, but Teresa was not to be deterred.

"How old are you?" Teresa asked from behind her.

"Thirty-eight."

"Eh, thirty-eight is young. You got plenty of good years left, but maybe not so many to find the right man and have babies. So, what are you doing sleeping alone?"

Truthfully, she would be ashamed to tell them. His name was Chris, he was ten years older than her, and Irish had loved him body and soul. So much so that when she found out, six months into their relationship, that he was married, she kept seeing him, reasoning that there must have been something wrong with the marriage for him to turn to her. Irish kept seeing him until he stopped seeing her and then she fled overseas rather than risk making a fool of herself begging him to come back.

She still ached for him so that Irish discouraged so much as a friendly smile from a willing man, rather than move on.

Irish would be ashamed to tell these strong Italian women such things about herself. She picked up the pace and said nothing.

Teresa skirted in front of her, managing to walk backwards despite the pace Irish had set.

"So how come?" Teresa's eyes were swimming with earnest.

"You're supposed to be walking."

"I am walking."

"Teresa, unless you're planning on running backwards when the time comes, you had better turn around."

"So, tell me already."

"Just before I came here to America, I ended … he ended … he left me. I came here." It was the best she could do.

Teresa turned around and fell in beside Irish. "Ah, big stupid bastard." She reached up and smoothed a lock of Irish's hair away from her face. "You're beautiful!" she cried. "Beautiful blonde hair, big blue eyes, nice big boobs." Teresa illustrated by cupping her own breasts, pushing them up then jiggling them up and down. "You forget about him. You don't want no Brit, anyway – too cold those bastards. No good for real women like us."

"I'm not British," Irish told her, "I'm Australian."

"Then how come you got mixed up with …" Teresa paused, contemplated the ground at her feet for a moment, wet her lips then continued. "I mean, how come you're called Irish then?"

"It's a long and ugly story. You're better off not hearing it." Irish couldn't help noticing how quiet and attentive the rear ranks were, or how closely they kept up.

Irish turned a corner, leading them into a street with a short but utterly ferocious hill she felt sure would put an end to the conversation. They would need every bit of breath they had for this monster. Once again, she had miscalculated.

Teresa tapped her on the arm. "Seriously. Your ideal man. Tell me. Maybe we help you find him."

"I honestly don't know, Teresa."

"Maybe you'd like a nice Italian boy for a change?"

"You mean like the ones we married?" Isabella said from behind.

Irish took a swig of water from the bottle in her right hand.

"Maybe not so good in one way," Teresa shrugged, "but then again–" She turned front on to Irish, slapped her hands either side of her crotch and thrust her pelvis forward, "very good here, si?"

Irish sprayed water on everything within a two foot radius.

"Very well built, the Italian men," Teresa said. "It's true."

There was a muffled giggling behind them. Eve had covered her face with her hand. While there was no mistaking the affection in Teresa's eyes, it didn't stop her cuffing Eve behind the ear.

"You think I don't like sex just because I'm older than you? I like sex. I like sex plenty!"

Irish turned an appealing gaze to Isabella, but she wasn't about to help her out.

"Yes, I like sex plenty," Teresa sighed again, turning around. "Hey, Bella?"

"Yes, honey?"

"I'm thinking… for Miss Irish… maybe Mister Ciccone's boy from the deli on South Street?"

"Alfredo? He's a little young, no? No offence, Irish."

"None taken."

Teresa shrugged and held up her hands. "These are modern times. Things are different for the young women now. And Alfredo, at least he's not mobbed up and he knows good food. Young man, good strong swimmers. Get you knocked up before you can say, *hey, where's my panties?*"

The sun fell through a gap in the trees, warming Irish's face. She closed her eyes for a moment. Maybe she should be aiming for more walking and less talking, then again, she reasoned, it was harder to walk and talk than walk and not talk, so maybe the talking added to their training. Besides, she enjoyed listening to them.

Irish took them along one of her favourite training routes. It was hilly and hard going, but it was also sweeping and beautiful, with wide, curving tree-lined streets and millionaire's mansions set back from the road on large properties.

They finished their six mile walk in an hour and three quarters – not bad for undernourished and unfit souls.

It was too early to eat cakes, but not too early to look at them.

Accustomed to being alone, Irish didn't think twice about stopping short at the window of Cicero's. She caused a three-person pile-up behind her.

"Hey, Teresa, how do they get that orange flavour in the cannoli without–"

The atmosphere changed so abruptly, charging up with the crackling electricity of an impending storm, that on instinct Irish almost drew her gun before she had even turned to see what was going on. Three large shadows blocked the sun.

Irish whirled around – *one, two three, count 'em and count them quick* – three faces from the family portrait tacked to her living room wall. *Draw? Show them you're carrying?*

Stepping in front of the women, Irish fronted the men. "Looks like it's been raining fat bastards."

"Your friend's got a mouth, Isabella."

Her friend's got a fucking gun, fatso. Push her buttons and watch her draw. Irish's right hand itched. She forced herself to smile.

Something crinkled. Irish smelled sugar, cream, almonds and vanilla. *Okay, breathe, but don't let them see it. Maybe they're just here to buy cakes.*

The man Teresa had described as a real head case, Cino Malatesta, spoke.

"Isabella. Teresa." He nodded at the women in turn.

The other two – Benito Recchio and Vittori Pavone – gave Irish two double barrels of cool disdain and followed Malatesta to the car parked at the kerb.

Irish felt the women trembling behind her. Little Eve mooched up close enough for Irish to feel her body heat. Irish willed their flighty legs not to run as she knew they were screaming to do.

"Oh no you don't, ladies," Irish breathed. "Nice and casually, we're going to watch these fine gentlemen get into their car, like we're seeing off old friends without a worry in the world." Someone came to stand beside her. Without looking, Irish knew it was Isabella. "And then we're going to turn around and go back to our leisurely inspection of the sumptuous cakes in this window." This, Irish said, even as she broke into a blinding sweat herself. "And now that our friends have gone, and we've finished looking at the nice cakes, let's saunter back to our apartment like the fearless women we are."

It was too much to ask.

Eve tried her damnedest, but her legs jerked pitifully. She broke.

When Eve ran, the other two buckled. Irish watched them bolt, eating up the pavement in front of her. Eve looked back over her shoulder but Teresa and Isabella never did once. That their entire attention was focussed on Eve in front of them gifted Irish with valuable insight: *They weren't running from the men; they were running to Eve.*

Irish let them go, not trying to catch them, not quickening her pace at all. This would be her chance to dissuade them. Now that they had experienced the terror of a confrontation, maybe Irish could persuade them to call the whack off and just quietly slip away to another country.

When she mounted the stairs to her apartment, they were already inside and had left the door ajar for her.

Irish pushed it open and stepped inside.

Eve had collapsed onto the telephone table seat, her legs jerking uncontrollably. Bent forward, Teresa and Isabella stood either side of her, palms on their thighs. All of them were rasping painfully.

"I'm sorry," Eve gasped.

"Not your fault," said Irish. "Isabella, what do suppose your former associates were about?"

"I think they were just buying cakes."

"Me too," added Teresa.

"I think you might be right."

When Irish, wrapped in a towel, came back from the shower to let them know it was free, she would regret having left them alone.

"We've been talking."

Already she had learned to hate those words. Irish waited.

"We want to start carrying our guns." *And there it was.*

"I see."

"Maybe we don't know how to shoot, but we stand a better chance with them than we do without them."

She had hoped to stop them going anywhere near the point of no return; now they were careening straight past it. Whether Irish liked it or not, it was time for the firing range.

Maybe the margaritas weren't such a hot idea given they would be hitting the firing range tomorrow. Then again, that they were hitting the firing range tomorrow was what made margaritas so very appealing.

Irish had cooked a Mexican banquet, from home-made, and labour intensive sauces, taken from the freezer.

Teresa regarded them with an ever so slightly raised eyebrow. "From the freezer," she said loftily. "Very convenient." Teresa was in what Irish had come to think of as her Sophia Loren mode. It was a mild form of gracious petulance.

For once, Irish wasn't hungry. The earlier conversation about her ex, and the prospect of tomorrow, had stolen her appetite. Even the sight of her guests enjoying her food couldn't pique her hunger. She pushed her plate aside in favour of her margarita.

The ice tinkled prettily in the margarita jug as she carried it into the living room. Irish lay on a sofa, legs dangling over the end, her glass propped on her chest, held by two fingers on the stem.

Noise drifted up from the street. A man and a woman. Irish stared at the window, wondering what they were arguing about. Whatever it was, the woman's wound was fresh and raw. She knew the tone all too well, having heard it often in her own voice.

"Do you know what I think men don't know about women?" Irish began, drawing a burst of laughter from Isabella and Teresa.

"It's easier to count what they do know than to count what they don't."

"They know as much as they care to, or as little."

Irish sat up and took a sip of her drink. Salt mingled with lime in her mouth. "I think men don't know how frightened we are."

"What are you frightened of, honey? You scared of being an old maid? Let Teresa fix for you."

Irish ignored her, struggling to find words. "I don't think they understand how frightening it is for us to love them the way we do, how frightened we are that they don't know just how much we love them." She looked at the floor. "I don't think they understand what it costs a woman to love a man. I don't think it costs them the same to love a woman. Why do they always take more than we have to give?"

Isabella pressed a finger to her lips and shook her head. Irish looked over at Eve. The sweets bowl had her undivided attention.

They fell into silence. Irish turned her glass to get to a bit of salt and sipped, regarding the floor while she rocked on the edge of the sofa.

Out of the blue Eve said, "They think we should toot sunshine. Like they pee rainbows."

When they all burst out laughing, Eve looked well pleased with herself, and as she looked at Eve, delight illuminated Teresa's face.

Irish had a sudden, powerful sense of impending loss.

She stared at her drink then put her glass aside.

She must be getting maudlin. It was time for bed.

Chapter Twenty-Seven

In the book of Michael O'Farrell, owner of the firing range, the world held two kinds of people: friends of Irish, and other. Any friend of hers was good people – a philosophy which rested heavily on the fact that he was more than half-crazy in love with her.

If it cost Mike an obvious effort of will not to do a double take when he clapped eyes on the two infamous mob wives, he made them no less welcome for it.

Irish crossed her arms against her chest, planted her feet apart and stood back, watching as Teresa, Isabella and Eve took in their surroundings, hoping against hope that they might show a flicker of fear or reluctance.

They turned three sixty degrees, nodding at the target silhouettes.

"I thought they'd be round targets," said Isabella, "with circles."

"Those are only good if you want to learn how to shoot a dartboard dead."

Forced laughter. Irish was very tempted to wipe the smile from Isabella's face. Isabella's gaze was steely. Irish sent it right back at her.

Mike turned to Isabella. "First you need to learn how to draw."

"Miss Irish already taught us how. Isn't that right, Irish?"

"It is," Irish smiled tightly.

"Okay, Isabella, show me your draw? That's great, although that new leather holster looks stiff. You might like to work on softening that up, or get a nylon one."

Damn you, Mike.

Isabella showed no reaction.

"Cross draw holsters... unusual. What made you choose those?"

"In the event they're needed, I thought they might buy the ladies a little time – precisely two seconds," Irish finished pointedly. Isabella's eyes were fit to strip paint from the walls. Irish's peepers were flamethrowers.

Like any man, Mike would sooner go to war than face angry women. Glancing from one to the other, he wisely declined to ask a follow up question. "Great!" His voice cracked. He cleared his throat while turning Isabella to face the silhouettes.

"Show me your empty check." Isabella did. "Good. We'll do a dry run. Acquire your target, arm fluid and a little bent. Arm straight up, but not straight. Make the gun an extension of your arm. You're a natural. Let's load."

Mike loaded the magazine, clipped it into place, then instructed Isabella to acquire her target again. She raised her Chief's Special to the silhouette. Her hand shuddered. Her aim floundered.

Irish sighed theatrically. *Isabella, Isabella, Isabella, you're not the killer you thought you were.*

Isabella glared at Irish, corrected her aim and shot the target clear through the head.

Ah fuck.

"Fluke!" cried Mike. "Do it again!"

Isabella did.

"Oh, come on! Third time's a charm."

Not only did Isabella hit the bad guy in the head, she was getting closer to smack in the middle of his highly unfortunate skull with every round.

"No way! You're too good, Isabella. Let me show the others."

Teresa stepped up.

"Shoot the bad guy right through his ugly head."

Teresa squinted, squeezed the trigger, lowered the Chief, unsquinted and made circles with her head. "Hey, where'd my bullet go?"

"About six feet to the right," said Mike. "Not to worry. We can't all be natural born killers ... um, I mean, try again, Teresa."

Teresa squeezed off another round.

"Something's wrong with this gun, I think. Where'd it go this time?"

Mike pointed. "You hit his brother, the guy next door."

Irish only knew a few Italian phrases and whatever Teresa said was not among them; regardless, it was the filthiest thing Irish had ever heard.

Mike said, "I'm sure the bastard deserved it, skulking in the shadows like that."

"Damned straight he did," blustered Teresa, sounding more like Eve than herself.

"Teresa, honey?"

"Yes, Bella?"

"Pretend it's a plate of grey? See it and taste it, yes?"

"Grey has no taste, Isabella! You of all people should know this!"

Teresa fired. If the silhouette had been a real man, she would have just blown his head clean off. Then she took out his heart for good measure.

"Whoa! Untapped talent! Teresa, I never doubted you," said Mike. "Okay. Isabella, Teresa, how about you start practising, while I start Eve on her way."

Watching Eve step up to the plate, gun in hand, a big nasty acidic whirlpool began to dissolve Irish's stomach.

Eve squeezed three shots into the heart of her target. Her face lit up like a Christmas tree.

One two fucking three Irish strode forward, broke her gun from its holster, acquired her target and emptied the magazine into her guy's groin. Breathing hard, she discharged the empty clip and reloaded. All eyes were on her.

Mike broke the silence.

"Irish, honey? I can't help but notice that yet again, every one of your shots has ended up in this guy's–"

"Yeah, I know. I really should start wearing my glasses when I shoot."

"You wear glasses?" Mike demanded, aghast.

"No. But I'm supposed to."

Chapter Twenty-Eight

Perhaps their new confidence was born from the surprisingly fair fist they made of their first shooting lesson, or maybe it was because they were now carrying. Teresa and Eve sheared off from the group to go home alone. Teresa wanted to get dinner on while Eve wanted to pick up some finishing touches for tomorrow's cooking project. The only basil they had was a day old, she said. Teresa beamed with pride and Irish couldn't help a lopsided smile. Eve may have been starting from behind, but she was gaining fast.

After they left, Irish glanced up at Mike in his office. His head was bowed over paperwork.

Isabella unloaded another magazine into her target. The guy was dust. "I thought that went well," she said.

Irish popped her guy in the groin again. "Brilliantly," she muttered.

Isabella laid her gun aside and whirled around to face Irish, hands on hips. "Something you'd like to say to me, Irish?"

Irish squeezed off another shot, tempted to ignore her. *On second thoughts, let's do this Queen Isabella.* Irish laid her gun aside too.

"Seeing as you ask, Isabella, yes there is."

"Shoot." Isabella's eyes were as cold as ice. That only added fuel to Irish's flames.

144

"I really can't help but wonder if you've put any thought into this little war of yours."

"This war of mine?"

"Well isn't it?"

"And what might you know about it, Miss Irish?"

"Nothing, seeing as you're not prepared to tell me anything. But I think plenty about it, and what I think is that you've got no damned right to be leading your friends into your vendetta."

"I am not leading anyone into anything." Isabella's voice had dived an octave. Irish's got higher, or at least louder.

"Oh come on, Isabella. Don't you dare tell me these women – well, more accurately *woman,* because the other one is still a child–"

"The hell she is."

"The hell she isn't. Don't kid yourself on that score, sister. She's more interested in lollies than she is in guns, and maybe if you left her to it, she might just find herself a life that doesn't involve blood on her hands and every good chance of getting clipped."

"You don't know what you're talking about."

"Maybe you don't know how selfish you are." Irish was getting hoarse. "What about Teresa? She's supposed to be your friend. On a good day she can barely keep it together, and you're talking about sending her to war."

"Maybe that war, as you call it, is the only thing stopping Teresa from opening her wrists."

"That doesn't excuse what you're doing to Eve, Isabella. She's just a child." Irish said again, and once again Isabella said, no she wasn't, that it had been a very long time since Eve had been a child, and if Irish was so sure that Eve and Teresa wanted rescuing from Isabella's war then maybe she would like to shut the fuck up and listen to their story.

Irish closed her mouth, stuck her hand on her hip and listened.

The subject of their discussion was at that moment waiting to cross at the lights, looking down as she scuffed the toe of her shoe on the ground, twisting her leg around like a diffident ballerina. Eve thought of the money Irish had spent on the shoes and almost dropped the grocery sack to clean off the scuff mark. She spit on her thumb and rubbed it over the leather. When the spit dried, the scuff mark came back. Eve resolved to clean it with proper polish soon as she got home, before Irish had a chance to see it.

When the walk signal came on, Eve scooped up her bag of shopping and scurried across the road. It was a lot darker ahead. There seemed to be fewer streetlights. Maybe they had been broken by kids, like they always were in her old neighbourhood. Those lights had been permanently broken. Once, someone kicked up a fuss because a girl had been dragged into a car right outside her apartment building and no one had seen it happen because it was so dark. They complained until the city came and fixed the lights.

Then no one in the street could sleep. The people were so used to the lights being broken, they couldn't handle it when they were working.

It went on for three nights. For three mornings, miserable sleep-deprived men and women trudged off to earn their minimum wages – at least those fortunate enough to be earning that much did – and those who earned less trudged off just as miserably and just the same.

On the fourth night, when the stones started pinging off the glass, Eve's daddy got out of bed, went downstairs in his shorts and showed them how to do it properly. When all the lights were extinguished, a cheer went up.

Now, at the sight of the menacing shadows looming ahead, Eve hesitated, hugging her paper sack to her chest.

The streets sure were empty.

A car cruised by, illuminating the shadows with its headlights. *Trees, they were only trees.*

Only. Trees.

Eve reluctantly edged into the darkness. The car turned left, brake lights reflecting red on tree bark as it departed.

Had she spent more time in the company of women, Eve would have known that her feeling was called woman's intuition.

She got a hurry on, lengthening her stride.

Maybe she had dawdled a little on the way home because she wanted time to think. Truth was, Eve had an awful lot to think about, even if she couldn't exactly frame the questions she needed to answer.

All she knew was a little while ago, things were very simple.

Now, things were not so simple.

Eve hugged the paper sack to her chest, mindful of the little pot of basil, and thought about the other goodies in there. She had been very strict with herself about not spending a dime of

Irish's money unless it was absolutely necessary. Tonight, she had made her first exception – a bag of chocolate sprinkles to decorate the tiramisu with. They only cost eighty-nine cents, but it was eighty-nine cents of luxury. It was a decision she agonised over, torn between her respect for Irish and the prospect of pleasing Teresa, before she reasoned that Irish would enjoy dessert all the more for having them.

Eve turned to reassure herself that the first shadow was just as a tree, as the headlights had revealed, then resolved not to look again. It was better to think about the things she needed to think about.

Camaraderie was not a word Eve knew, but she knew what it was: that glowing feeling in your chest that made you sleep well and happy at night and made you want to wake up in the morning. And therein lay the heart of Eve's problem.

A little while ago, while she was still in the pen with no prospects when she got out and nothing to look forward to – save the sweet relief of doing junk again at the first available opportunity – life had at least been simple. Then along came the opportunity to do the mother who killed her daddy and for the first time since his death, she had had something to look forward to other than junk.

But that's when things got complicated. Something had come her way that was even better than the idea of avenging her father: the women. Sometimes when they all laughed together or did kind things for each other, Eve wanted to plead with them to call the whack plane off. Eve loved being with the women so much that she wanted to stay with them forever, and not do anything, anything at all, that might put them or their good thing in danger.

Sometimes she didn't speak for the sheer pleasure of listening to them talk.

Eve had something with the women she had never had before, not even with Desiree, who had been her dearest friend in the world. Friendship in the pen was one thing, but this thing she didn't know the name for, this was something else. It made you take the most beautiful scarf out of all the beautiful scarves someone had given you and give it back. You could wrap it around their neck and kiss them on the cheek without being afraid they would laugh at you, and they would accept that beautiful scarf like it was something you bought for them instead of something they had bought for you with their own money.

That had been the first gift Eve had ever given anyone. Before that, she had never had anything to give.

Then there were all the gifts they gave her, the sort which had nothing to do with money or presents. They trusted her, gave Eve her own keys to the apartment. They cared whether she had enough to eat and whether she liked what she ate. They knew what her favourite cakes were and brought them home along with their own favourites. Most of all, they saw in her something no one, besides her father, had seen in her before: a future.

Teresa and Isabella showed her how to cook, how to taste food, and how to make food taste. With every step she took, with everything she learned, they told her what she could be, the person she could become if she wanted to. She could be a great chef. She was young and beautiful, they said, with the world at her feet. She could take Paris by storm. When Eve told them that sort of thing didn't happen to people like her, coming from where she came, they replied, "Then you will be the first."

Then there was Irish. In quiet moments, at the times when Teresa wasn't so well and Isabella took her to the bedroom to wait it out, Irish came to her whispering fine things, things that dreams were made of. She was young, with her whole life ahead of her. Would she perhaps like to go to college? What might she like to study?

Most of all, what the women gave her was their time.

Which took her straight back to the only other person to have had that sort of time for her – her daddy. He had worked like a dog but he always found time for her.

Her father stuck around to care for her long after her mother left. He made sure she had clothes. Eve had the luxury of tights in winter, of polished shoes even if the soles were worn. Leroy buffed them until they shone and every Monday morning when she set off for school, Eve looked down and smiled.

Her father taught her that they were better than their circumstances.

An educated man with a genius I.Q., Leroy worked in the public school system because he wanted to make a difference. He was more saint than sinner but he also refused to be a victim. Leroy wasn't above playing a system stacked against him, if it meant keeping a roof over their heads and food on the table.

For the most part, Leroy earned their way honestly. To make ends meet, he did a few little things on the side. Nothing too serious, but sometimes things happened at home Eve knew better than to tell anyone about. She might come home from school to find boxes in the living room, stacked almost to the ceiling, and in the dead of night, when she should have been sleeping, hear rustling noises which meant in the morning, the boxes would be gone.

That's how Leroy had met Teresa's son: dealing in boxes.

Eve had taken an instant liking to Gabriel for two reasons. One, when he spoke to her, he always ducked down to her level. Two, he asked her how she was. Boys of his age didn't ask girls of her age how they were. He listened and he cared. And when he wasn't doing any of those things, he teased her mercilessly and she teased him right back.

Gabriel was killed in the street, Leroy in their home. Eve had been there but she couldn't remember it. The memory was like that frosted glass they put in windows for privacy, the type that let in light but you couldn't see through. When Eve tried to remember seeing her father killed, she could see movement and colour behind the glass, but nothing more distinct.

Sometimes she thought that was a shame because she wanted to see his face again, but Leroy lived behind the glass, obscured from view.

Eve realised she had come to a standstill. She started walking again.

If she could have a real future like the others talked about, maybe she wouldn't need junk again. Maybe she could bear for her daddy to see her again and maybe she could see him too.

Elroy deserved to be avenged but would he want her to avenge him? Or would he want Eve to be better than her circumstances?

Eve was too preoccupied with her own thoughts to notice when a shadow separated from a tree. "Hey."

Eve jumped and picked up the pace.

"Hey! I'm talking to you." A man stepped into the thin yellow light surrounding her.

"How ya doing?" She had seen that smile a hundred times on the street. It wasn't about anything happy and it always ended badly.

She tried to keep walking. He cut her off.

"Don't you remember me, baby?"

Too late, she realised he was one of the men from the family portrait tacked to the living room wall.

It didn't occur to Eve to scream. People like her didn't scream. People like her endured.

Eve held the paper sack closer to her chest, ducked around him and picked up her pace. An alley lay up ahead. Part of her mind realised the danger but it was shouted down by the urge to move forward. Forward meant *home* and *safe*. Forward meant the women.

"Don't you walk away from me, whore." Her head was yanked back. Her mouth peeled open in a rictus of pain as he wound her hair around his hand and forced her into the alley. The grocery sack crackled loudly as she clutched it tighter.

"You really don't remember me, do you?"

Terrified, she shook her head wildly. He pulled her hair tighter.

She shook her head hopelessly, already knowing how this would play out.

He pushed his face into hers. Whiskey fumes wafted over her face. "Well maybe I should remind you."

Eve's terror released her bladder. A hot stream burst down her legs.

Swearing, he jerked his foot back, disgust darkening his eyes.

They came to her then: threes words Eve had long forgotten and thought never to have use for again. "Please, mister – don't."

Irish hung her head. The world suddenly seemed a much darker place.

"So, the man who killed Eve's father…"

"Yes."

Irish said it anyway. "…killed Teresa's son."

Isabella nodded.

"And that man was Teresa's lover?"

"Yes."

Irish glanced at the silhouette on her right and rocked on her heels for a while.

"How did Eve survive?"

Isabella answered Irish in the same way Eve had answered her. "How do you think she survived?"

Irish clenched her jaw. Her eyes kept finding their way back to that silhouette.

"Let me guess. Would this man's name be Carlo Scatera?"

Isabella inclined her head.

Irish seized her gun and emptied the magazine into the target. Every round was a headshot.

"Let's go home," she said.

Chapter Twenty-Nine

They paused on the stairs.

"Did you hear that?" Irish asked Isabella.

"What?"

"I thought I heard a woman scream."

They listened.

"I must have imagined it."

Ears straining, Irish turned the key and pushed the door open. It hit a paper grocery sack on the floor. Beside it lay a pair of torn panties and a pile of bloodied clothes. Irish drew her gun.

Isabella drew five seconds behind her.

From the bathroom came the sound of a woman's low groan.

Silently, Irish and Isabella rushed forward. Guns in hand, they filled the bathroom doorway.

Eve took one look at the guns and screamed. She was in the bath, her knees drawn tightly to her chest. Teresa knelt on the floor beside the bath.

Isabella and Irish holstered their Chief's.

"What happened?"

Water splashed as Teresa sponged Eve's back. "Sergio Virrini cornered her on the way home. He tried to rape her."

"Tried?"

Teresa turned large, solemn eyes to Irish. "She stopped him."

"Whose blood is on Eve's clothes?"

A heartbeat's silence.

"His."

Irish crouched down beside the old, claw-footed bathtub. Eve stared into space.

"Eve, can you tell me what happened?"

"I scuffed my shoe!"

"That's okay baby. Eve, was he alone?"

Eve nodded, screwing up her eyes. Irish turned to Isabella. "What would the chances be of him telling his friends where he was going and what he was going to do?"

"I don't know."

"Where did this happen? Was it nearby?"

Shuddering, Eve nodded again.

As if on cue, sirens rent the night. With a thundering heart, Irish cocked her head to listen. The sirens went past, faded into the distance then stopped. "Police," Irish said to Isabella. "Not paramedics. If his friends found him, would they call the police?"

"Not a chance."

"So, maybe that tells us someone else found him, someone who wasn't looking for him, just a passer-by."

"They're still gonna hear about it, Irish."

"I know, Teresa. I'm trying to work out what they're going to make of it."

Isabella said, "What does that matter? This tells us they're already coming after us. They attacked Eve because she's with us."

Eve shook her head. "No. He said he knew me from before."

"You mean, from the street?

"So he said. I didn't remember him."

Irish stood up, running her hand over her hair. "I ... are you saying this is just a co-incidence–"

"I don't know!" Eve shouted.

"That's enough Irish," Isabella said. "She's been through enough. Leave her in peace."

Irish ignored her. "Eve, do you think you left anything behind?"

Eve shook her head. "I checked twice. I didn't leave anything. Not even my panties."

Eve sounded so much like a little girl, faltering on the word *panties,* Irish thought her heart would surely break.

"We're just going to have to tough it out, see if they come."

Eve raised her solemn brown eyes. "I shouldn't have come back here."

Isabella joined Teresa kneeling beside the bath. "Don't you dare say that, Eve. The three of us are in this together."

Irish flinched then told herself to suck it up. There was work to be done in the living room.

Scooping the grocery sack from the floor, she inspected its contents: a much worse-for-wear potted basil, a Chief's Special and a blood-spattered packet of chocolate sprinkles. Irish lifted the packet out and held it in her fingers.

Eve's voice carried from the bathroom. "Where does this leave us, Isabella?"

Irish stared at the bloodied chocolate sprinkles, hoping against hope the women would go to the cops and plead self-defence, but knowing the truth in her heart: *It leaves you, ladies, with one fat bastard down and twelve to go.*

Chapter Thirty

There was a body of water just begging to swallow that grocery sack.

Irish rummaged around in the early morning dark for the first tee shirt and sweats she could lay her hands on. After last night, she figured the others could do with their rest.

On an empty stomach, she clicked the apartment door closed quietly and went out to pound the pavement like the angry woman she was.

What sort of a world made thirteen-year-old girls sell their bodies to survive? What sort of a world made twenty-year-old girls go through what Eve had gone through last night? And who the hell made the world that way?

A solitary early morning driver made the mistake of failing to give way. Irish rounded on him so ferociously – bobbing her head to let him know she was reading his number plate and running straight at the car – that he slammed on the brakes and gestured for her to cross.

She pounded away until she left the pavement for the river bank. Irish slowed to a walk. It was too early for other runners and there was no running track here anyway. She pushed through the trees, holding their wet branches back to gain access to the river.

Slipping the backpack from her shoulder, Irish loaded it with a couple of good sized rocks, hurled it into the river and watched it sink, the nylon straps streaming through the water like a parachute.

The tree branches yielded as she brushed them aside again, walking along the river bank and daring the big bad nasty world to send a mugger or rapist or anything in between her way for Irish to make short order of. Maybe the world was too afraid of her in her current mood, but no one materialised.

Irish took off at a punishing pace, belting it out for an hour. Opening up for a final blast, Irish turned into the road she had led the others along – millionaire's row, as she thought of it. As she pelted down her favourite, steep, tree lined street, a black car sailed past her, gliding around the next corner and out of sight. Something told Irish it hadn't kept going once it turned the corner.

Her endorphins shook hands with incoming adrenalin, then cleared off.

Irish slowed.

And Irish unzipped her jacket.

She was fifty feet from the corner when Teodore Saracini and Cino Malatesta stepped into her path. Irish set her expression to neutral, save a vague smile, and kept running toward them.

Running.

Running.

Running.

Saracini and Malatesta each folded one hand over the other in front of them. Irish's racing mind helpfully pointed out to her that it was the same posture they had adopted at the funeral where the A3 portrait had been taken, that it was, in fact, their habitual posture. At least at funerals.

Teodore Saracini nodded cordially at her. "Good morning, Miss Irish."

So you know my name. Who have you been talking to?

Irish gave him a bright, unsurprised smile and nodded back. She had to hand it to him – the guy had presence, and he was a snappy dresser.

"Good morning, Teodore." *Swings both ways, prick.* She turned to Malatesta. "Cino, Cino, Cino, we really should stop meeting like this."

"What, you think I got a hard on for *you*?"

"I think if you did, you'd never see it over that fat gut."

Irish caught the movement out of the corner of her eye: Saracini's smile before he smothered it.

Malatesta retaliated by copping an eyeful of her breasts. Irish decided to let him know how unfazed she was. She looked down as if to say, *What, these old things?* and realised that as luck would have it, she had pulled her *No Fat Dicks* tee shirt out of the drawer this morning.

"Heh heh heh, you're a very funny lady."

"Heh heh heh, you're a very fat bastard."

Cino's right arm jumped. Irish gave him a flamethrower of a smile. "If you'll excuse me, gentleman, now that we've exchanged pleasantries, I'll be on my way."

Saracini stepped forward. "If I could trouble you for a little of your time, Miss Irish. Mister Albrici would like to see you."

"Good God! You're not going to take me for the proverbial little ride, are you?"

Saracini shifted his feet comfortably. "Mister Albrici wishes only to know of your interest in his wife. He simply requests the pleasure of your company."

"Well then, he'll have to send a proper written invitation for me to R.S.V.P. to. Where I come from, boys ask girls for their own dates. They certainly don't send their boyfriends to do it for them."

Saracini's face darkened, but his voice was well-modulated. "Let's not have any unpleasantness."

Malatesta brushed his lapel aside to expose his piece. Irish smiled coldly and flipped her jacket open. *Fucking snap.*

"Let me tell you something, Cino: you do not want to get into a shootout with me when I'm not wearing my glasses. If the good Don wants to talk to me, he knows where to find me. Now, if you'll excuse me, I have an appointment with a bakery that just can't wait." She cast a lingering gaze on Malatesta's paunch. "Some of us can hold our sugar."

Irish started to skirt around them but they stood back to let her pass. Her slow run was made difficult by her held breath, waiting, as she was, for a bullet between the shoulders that didn't come.

This time.

Chapter Thirty-One

That evening, The Whack Club convened an emergency meeting.

"I'll see you and I'll raise you."

Jesus, I'd kill for a cigarette. Irish dared not voice it. Considering what Eve had been through last night, it was better not to tempt her with thoughts of her own.

Teresa reminded Irish it was her go.

"Sorry." Irish needed a cigarette as badly as she had ever needed anything in her life. She picked up a pen and put it to her lips. Pulling it away, she drew a breath and pretended it was something better, something that carried a belt of nicotine.

"He didn't want to kill you," Isabella offered conversationally. "If he did, you'd be dead by now."

How reassuring. "So today was about … ?"

"Curiosity," Isabella shrugged. "Maybe it would be better if we went out together from now on."

"No," said Eve. "That's no way to live a life – being afraid all the time – and we shouldn't let them know we're afraid."

"Besides, this way, they take one of us out, some of us still stand. And those some of us kill the sum of them. I still say we whack 'em all in one day." Thus, Teresa tabled her cap plan for board approval, before pleasantly reminding Irish again it was her go.

Irish inspected her hand and folded. "I'm out. You know, about that Teresa? How would you get them all in one place at the one time?"

"Oh, that's simple." She shot Isabella a glance. "Strip club."

"Whore house," supplied Isabella.

"Charming," rejoined Irish. "They're real class acts, these blokes of yours." Irish gave it a moment's thought. "Witnesses. Potential casualties – of the innocent kind, I mean," she added as an afterthought.

Isabella glanced over her hand. "So, we don't do them in one sitting."

"But we do them in one day," insisted Teresa.

"To avoid blowback," contributed Eve.

Irish sighed. Any minute now she would roll the linen tablecloth into a giant stogey and smoke it.

"Maybe, before we make the whack plan, we should work on the escape plan. Maybe having a proper escape plan will help us formulate the whack plan." There. That was almost as good as a drag. Oh, the hell it was. "Teresa, Isabella, you got passports?"

"Si."

"Sure."

Irish slid the splayed cards toward her for a shuffle. "How about you, Eve?"

When she didn't answer, they all looked at her. Her eyes were full moons; at their depths were lakes. "Why can't we stay together? Why do we have to break up?"

The three older women started to get to their feet then sat down again.

"Honey, we won't be breaking up," said Isabella. "We'll just need to go separate ways for a little while."

"To avoid that blowback you talked about," said Teresa.

"Or, as we say at home: payback is a bastard. Do you have a passport, Eve?"

She shook her head. "Uh-uh."

"See, ladies, this is what I mean about the importance of a plan. I believe our young friend Eve is not entitled to hold a passport. So how do we get her one?"

"I know some people," offered Eve.

"And if you go to those people and you get caught, then you go back to jail, right?"

"No other way."

"Yes, there is. You tell me who they are and where they are–"

"Won't talk to you if they don't know you."

"–and you introduce me to them as a friend then be quiet as a mouse. I'll get you a passport, or if not, at least I won't go to jail for a first offence. Capice?"

"Eh, Godmother?"

"Si, Teresa?"

"You very funny lady. Where you going, funny lady, when the fun's all done? Back home to Australia?"

"No, there's nothing left for me there." Irish gave it some thought. "Maybe I could finally go to Ireland. I've always wanted to."

Isabella's brow furrowed. "You mean you've never been?"

"No."

"But why... Why are you called Irish, then?" Teresa enquired diplomatically.

"It's a long story."

"So, tell us, we've got all night."

It took a few moments for Irish to realise she had been asked a question. "Sorry. I'm just a bit distracted because I'm waiting to hear from my agent."

"Your agent? Like, your handler or something?"

Irish tore her gaze from the clock to look at Isabella. "No, like my agent. I finished a book just before I got bus–" Irish started to say *bushwhacked* but caught it. "...busy with you. My agent it put it up for auction. The bidding was supposed to start this afternoon."

"So, you're a writer?" asked Isabella.

Irish glanced at the clock again. "Yes. Not that I really need it, but I've got a feeling this book could be big."

"So, you write as well as... the other?" persisted Isabella.

"The other what?"

"You know... the other thing you do." Slowly, Isabella and Teresa got to their feet.

"What other thing? I don't do anything else. Only write."

"You mean you're not I.R.A.?"

"You mean you're not Catholic?"

"You mean you're not black? What are you two talking about?"

"I.R.A.! Why would you say such a thing?" said Irish.

"Because you distinctly led me to believe it."

Eve got to her feet too. "Whoa, ladies. Maybe you were thinking that about Irish because of where you come from. Know what I'm saying? I never thought she was I.R.A."

"Well maybe that's because you've never seen her hope chest, Eve. What are you doing with so many weapons?"

Eve came to stand beside Irish. Irish shifted her weight. "They make me feel better," she muttered.

Isabella stared at her. "They what now? Why would one woman need such an arsenal?"

"When I came to America I landed in New York," Irish said, as though that explained everything.

They waited.

"Do you know what a reputation New York has? I was vulnerable–"

"Vulnerable? With that cache, the closest you'll come to vulnerable is fucking invincible."

"Chris had just dumped me. I get here – no sooner do I get off the plane than I'm mugged."

"That explains one gun, Irish!"

"Then on the way back from the police station where I reported it, I was mugged again!"

"Two guns! That explains two guns, Irish!"

Eve spread her hands. "She already told you – they make her feel better. Some people collect teddy bears."

Silence. Very uncomfortable silence.

Hand on hip, Isabella was doing that Italian bouncing on the foot thing which Irish knew to mean *incoming*.

"Wait a minute, what do you write?"

"Novels."

"What sort of novels? Name one."

"I'd rather not say."

"I'd rather you did."

"You wouldn't know my books. I write under a pen name."

"Which is?"

"Madonn'. How many names you got?"

"I don't usually disclose my pen name, except to those who really need to know."

"We really need to know." Isabella rubbed her fingers against her thumb. "Let's hear it.

"You wouldn't have heard of me."

"Try me."

Irish lifted her chin. "Imogen Devereaux."

Three heads bowed while three brains puzzled over the name. Isabella was the first to raise her face.

"Hey, I know that ..." began Teresa, understanding dawning in her eyes like a sudden sun.

"What?" demanded Eve, looking from one to the other.

"You're a ...." Isabella couldn't bring herself to say it. "No!"

"What? What?" said Eve. "Someone tell me."

"Please tell me that we're not being trained for a mob war by a fucking romance novelist!"

Irish blushed then immediately rallied. "Hey! I can shoot!"

"Yeah, through the dick."

"Isabella, what man's going to return fire when his dick's just been shot off? You're splitting hairs, girl."

Isabella ignored Eve in favour of giving her full attention to glaring at Irish. It was unbearable.

Irish looked down, giving her shoes a mental shoe shine. The silence was thick enough to choke on. She looked up again. Their expressions hadn't changed. With nowhere left to go, Irish went native.

Waving her hands, she exclaimed, "Madonn!"

With two lengthy strides Teresa crossed the space between them to deliver a resounding whack to the back of Irish's head.

"You Italian?"

"OW! No–"

Whack!

"Catholic maybe?"

Whack!

"Shit! Ow! No!"

Whack! Whack! Whack!

A stream of Italian invective poured from Teresa.

"Hey! I thought you didn't speak Italian!"

"I do today!"

Whack!

"JESUS!"

Her open hand suspended mid-air, Teresa's eyes widened then narrowed to that look she reserved for bad cooks, or worse – cooks who didn't use salt.

When Eve put herself in the firing line, Irish was not too proud to take shelter behind the young woman's back.

"Just wait a minute here! Are we forgetting this fine lady took us in? Are we forgetting every fine thing our friend Irish has done for us?"

Isabella locked two withering barrels onto Irish's face. "Why the hell did you?"

"Because I didn't want to see you hurt!"

Teresa stood shoulder to shoulder with Isabella. "Nobody does such a big thing as this for such a small reason as that."

Irish stepped out from behind Eve and fronted the mob women. She stood at Eve's shoulder, as Teresa stood to Isabella's.

"Maybe not where you come from."

Isabella flinched. Teresa blanched. Irish smiled, letting the statement hang. *Time to press the big button.* Irish looked meaningfully at Eve. "But some of us care more for others than that."

There was a distinct tightening of jaws from the women of La Casa Nostra.

Eve slung an arm over Irish's shoulder. "Come on, Irish. There's a couple of nice big soft cosy beds with our names on them – thanks to you, sister."

In the night that followed Irish tossed and turned, and every time the back of her bruised head met with the pillow, she wondered yet again just how the hell her cannoli lust had led to this.

Irish had ducked their questions because the truth, too raw and too awful to be admitted, most of all to herself, was closer to home, and it had nothing to do with cannoli: for all her fabulous wealth, her fabulous apartment, her fabulous career, her beauty and fame, Irish was the loneliest, most vulnerable woman on the planet.

Irish was, in fact, so lonely and terrified by the world at large, that she may well have been scared of her own shadow, had she not been so grateful for its company.

Chapter Thirty-Two

The next morning, Irish went for an early run alone. When she returned home, lined up in a neat row on the kitchen pass-through were three Chief's Specials, aligned dead centre, at perfectly spaced intervals, all pointing in the same direction and all polished to a spiffing finish.

Organised crime had just taken on a whole new meaning.

"How come the pasta's not dead?" This, from Irish.

"How do you mean, *dead*?"

From the guns lined up in the pass-through, Irish had correctly deduced the women wished to go to target practise.

"Well, dry, I suppose. Something other than al dente. I mean, you cook it, fridge it, bake it–"

"No, no, no," said Isabella. "Listen."

Head. "You sauté your mushroom in a little butter."

Groin. "Uh-huh.

Following last night's revelations, Irish wouldn't have been surprised to find them gone this morning. That they weren't, she suspected was owed to Eve – the most disadvantaged, youngest and the smallest of them all, and in the social structure of their small group, also the most powerful – a fact Irish alone recognised. She intended to keep pushing that button called *Eve* until they called the whack off. A pleasing divide had begun last night, now all that remained was to conquer.

Heart. "Then you make a roux from your butter and flour, add some salt..."

Groin. "Right."

Head. "Add your chicken broth and cream. Keep stirring until it's thick."

Groin. "Okay, like a white sauce."

Chest. "Right... right. Then to your sauce you add your cooked chicken, mushrooms and your sherry. Heat it through. Then put your cooked noodles–" *head, head head,* "...or your spaghetti, whatever you like to use–" *shoulder* "–shit! ... in a buttered casserole, pour on the sauce..."

Groin. "Okay."

By way of compensating Mike O'Farrell for these out-of-hours sessions, they had taken to arriving with enough tin foil covered casserole dishes so that he didn't have to cook for himself all week. When he gained ten pounds inside a month, they cut back on the cheese.

But not the butter.

And certainly not the cream.

Today's delivery included tetrazzini, a dish Irish had never heard of before, but which had her mouth watering from the moment her nose clapped eyes on it. Isabella graciously consented to give her the recipe.

Stomach. "Top with parmesan..."

Groin. "Reggiano?"

Head. "Of course. Sprinkle with a little paprika, then into the oven until it's bubbly."

Groin. "So, you wouldn't prepare it in advance and fridge it?"

Heart. "No no no no." *Head.* "Always straight from the pot to the oven. Then it's okay to reheat it. Capice?"

Groin. "Si. So, there's no garlic in it?"

Smack between the eyes. "No. We don't put garlic in everything, you know."

Groin. "Just asking. No onion either?

Heart. "Nope."

Groin. "Interesting. Thanks, Isabella."

Head. "You're most welcome, Irish."

Now Irish was in her favourite place in the world: with a head full of endorphins, a gun in her hand, her best shooting range song, *Single Ladies* playing in her head while she thought about food. Life didn't get any better.

Teresa and Eve had taken off for home, leaving Isabella and Irish alone.

Groin. Irish plunged. "What about the diamonds, Isabella?"

Heart heart heart head head head then Isabella's shots went wide. Irish put down her gun and faced her. Isabella did the same.

"What about them?" she returned flatly.

"Do you know how they disappeared from evidence?"

"No, I don't."

"Do you know *why* they disappeared from evidence?"

"I don't know that either."

"Have you speculated?"

"At first, I thought maybe Domenic had maybe… found a way to make things right. But I think it's more likely… maybe he just found a way to get his diamonds back. Maybe someone got to them before him. Or maybe, it really was a screw up by the cops." She smiled wryly.

"Have you wondered why your husband did this to you in the first place?"

"Oh, that I know."

Then it happened: Isabella opened up to her.

She told Irish everything. About Domenic and his pet F.B.I. agent, the set-up.

Irish dared do something she would not have dared before: she offered Isabella her shoulder. Isabella fell forward.

Irish stroked Isabella's hair while she cried, knowing what sobs like Isabella's meant: getting it out of your system.

But Isabella hadn't finished. After she had cried that lot out of her, she told Irish about jail, about Bobby Hernandez.

About Desiree.

About Domenic's mistresses and whores. About Domenic trading her in for the mistress who gave him a son, about her crisis of faith and wish to redeem herself. Of these profound admissions, Irish had only one enquiry:

"How much younger than you was this bitch?"

Groin groin groin groin groin groin groingroingroingroingroingroingroin – Irish snatched up her weapon and unloaded the clip.

The call from her agent was cause for celebration.

Dinner out, then a nightclub, said Irish. But first they would shop – her treat – for new dresses.

They walked back to the apartment swinging large, glossy paper bags the likes of which Teresa and Isabella had thought would never mean anything to them again, the likes of which had never meant anything to Irish until now, the likes of which had never slipped over Eve's beautiful long brown fingers.

They took turns in the shower. Those who had finished showering broke out hairdryers, make-up, curling wands, perfume and silk stockings. The women took their time getting ready, wandering from room to room to compliment each other on their purchases and to enjoy watching each other's progress as they made up and did their hair.

Irish mooched around looking at the others laying their nice things out on their beds. "Hey, who'd like a glass of something before we go out?"

Eve shook her head. "Not for me, thanks Irish."

"No, I know, honey – you prefer sweets."

Not tonight she didn't. Eve didn't have eyes for lollies, only the new dress that lay on her bed. The look on the kid's face was priceless.

"How about you ladies?" Irish called, sashaying into Isabella and Teresa's room in her silk robe.

"No. You wait for dinner like a good girl, Irish. Maybe tonight we find you a man. You get laid, you don't need no wine." Teresa fished her dress from the tissue paper. "I still say this is too young for me."

"We've been over that," replied Isabella.

Teresa had to be talked into the dress. "Honestly, Teresa, do you think any of us would let a woman we like be seen in something too young for her?" asked Irish.

Teresa muttered something about jiggly bits.

"Sorry?" said Irish.

"What you get after you have babies, capice?" Teresa stepped into her dress and faced the mirror sternly, hands smoothing the material anxiously over her hips. "Hey, it's not so bad."

The other two exchanged smiles. "See? We told you. You get lots of exercise, you got no jiggly bits, capice?"

Teresa caught her eye in the mirror. "You speaking Italian again, Irish?"

"Uh, no Teres–"

"Good. 'Cause I'd hate to have to smack you in the head tonight, Godmother."

Smiling shyly, Eve came into the bedroom in her new dress. *Oh God – the kid was a knockout.* Isabella gazed at Eve with motherly love in her eyes.

"You're so beautiful!" Isabella bit her bottom lip.

"Let me see!" Teresa whirled around. "Ahhhh!"

Poor Eve's cheeks were squeezed between Teresa's hands while she rained kisses all over her face. Then Isabella took a turn.

Irish started laughing. "Why you laughing, Irish?" Teresa demanded.

"I'm laughing because…" *I'm laughing because I'm in the company of women who can love a girl for being pretty.* "I don't know why I'm laughing."

"Well hurry up and stop it. There's a good time waiting for us to have it. Go get dressed," snapped Teresa, then went back to raining kisses on Eve.

Irish slipped out of her robe and into her dress and shoes. The others waited for her in the hallway.

"Irish, Irish, Irish," Isabella raised her eyebrows. "What would your mother say?"

"She'd say, that's a nice dress you're almost wearing, Irish. Or, Where's the rest of it, Irish? Or, nice handkerchief. Pity you don't have a dress to go with it, Irish."

"Your mother called you Irish?"

"Don't ask."

Eve turned from checking her reflection in the hall mirror. "Hey, look at us. We all chose red dresses."

The others looked down at themselves then at each other.

"I hadn't noticed."

"Me neither."

"We look like some sort of club, maybe," said Teresa.

"A club of what?" This, from Isabella.

"A club of women like us," returned Teresa.

"Then what shall we call ourselves, ladies?"

Eve gave it some thought. Her eyes grew wide. "I know! How about *SICA*?"

"I give up," Irish said.

"Society for The Intention of Cruelty to Animals."

Irish laughed. "We'd need to find a way to turn it into *SIC 'EM*."

Teresa gave her a look that said, *stupid*. "*SIC 'EM* is Italian for *SICA*, obviously," she said, with much emphasis on the *obviously*. "Let's go. There's a good bottle of champagne out there with our names on it, si?"

"Si!" said Irish.

"You speaking Italian again, Irish?"

"No, Teresa."

When they opened the street door, the other three stopped laughing. Irish looked up sharply, her myopic eyes struggling to see what the others had already seen.

Her first impression: *what a fine looking pair of men.*

Domenic Albrici and Dante Alessandri stood eight feet away, hands crossed in front of them in that now familiar undertaker posture.

The men walked forward nice and slowly, almost formally. Irish's heart raced – and it had nothing to do with fear. If she thought Teodore Saracini had presence, he was ether compared to these two.

"Isabella," Domenic Albrici greeted his wife. "I can't say I approve of your hair." He gave her a stern semi-smile.

"I can't say I give a shit."

The Don raised his eyebrows. "Such language. Do you learn this from your new friends?" He took a step closer. His face almost touched Isabella's.

"What do you want, Domenic?"

Irish caught herself staring at Dante Alessandri. He returned the favour. Turning his cool blue eyes to her, his gaze roamed over her nearly there dress, or more accurately, at the considerable amount of flesh it didn't cover. The son-of-a-bitch had the nerve to look like he didn't approve.

"I wished merely to meet your new friends. Won't you introduce me to Miss Irish and–" he nodded in Eve's direction but did not look at her– "the other?"

Isabella gave him a smile hard enough to break rocks on. "My friends are no longer any of your business, Domenic."

"Your welfare is always my business."

Irish was taking in too much detail – their shoes buffed to

a parade gloss shine, the cut of their double-breasted suits, their silk ties. Someone favoured Paco Rabane aftershave, the other, Christian Dior.

Isabella's voice quavered. "I should punch you in the mouth, Domenic."

Dante Alessandri put himself between Isabella and the Don. "Don't be foolish, Isabella."

"And as for you, Dante Alessandri, if I weren't a lady, I would spit on you."

"We live in modern times, Isabella," Teresa offered helpfully.

"Damned straight, 'Bella," rejoined Eve.

For once in her life, Irish didn't have a bit of lip, a hint of sass, a dash of vinegar in her. Teresa reminded Irish of her tongue by way of a short sharp jab to the kidneys but, unable to tear her eyes from Dante Alessandri, Irish could say nothing.

Behind the men, the women's limousine slid up to the kerb. While Isabella and Dante faced off, the Don stood perfectly at his ease behind Dante. Irish only wanted it to be over. It was all she could do not to break, dive around the men and usher the women into the car.

The men stood aside to let them pass.

In the back of the car, Irish looked to Isabella. "You okay?"

"Sure."

When next the subject of escape plans and visas was raised, Irish was pleasantly surprised to find Isabella agreeable. Plans were put in place, Swiss bank accounts arranged with a minimum of fuss.

Of course, Irish had no way of knowing that they had just

slipped quietly past the point of no return, that Isabella had just cleared the last hurdle – Dante Alessandri – to open whack season.

They made their way through an elegant three course dinner then headed to a basement nightclub. Heads turned when they sashayed down the stairs.

A handsome young waiter glanced up.

"Be right with you, ladies," he grunted, struggling to open a bottle of beer.

Irish took the bottle from him, twisted the cap off and handed it back. He stared at Irish's all but exposed breasts, his eyes tracing their curves.

"Thanks, lady." His voice cracked.

"No worries."

Needless to say, a very good table was found for them.

They ordered frozen strawberry daiquiris and settled back to watch the action on the dance floor.

A man carrying a camera approached their table. Irish watched his approach warily before realising he was one of those photographers who earned a living selling people pictures of themselves on their nights out.

Teresa waved him off.

"Wait! Come on, let's!" Irish shouted above the music.

Eve bobbed up and down. "Please, Teresa?"

That was all it took. "Si," said Teresa.

Isabella, Eve, Teresa and Irish raised their glasses in a toast.

"Cheers."

"Here's to us."

"Salut."

"You speaking Italian again, Irish?"

The flashbulb erupted.

The women put their glasses down, slung their arms around one another and faced forward, offering brilliant smiles to the camera. The flashbulb erupted again.

They turned in almost as soon as they got home, strewing dresses and stockings over furniture as they passed.

On her way back from the bathroom, Irish caught Isabella staring at the A3 portrait in the living room.

"What's up, Bella?"

"They've got a lot more muscle then we have," Isabella replied quietly.

"Yeah, well, you've got two muscles they don't have, sister, and that's all you need to make every one of theirs do anything you want."

When Irish curled up under her eiderdown, her sleep would be disturbed by dreams of Domenic Albrici and Dante Alessandri. They were the most fiercely erotic dreams she had ever known.

Chapter Thirty-Three

"Maybe I don't want a man."

"You're a healthy woman. You want a man all right."

"Enough of this talk of men," Irish said. "Glorified vibrators, the lot of them."

"Hey, Irish?"

"Yes, Teresa?"

"You got one of those things?"

"No, Teresa."

"I was just wondering. Maybe one of those other things without the batteries? What are they called ..."

"I wouldn't know, Teresa."

Teresa eyed her. "You go to hell for telling lies."

"Only if you're Catholic."

Irish really should have known better. When the whack to the back of her head came, she sighed.

When they weren't stair-training, walking or running, Irish had them doing light weights.

"Man, I feel like a woman," Isabella huffed the first time she tried it.

Eve had been equally unimpressed. "Girl, why we gotta do all this?"

"So when the time comes, you won't look like *Charlie's Angels.*"

"Hell's Angels more like it," said Eve. "We're gonna end up all muscly."

As Irish finished her curl, inspiration shot into her brain on a tide of endorphins. "Hey! I know what we should call ourselves – our little red dress club, I mean."

"What's wrong with *SICA?*" demanded Eve.

"*SIC 'EM,*" Teresa corrected, "You speak Italian like a good girl now."

"Let's hear it," invited Isabella.

"Hell's Belles!"

Teresa dropped her weight. "You can call yourselves whatever the hell you like, but I call myself hungry." The dumbbell rolled languorously across the floor, as though to follow Teresa into the kitchen.

When they weren't stair-training, walking, running or resistance training, they were cooking. Both Cicero's and Alfonso's stocked their fare, on condition that no-one learn of the arrangement, lest it arouse the Don's displeasure.

When they weren't stair-training, walking, running or cooking, they were shooting the living bejesus out of inanimate targets, but the Whack Club had taken an unofficial sabbatical, its members too busy in the living of daily life, just as Irish had planned.

Irish was running late to meet her agent. She dived into the kitchen and proffered her back for inspection.

"Can you see my panty line through my skirt?"

They gave her butt the serious attention the question warranted.

"No."

"Uh-uh."

"You're safe."

Irish slung on her jacket. "What about my gun? Can you see my gun through my jacket?"

"No. You're fine."

She tore from the kitchen. Teresa called her back.

"Irish?"

She bounded back in. "Yeah?"

"You gonna wear that holster with those shoes?"

Irish looked at her feet. "I was. Why?"

Teresa shrugged. "Doesn't go. Holster's black, shoes are tan. Change the shoes maybe."

"But I was going to take my tan bag with me."

Isabella spread her hands. "What difference does it make? You're not going to see the holster under her jacket."

"She'll know," insisted Eve. "Won't do her confidence any good. She won't be able to concentrate, thinking all the time about how her holster doesn't match her shoes, even if it is beneath her clothes. Make her feel like she's dressed from the opportunity shop."

"What is this, Charlies' Angels?" Flouncing around, Irish settled into an exaggerated, ineffectual shooter's stance then cocked her finger and thumb into a mock gun.

Eve clutched her chest and fell to the floor.

"Shit. Sorry, I didn't realise it was loaded."

"Irish, holster your weapon," Isabella commanded. Irish uncocked her fingers.

"Besides," said Teresa. "What if she's in an accident and has to go to the hospital? They take her jacket off – *pfft* – then everyone sees her holster no match her shoes."

"But if I change the holster, I have to change the gun."

"So change it already. What's the problem?"

"The only tan holster I've got is for the .357."

"So, take the .357."

"But the .357's black. I mean–" Irish motioned toward the window. "It's spring outside. Black in a gun is so winter."

They dropped what they were doing and followed Irish into her bedroom.

"I've been thinking," Irish said. "Maybe we could do with some sort of engagement training."

"Like fighting mercenaries or something?"

"Maybe I can get us some time playing war games with your fine U.S. Army."

"You're kidding. How?"

"Research opens all sorts of doors. You'd be amazed at the things people want to tell you and the things they'll do for you when they learn you're a writer."

"Like things that go in holsters?"

"Absolutely. And war games. I bet when I tell the P.R. department of the U.S. Army I'm writing a book they'll bend over backwards to help me. What do you think?"

It took three changes of clothes and shoes before they could all agree on an ensemble: black bag, black shoes and black holster housing the Walther, which being tan and black, would go with most anything.

When Irish let herself back into the apartment two hours later, she was more than a little tipsy on good champagne and drop dead drunk on the cheque she held. She raced up the stairs, dying to share it with the others.

Irish flung open the door. Everybody was in the living room, taking a break. *Oh good.* And even more unusually for that time of day, all of them had a drink in hand. *Even better.*

"Oh boy, let me at one of those and let's talk about what we're going to do–" Irish followed their collective gaze to the small white box on the living room floor. The lid lay on an angle, one edge on the floor, one edge touching the box rim.

Irish stepped closer and peered in, squinting without her glasses. *Something dark and… furry.*

Her heart stopped then took off like a racehorse threatened with the glue factory.

Dead rat. Ah shit.

"It's started," said Isabella.

Chapter Thirty-Four

The Whack Club reconvened.

Isabella worried about the possibility of bugs planted by Domenic's pet F.B.I. agent Lance Jameson, (or as she called him, Lance *fucking* Jameson, which she did so often that Irish had to remind herself that *fucking* wasn't a middle name), so they put music on to cover their conversation.

They rehashed the old arguments: how to whack and not be whacked? Was it better to start at the top or at the bottom? Maybe to start with the lower ranks, the soldiers and associates, would be to arouse less suspicion.

Maybe.

Then again.

Maybe to start at the bottom was to tip off the top, the people they wanted dead most of all.

Irish, trying to undermine the whack plan in favour of escape, spoke of telegraphed punches.

They argued well into the night, finding more questions than answers, then got up first thing in the morning to do it all over again.

While they argued in earnest, they trained harder, going to target practise twice a day. They arrived in the dark, left in the dark, returned in the dark to do it all over again.

The women concentrated most of their physical training on running and got serious about diet, taking the pledge by swearing off cakes for the duration.

Sometimes, while they were out running, they made it past a pastry shop without stopping to look in the window.

Sometimes, but not often.

Sometimes, it seemed they would make it past the window cascading with dainty delectables all dusted with snowy sugar turning prettily on round stands. Led by Irish, whose head pointed resolutely forward, they ran past, only to return led by Irish turning them in a tight circle.

And so it was on the morning in question.

On the morning in question, the unthinkable happened: the women's menstrual cycles synced.

So it came to pass that four hormonally psychotic pre-menstrual women went running with heavy, painfully swollen breasts. So it came to pass that four pre-menstrual women who were trying not to eat cake, stood salivating at Cicero's window with those painfully swollen breasts, made more so by their running.

It was into this scene that Paolo Discenza came.

Paolo Discenza, the youngest and fattest of Johnny Acerbi's crew.

It was into this scene that Paolo Discenza, the youngest and fattest of Johnny Acerbi's crew came, and said – this is what he said to those cake-deprived women with their swollen breasts and their bloated, sweating bodies and their limp, hormonally oily hair – he said:

"Jesus. You sluts maybe should take a freakin' shower and put on some make up."

This, he said to the Hell's Belles.

He was twenty years junior to three of them. The other one, in a fit of hormonal esprit de corps, gained two decades in three seconds.

If only he hadn't been carrying cakes, things might have been different.

Maybe.

The late afternoon sun filtered through the living room window, illuminating a rainbow of dust motes dancing in the air and warming the living room where the women lounged in companionable silence. The television was on in the background.

They idled the time away doing odd bits and pieces. Isabella leafed through a magazine. Teresa tweezed her eyebrows using a small hand-held mirror. Eve polished her nails.

Irish reached for the remote and turned up the volume to save Eve the trouble.

"In an incident described by police as *bizarre*," said the newsreader, "a man died today as a result of being," she paused for effect, "ironed to death. The man, who appears to have died as a result of multiple wounds inflicted by a domestic iron, was found with a curling iron inserted in his–" The newsreader's eyes flitted rapidly back and forth. She winced. "Oh my God! And it was turned on!"

Eve nodded at Irish. "Love the new look. It suits you straight."

"Thanks," said Irish, and passed the cakes. Eve blew on her nails and selected a cannoli.

Popular, those cannoli.

Chapter Thirty-Five

Last night's debate had effected a little progress: in order to learn their targets movements, they would need disguises.

"Hats, sunglasses and wigs?" Irish ventured. "What are they going to think if they notice us capering around in our Jackie O's and Tina Turner's acting all furtive?"

Teresa didn't hesitate. "They're going to think we're trying to hide. Which is true, no? For all sorts of furry reasons."

"Good point," Irish agreed uncomfortably.

"Maybe we need to do something about make-up too, like movie make-up or something. You know, make us look different," Eve offered.

"Great idea," said Irish.

"And maybe we should all have false passports." said Eve. "Not just me."

"What are Isabella's and Teresa's chances of getting away with that? They're too high profile. They get noticed at the airport when the Jersey morgue's suddenly holding more clippings than a lawnmower's grass catcher. Our customs guy decides to take a nice leisurely look at their passports, and he's got reason to hold them when he didn't before. Falsifying a passport is a serious offence. I think they've got a better chance of getting away by being themselves."

"If being themselves don't get them clipped in the meantime."

Irish glanced at the clock. "How about we start with wigs and hats?"

Now the others had gone on disguise reconnaissance, leaving Irish alone to work on the edits for her new book.

Try as she might, she couldn't concentrate.

The problem, she concluded, was that she hadn't exercised. Endorphin deprived, she couldn't think straight.

Irish gave it one more try then gave up.

Only a run would cure her.

The mid-afternoon sunshine was glorious but a little too warm for a run. Irish promised herself she would take it easy, but she soon hit her runner's high and opened her stride to its usual punishing length.

Ah, that's the ticket. Who needs nicotine?

Don't kid yourself Irish. You'd kill for a cigarette and you know it.

She was too lost in her own thoughts to notice the car slip quietly by and turn into the street ahead.

Had Irish noticed, she probably wouldn't have thought much of it. It was just a car, after all. Just a car turning into a street like happened hundreds of times every day.

Maybe Irish would have thought more of it had she noticed the car that immediately followed the first, accelerating smoothly to catch up and tailing it closely around the corner.

Maybe she would have thought more of it had she noticed the third car that shot out of a side street and accelerated to close the gap to the two ahead.

Maybe then she may have wondered why so many people

were heading to her favourite park at this time of day, when school was still in; she might even have noted the cars were not of a typical make to ferry children.

Irish was a writer. It was her job to notice things that other people didn't. For the same reason, she didn't always notice the things she should.

Consequently, when in the seclusion of the park, eight of Domenic Albrici's men stepped from the foliage to surround her, Irish didn't even have time to go for her gun.

Heretofore being ladies of discernment, Isabella and Teresa, guided by eighteen-carat internal compass, gazed into the window of the most exclusive wig couturier in town.

"Shall we go in?" suggested Isabella.

Less than thirty seconds later, they ejected themselves from the shop like the proverbial scalded animal.

"Fifteen hundred dollars for a wig?" Teresa had demanded of the proprietor.

"It's human hair," he replied.

"For fifteen hundred dollars, I'd want the kidneys as well."

Now they stood on the street.

"What do we do?"

"Maybe go find some synthetic ones."

"I don't think they look as good," counselled Eve.

"We're not out to look good," countered Teresa.

"No, but from my time on the streets, I know they look like wigs."

"Ah."

They stood around uncertainly.

"Maybe we should go home and ask Irish before we decide."

"She's working on her book. Let's go and find some cheaper ones, at least have a look before we trouble her."

Irish's run petered out like an inopportune laugh.

Ah shit ah shit ah shit. Maybe the curling iron hadn't been such a nice touch after all.

They closed in. Four in front, she didn't know how many behind. She sensed them but no way would she turn around. Irish lifted the bottom of her tee shirt to wipe the sweat from her eyes, the way men with cut abs always do when another runner comes into sight.

She nodded in Teodore Saracini's direction.

"Afternoon, Theo. How they hanging?"

He nodded solemnly. "Miss Irish."

Not counting the goons behind her, it looked like Cino Malatesta was absent from the semi-circle closing in front of her.

"Boyfriend not with you today, Theo?"

A tick hammered Saracini's jaw. "I would caution you against saying that again, Miss Irish."

"What can I do for you glorified jar openers this fine and sunny afternoon?"

Saracini shifted his feet comfortably and rearranged the hands folded in front of him.

"Mister Albrici once again requests the pleasure of your company."

"I believe I've already mentioned–"

"And I would caution you against mentioning it twice, Miss Irish. Unless you're prepared to draw your rather fetching .357 from the shoulder holster beneath that running jacket."

Hot breath lapped at her neck.

"Alas, the things you see when you're out without your gun." She didn't expect they would believe it for a second.

Saracini adjusted his stance and ran his tongue over his teeth beneath his lips. Irish thought of the red ochre dust of home, the way it stuck to your teeth on road trips.

"When the Don tells you to come, you come."

"Now there's the poorest excuse for fudging cunnilingus ever I've heard."

Another's breath had joined the first lapping at her neck. This guy liked his garlic roasted.

"Miss Irish, be reasonable. Mister Albrici merely wishes to learn a little more about the beautiful young woman who has taken such an interest in his wife."

"Uh-huh."

Number three seemed to prefer white onions and goat's cheese.

"We wouldn't have troubled you, but we can't seem to learn your real name and we are so interested in knowing all about you." He shrugged. "So the Don asks you to come along and tell us all about yourself."

Number four had a predilection for sun dried tomatoes and balsamic vinegar.

Eight eight eight eight and all of them carrying. She would never take them.

"Well, I'm sorry, Theo, but I really can't do that."

"I think, Miss Irish, that you don't know how things work in our world."

Maybe not, but she did know a thing or two about saltwater crocodiles.

Irish took a deep breath, fixed Saracini in her sights and roared.

After two hours of traipsing, Isabella, Teresa and Eve found another wig shop. Footsore and in need of afternoon tea, they inspected the window.

"What do you think?" asked Isabella.

"The price is right," said Eve.

Teresa curled her lip. "The colours are..."

"A little brassy, maybe. Let's go in and look."

They were the sort of wigs that really looked like wigs. Tina Turner and Cher would have had a field day. Actually, these wigs looked like the love children of their wigs.

Looking for better ones, Eve and Teresa scouted the walls while Isabella searched the back of the shop.

"Well? What do you think?" Eve had donned a wig.

"It looks like you're wearing a wig," Teresa said.

Isabella said, "Of course it does. It's blonde."

"So?"

"You're black, Eve. How many blonde sisters do you know, sugar?"

Eve slipped the wig from her head. "I forgot."

Isabella's green eyes were indulgently soft. "That you're black or–"

"Wait a minute," Teresa said. "Isn't there something about… the best way not to be seen is to be seen?"

"Huh?"

"Some saying of spying or espionage or something… about the best place to hide is in the open…"

Her cry was light years away from the terrified screams of the terrified woman she really was. It was the blood curdling roar of a warrior lost to battle lust.

Saracini looked like reaction was beneath him. He merely resettled his feet comfortably and set his dial to implacable. Irish hurtled forward, her impetus as unstoppable as the pee demanding to get of her. She was close enough to see the lines of Saracini's forehead when something flickered in his eyes.

And Irish smiled.

A moment before she would have barrelled into him, he stepped aside. Suddenly, miraculously, she had a clear path and she was through.

Assuming a slow, even stride Irish deliberately took her time leaving the park, while her flight or fight instinct screamed at her, *What the fuck are you doing? RUN RUN RUN RUN OH YOU*

STUPID BITCH RUN FAST AS FAST AS YOU CAN FASTER
and her ears strained to hear the thunder of sixteen angry feet
closing in on her while her pee reminded her it wanted OUT
and her back tried to shrink away from the bullet that would
come any second now–

She was out of the park.

Irish managed to get around the corner and out of sight
before sheer terror overwhelmed her and she couldn't run
for trembling. Her lungs pumped overtime, sucking in great
bellowing draughts of oxygen. She bent forward, resting her
palms on her thighs.

Irish didn't know anything about mob etiquette, but she did
know something about saltwater crocodiles.

Many years before, a solitary woman in a small boat was
exploring a river in the Northern Territory when a crocodile
attacked her boat, capsizing it and tossing her in the water.
Seizing her in its jaws, the crocodile thrashed her through the
water in a death roll, then, for reasons known only to itself, let
her go.

The woman knew she had to get out of the water. Two poor
escape routes were available: she could go for the muddy river
bank, where she would undoubtedly sink and get stuck – ergo
become a light lunch for the croc which would not get stuck – or
she could scramble from the water into a mangrove tree.

Saltwater crocodiles are not known for their ability to climb
trees. Sensibly, she chose the latter.

The crocodile rose gracefully from the water, neatly plucked
her from the tree and thrashed her in a second death roll.

Again, it let her go.

As before, she went for the sanctuary of the mangrove tree. As before, the crocodile plucked her from the branch, thrashed the woman in a death roll then let her go.

Incredibly, she had the presence of mind to realise that between them, they were establishing a pattern, that the crocodile was fast learning this new method of hunting for food – *Okay, you climb in tree, I get you out of tree. Ooh, you taste a bit like chicken* – and that having survived the death roll of a saltwater crocodile three times, if she wanted to live to tell the tale, she was going to have to do something different, something the crocodile didn't expect.

She went for the river bank, where she promptly sank and got stuck.

Surprised by this new development, the crocodile blinked, watching the woman for the considerable time it took her to extract herself from the mud and wade out.

Irish took off at a fast jog, though her tortured lungs felt fit to burst. Halfway home, relief displaced terror and she started to laugh.

She was still laughing when an arm shot out from an alley and covered her mouth. Turning her wide terrified eyes to Cino Malatesta, Irish realised, too late, that she was looking at plan B.

A man walking his dog crossed the alley in time to see a pair of violently fluorescent runners disappear around the corner. He would never forget the sight of them, nor the woman's scream that followed. It was the guttural cry of a mortally wounded animal going to its death.

The sound was so terrible that his little dog jumped and pricked its ears, first looking at the corner then up at its master with solemn dark eyes.

The violently fluorescent runners reappeared as the body they were attached to thumped to the ground.

The man stared for a moment longer then yanked on the little dog's lead.

In Jersey, it was better not to get involved.

"Eh, I can't remember," Teresa sighed impatiently.

"Maybe we should go home and talk to Irish about it," Isabella said.

"We rely on Irish too much. We're three grown up women with good minds. We should be able to work this out for ourselves."

Eve said, "Okay, let's talk pros and cons."

"The thing about not being seen by being seen, whatever it is," muttered Teresa. "Nobody who knows us would expect to see us in such garish things." She picked up a platinum blonde wig and regarded it as though it were the pelt of skinned road kill.

"True. But the more expensive ones would blend in better and I think you could do more with them. Maybe we could get away with just buying one of them each and set them in different styles."

"That reminds me," murmured Eve, fishing a notepad from her purse. "Gotta pick up a new curling iron for Irish."

"You'd never know it's the one wig, whereas…" Isabella held up a nylon red number styled in slashed bob.

"Yeah, you're right, Isabella. And I think you can probably colour the better ones, too."

Isabella said, "You know what? I think we're going to need some of each, as much as any of us hates the idea of spending any more of Irish's money than we need to."

They picked up a gaudy one for each of them and one for Irish, and another four less so, then headed back across town for a second look at the upmarket wigs.

Irish had nothing left. Every breath was torture. Her agonised lungs struggled to fill themselves. She lacked the strength to crawl.

But she had to try. If she didn't, she would die here.

With a tortured grunt she tried to rise, then collapsed defeated, the back of her head colliding painfully with concrete.

Struck down in that lonely alley so far from home, Irish, struggling for every breath, her lungs burning, pondered life's big questions, like: *what sort of God gives your enemy a glass jaw then lands him on top of you when you deck him? Particularly when you're screaming to PEE?*

A very funny bastard.

Cino, like the saltwater croc, made the mistake of releasing her from his grasp.

"Aren't you going to draw on me, bitch?"

"Ladies first. I insist, Cino."

That's when he had swung for her. She was faster but he was fatter.

If only the fat bastard hadn't landed on top of her, it all would have worked out beautifully.

PEE! cried her brain.

She needed something to hang onto for leverage. Irish tried for the wall but there was nothing there for her to grasp. She only succeeded in skinning the tips of her fingers and *shit!* maybe breaking a nail.

"Cino, if you've made me break a nail, then I'll put a bullet through your bloody head, mate." Then, as an afterthought: "And if I have to pee in an alley, I'll kneecap you as well."

Irish couldn't bear the thought of Cino lying on top of her for a moment longer. With a supreme effort of will, she slid her upper body free, the concrete abrading her skin nastily through her clothes.

Oh, sweet relief. She could breathe. Now if only she could pee.

Cino's head lolled, landing on her groin. Taking one look at his lips over her fun spot, Irish slid herself free with an effort worthy of Wonder Woman.

Nothing felt broken but everything felt battered. Her sweats had saved her skin from the worst of it, but everything beneath protested. Her lungs hurt worst of all – the poor old lungs she had promised to take it easy on going out in the heat of the day like she had. *Ouch.* So much for that plan.

Then she noticed Cino's feet sticking out from the corner. She would have to drag him out of sight.

Her grimace was heartfelt. "Cino, you miserable son of a bitch," she hissed.

Irish staggered to her feet – *PEE!* cried her brain – and swayed on the spot while her spinning head tried to level the horizon.

"Okay, let's get this over with."

Irish heaved his arms over his head. Cino's jaw clacked ominously; his head lolled; his mouth fell open. It appeared the upper and lower parts of his jaw were no longer intimately acquainted.

"Now, that's not good."

Irish tugged on his arms.

"Jesus!" She dropped his arms. Hands on her thighs she stood panting. *Impossible.* She would never move him this way. What if she went to the other end, tried pushing him like a wheelbarrow? *Worth a try.*

Irish stuck her head around the corner. *Clear.* She jumped out and hoisted his feet. It was then she noticed that his runners were the same as hers.

"Well, Cino, if you thought being flat-footed was a bastard, then that jaw of yours is going to put things nicely into perspective when you wake up, prick."

Irish hefted his legs over her shoulders and pushed forward with all her might. She almost burst out laughing at her own wishful thinking. *Why would pushing be any easier than pulling?* His legs dropped to the ground, wobbling as they hit.

Hand on hip, Irish stood huffing and puffing.

PEE! cried her brain. *PEE PEE PEE PEE PEE!*

She propped one of Cino's legs against the wall. It slid

down to the ground, bounced once then settled. *One more time.* It stuck; the heel of his runner caught on a groove between bricks and held fast. Irish hefted the other leg. The movement dislodged a pack of cigarettes from his shirt pocket, sending a red alert to her brain, which stopped crying, *PEE!* in favour of *HELLO!*

Irish dropped Cino's leg and fell to her knees. She eased the cigarettes from his pocket like they were a religious artefact.

A full packet, less one. She dug in his shirt pocket for his lighter. It wasn't there. She slapped his face.

"Hey, paesano! Where you friggin' lighter, mate?"

Irish cast about. It wasn't on the ground.

That could only mean one thing: back pocket. Irish looked to the heavens.

Palms on his flank, she pushed. *Here goes here goes here goes yes!* She rocked and *voila!* over he went. Something popped loudly in the alley, the sound echoing off the wall. The sound had come from the direction of Cino's hip. His leg was at an impossible angle.

Her eyes lit on the bulge in his back pocket. *JackPOT!*

Irish slid the lighter free, eased a cigarette smoothly from the packet and slipped it between her lips.

Her gaze fell to his other foot, still exposed to the street.

"Bugger you, Cino, you inconsiderate bastard." Hefting his leg, Irish pushed it to the wall. Willing it to stay there she pressed it once for good measure then motioned with her hands for the leg to *stay.* His foot slid down then stuck in a groove.

Irish drew a few steady breaths to salve her tortured lungs, then promptly filled them with cigarette smoke.

She put the cigarettes and lighter back in Cino's pocket, for he would surely want them when he regained consciousness, (although Irish pondered the logistics of smoking with a dislocated jaw.)

Taking a deep, contented drag, Irish resumed her run, cigarette between her lips.

Chapter Thirty-Six

"I think they're onto us!" Irish cried, bursting through the apartment door.

Three strange women with fluorescent hair swam into view. Irish did a double take and glanced over her shoulder to check the apartment number.

"See! Irish didn't recognise us!" said the voice of Eve.

Irish squinted and thrust her nose forward.

"That's only because on a good day she can't see her own boobs, and look at the size of them." Judging by the flailing hands, that would be Teresa.

"Why do think they're onto us?" the voice of Isabella demanded from beneath a platinum blonde mop.

"Domenic's men cornered me in the park."

"How many?"

"Eight of them."

"That's not good," Isabella remarked casually.

Teresa's nose twitched like a rabbit's. "I smell cigarette smoke." She turned to Eve. "Can you smell cigarette smoke?"

"You weren't hurt, were you?" asked Isabella.

"A broken nail."

"Madonn!" They gathered around to inspect the damage.

"Irish, have you been smoking?"

Irish ignored Teresa. "I think they're onto us," she said again.

"I doubt it."

"Irish, answer me like a good girl now. You been smoking?"

"If they're not onto us, why would Domenic send eight of his men to pick me up?"

"I said, I don't think they're onto us. I didn't say you weren't bothering them."

To Irish's mind, Mob + Bother = Dead.

"I'm not really seeing the distinction."

"You're an outsider. He doesn't have your measure, doesn't know what to make of you. He's uncomfortable because you're not within his control and you haven't responded to his intimidation."

Irish ran her fingers through her hair. "Saltwater crocodiles," she muttered.

"What?"

"Never mind."

"Excuse me, but I think there's a question not being answered here." Teresa had channelled Sophia Loren.

"I agree," said Irish. "I'm still not convinced that's all there was to it."

"If he wanted you dead, you'd be dead. This was more of a persistent invitation."

"So, *you* get a dead rat and it's something to be worried about. Tell me what the difference is between that and this, Isabella."

"Your message was from Domenic. Ours won't be. And we won't get to see them coming."

Irish thought of Cino and paled. "In that case, I may have miscalculated."

"What do you mean?"

"I mean, maybe we should get out of town."

And yes, at last, Irish got to pee.

Chapter Thirty-Seven

"I wonder who cleans up crime scenes?" This, from Irish.

Isabella tossed a bag into the car. "I presume the cops would."

Teresa came out carrying a bundle of cosmetic bags. They had parked the car in the alley and were loading it by way of the building's rear, unused stairs.

"You think?"

"Well surely they wouldn't leave the victim's families to do it?"

"What are we talking about?" asked Teresa.

"I was wondering who cleans up the mess at crime scenes."

"Huh, never a man," Teresa muttered, her head disappearing into the car.

"That's my point," said Irish.

"Not following." Isabella gave her head a small shake as Teresa thumped about, rearranging bags for a better fit.

"I mean, given that most cops are men–"

"Right?"

"Then it seems likely that most crime scenes would be cleaned up by men."

"So?"

"So, if they can clean up grey matter, viscera and splattered blood, how come they can't use a coaster when they're at home?"

Isabella laughed softly. Inside the car, Teresa banged her head.

"No, think about it. They can comb an entire house looking for a single human hair, but they can't put the toilet seat down?"

Teresa backed out of the car.

"Well doesn't that strike you as a somewhat selective attention span?"

Isabella and Teresa took one look at her earnest face then collapsed laughing.

"I'm serious!"

That only made them laugh harder.

It seemed the worse things got, the darker the mob women's humour became. The evening before, as they were packing, Irish had asked them in all earnest what they thought would be happening in the Albrici camp. What would the Don make of his disappearing men, particularly in light of her sparring match with Cino Malatesta? Surely that would cast an illuminating glow over the other two disappeared? Or at the very least, a little niggling question mark?

Isabella had been supremely unperturbed.

"Why would they put the two together? Cino, he was sent after you. But the others, they just went out to get the cannoli."

Teresa folded her hands in front of her in that familiar funereal stance. "We need your wisdom, Godfather. Something is happening to our associates. Every time they go out to buy cannoli, they come back in a body bag."

Isabella didn't miss a beat. "Consiglierie, these cannoli – they must be killers."

"Si, si, Godfather, the cannoli, they got Jimmy Hoffa. Is little known fact."

"They've been known to eat whole horses, leaving only the heads."

Teresa fell to her knees laughing.

"Perhaps I could trouble you to be serious for a moment," Irish said dryly.

Teresa bounded across the room to seize Irish's earlobe.

"Serious? You want serious? Let me smell your breath, girl."

Eve floated through the room, giving Irish a high-minded look on the way past. Irish disengaged her earlobe from between Teresa's fingers and flipped Eve a mental bird.

Isabella stood up. "Let me ask you this, Irish. Cino Malatesta weighs... how much, you think?"

"Too much."

"But how much to your much?"

"A Sherman tank more."

"Right. And he's how much taller and wider than you?"

"A head and a bus front."

"Okay, so you're him, with a reputation to maintain, and you've been sent out to retrieve one solitary, comparatively slight little woman. You come back with a ... what did you say you did to him?"

"Dislocated jaw, I think." Irish left out the hip.

"Right. So, what are you gonna say about how it happened? You think he'd say that a woman did that to him?"

Irish thought about it. Hard.

"Trust me, Domenic is none the wiser about what happened to Cino and who did it. There's some gang of imaginary toughs out there tonight who'd be shitting themselves, if only they were real."

Just the same, Irish thought it would be a good idea to break camp. She had already made tentative arrangements with the U.S. Army's Public Relations Department for engagement training. Now seemed a very good time to take them up on their offer.

They would take turns driving, except Eve who had never had the chance to learn. Teresa went first.

"Where we headed?" Eve fitted the last bag in the trunk and climbed in the back.

Irish glanced at her in the sun visor's rear vision mirror. "Upstate New York."

They bumped from the alley onto the street, Irish bracing for a head shot the minute they were in the open. Teresa glanced at her.

"You look nervous, Irish? You nervous?"

"Yes," she admitted. "I never could get used to driving on this side of the road. Every time I look up, I expect to see a car hurtling toward me a split second before we collide head on."

"So, you don't drive here?"

"Not often, no."

"Then how come you got a car?"

Irish shrugged. "Why not? It's there if I want it and it's not as if I can't afford it."

"Irish?"

"Hm?"

"Mind if I ask, just how rich are you?"

Irish felt the real question, the lingering suspicion, hanging in the air. *Just why was she helping them?*

"Filthy," she said. "I'm filthy rich."

"Must be nice to be rich," Eve said quietly, staring out the window.

"All from writing romance novels?" This, from Isabella.

"Plenty, but not all. My family owned an outback cattle station."

"One of those places where you have to ride three days to check the boundaries?" asked Isabella.

"Yes, but we call them fences, not boundaries."

Isabella's expression told Irish she had dreamed up the stuff of movies: fierce sunrises and blazing sunsets, dusty cattle drives, kangaroos, snakes, bushfires, endless adventure.

The reality was less romantic and more isolated.

In her home town, boys were boys and girls were girls and any challenge to the status quo was paid for by loneliness.

Irish was raised by a joyless mother whose hair was permanently plastered to her forehead by steam or sweat. When her mother wasn't immersed elbow deep in the old copper boiler, she dished up grey serves of boiled mutton and overcooked vegetables to the station hands she was obliged cater for. And she resented every moment of it.

Irish was a precocious student whose intelligence attracted the ire of dull boys and lazy girls alike: both disapproved of smart girls. By high school, Irish was an early bloomer hated by girls who resented the unwelcome attention she attracted from boys.

So relentlessly was Irish bullied by the girls she wished only to befriend, that with two years of high school left, her father sent Irish to an exclusive private girls' school in the city. There, the girls snickered at her unaffected country nature and natural speech, while themselves sounding out rounded vowels in plummy accents acquired with daddy's money.

Irish gave up on making friends, instead befriending the characters she met in books, who liked her just fine the way she was. The school photo of her final year captured a buxom, blue-eyed blonde with a sunny countenance and undiminished smile, leaning away from a class of girls with upright posture and carefully composed expressions.

For all her wealth and success, throughout her lonely, isolated life Irish craved the one thing she had never known: the friendship of women. Though wild horses wouldn't drag the confession from her now.

Out of the blue Eve said, "Had a cousin once in upstate New York."

Isabella was quick to show interest. "Really? Mother's side or father's?"

"Mother's." Eve said *mother* like it was a dirty word.

"Maybe your cousin might know where to find your mother."

"Why would I go looking? She left us."

"She was very young," Irish reminded her gently.

"So was I," Eve said.

"People do things for all sorts of reasons, Eve."

Eve made a show of interest in passing objects. Any second now that bottom lip was going to break Irish's heart. "Went to my cousin's once. Little place called Willow Falls."

Irish reached into the door pocket to retrieve a road map. "I think that might be close to where we're headed. Maybe when we get there, you might like to reconsider. No harm in thinking about it, right?"

"Maybe."

Isabella said, "I've been thinking, what happen after? I mean, if it comes out these soldiers helped train us?"

"What would your boys do to the solider boys if they find out? I think our soldier boys are equipped to defend themselves. The guy I spoke to sounded seven feet tall."

One Lieutenant Daniel Sutcliffe, the guy Irish had spoken to last night who sounded seven feet tall, had suggested they use paintball guns for their war games (*unless you'd prefer to use real guns and live ammunition – ha ha,* he said. *Oh no!* Irish replied. *We might break our nails!*) A paintball war would prove interesting, said Sutcliffe, as his men would be as unfamiliar with the weapons as the women, which should, in theory, level the playing field.

"What did you tell them about us? About our reasons for wanting to play war games?"

They had left the city behind them now. Houses were fewer and further apart.

"I said I'm researching a book about women taking on men at their own game, women who went to jail for a crime they didn't commit. I'm trying to establish how feasible it would be for untrained women to take on highly trained men."

"Isn't that a little close to home?" asked Isabella.

"Hide out in the open," offered Teresa.

They all thought about that for a while. Eve broke the silence.

"The closer it is to the truth, the less likely we are to slip up."

"I think it'll hold water. Though I'm concerned about him recognising you. What's he going to make of me bringing a couple of mob wives with me?"

"I resent that description, Irish. We do have interests outside the home, you know."

"My apologies, Isabella."

They stopped once at a diner for some memorably good hamburgers – so fresh they were as good as homemade – and ate them taking in the mountain view.

When Irish tried to take a turn driving, there was a spirited discussion about her eyesight and reluctance to recognise the right side of the road. She was declared a last resort by Teresa and evicted from the driver's seat in favour of Isabella.

The scenery grew more beautiful as the miles fell away. The base wasn't sign-posted but the lieutenant had described the turn-off to Irish. Several hours after leaving home, they bumped down the dirt road. The place was gorgeous.

"You American taxpayers are very generous to your army. We give ours a water canteen and toss them into the desert."

The base was in a valley, a deep, densely wooded and beautiful valley. They were surrounded by mountains. There was no discernible fence, but after a little while they came to a gatepost.

As they approached, creeping along the dirt road, a fresh-faced young man stuck his head out of the little sentry house to give them directions.

They were to follow the track – *don't worry, it's two wheel drive all the way, your vehicle can handle it* – for about fifteen minutes, all the long way round – *please not to run over anyone on the way, unless they were in a uniform other than worn by the United States military, in which case, please feel free* – and, if they happened across any men out of uniform coming from the shower block, *well, please excuse* – *Lieutenant Sutcliffe had put out the word company was coming, but some of the men might not be expected to remember that until they had been reminded a few times by way of Lieutenant's judicious boot targeting their ass* – *begging your pardons, ladies* – and as luck would have it, the resort had *four* – *count 'em* – *four ladies! self-appointed luxury units currently standing empty awaiting the ladies pleasure at the end of the driveway* – *can't miss 'em* – and the Lieutenant expected they would be much more comfortable there than in the proximity of the barracks, *also known as the zoo* – *all those hairy animals snoring their heads off after a hard day's slobbering, I mean soldiering* – *you understand, don't you ladies?* And if the huts were a little isolated, well then *at least the ladies will have their peace and quiet and privacy, and the Lieutenant would be along as soon as his duties permitted to show them around.* They were to make themselves at home in the meantime, *but please to avoid the firing range which could be identified by the high fence, signs warning of Danger* – *Firing Range* – *and certain sounds that maybe would sound to the ladies like popcorn popping in the pan.* The smile falling from his face, the young man drew a breath and barked, *Move on! (please ladies)* shot up his knee, stamped his foot beside the other one and removed himself to the sentry box where he regarded the road with a ferocious scowl.

The bark had its desired effect on Isabella at the wheel. She lurched the car forward in a way she hadn't since learning to drive. She calmed down, touched a foot lightly to the brake and resumed at a more circumspect pace.

The vista surrounding the base was majestic.

Irish could hardly wait to get out and look around. They didn't see any naked men as they passed the shower block – even though Teresa twisted in her seat to give them a second chance – but they did see men in sweats and runners climbing a steep hill before disappearing from view. Every so often, flashes of colour appeared through the trees.

"Hey! I think that's a running track up there. I bet it follows that ridge all the way around."

Isabella brought the car to a halt outside a row of four quaint huts. Everyone got out and stretched their legs and backs gratefully. Isabella popped the trunk.

"How about we leave the unpacking for now, throw on our sweats and follow that track?"

"Irish, you're a glutton for punishment, woman!" Isabella said, arching her back.

"You go for a run, Irish. The rest of us will unpack the bags."

Irish had dived into one of the huts and exchanged her street clothes for sweats in forty-five seconds flat.

"Take care, flash," Isabella said.

"Back before dark," she told them.

The incline almost stopped her in her tracks. She must have become to accustomed to the hills on her usual routes. It was nice to be challenged, to feel the burn. At the top of the hill, the track abruptly levelled out and turned right, following the ridge, as she had thought. Irish looked forward to a bird's eye view of the valley, at least what could be seen through the trees.

Irish took off, careful to avoid the tree roots that intruded under foot, lest she be sent sprawling. Soon she was half drunk on fresh air and the scent of pine needles crushed underfoot. She thought she smelled wood smoke wafting up from the valley.

The track suddenly narrowed, crowded by trees on either side. It became a sort of a tree-tunnel. There was only room for one person, the lower branches clearing her head by about a foot. The tunnel seemed to a clearing on the other side. Ignoring the claustrophobia induced by the encroaching trees, Irish focused on the open space.

She broke free of the tree tunnel just as a flash of khaki disappeared around a bend ahead. Eager to make acquaintance, Irish sprinted to catch up. The young soldier picked up his pace. Irish caught him anyway. He sped up. Irish pulled alongside him. He cast an annoyed sideways glance at her. Eyes lighting on her breasts, he did a double take, frowned and pulled away again.

Okaaay. She hadn't intended to race him, but if that's the way he was going to be…

Irish pulled ahead of him. By now he was grunting in earnest.

It looked like the track finished about a hundred metres or so further on. She opened her stride. Behind her, the grunts and thuds told her he didn't have anything left. Then again, he had youth on his side.

Irish grinned and gave it a little bit more, by no means all that she had. She estimated he had fallen a good ten metres behind her now. Irish decided to ram the point home and make it a little more.

About twenty metres on, she heard him fall to his knees, rasping painfully for breath.

Grinning, Irish doubled back.

"Let me tell you a story, son," she said by way of greeting. "An old bull and a young bull are standing at the top of the hill, when they sight a herd of cows down in the valley. The young bull turns to the old bull and says, *Let's charge down there and have us one of those cows!* Irish raised her eyebrows suggestively. "The old bull replies, *No. Let's walk down there and have us all of those cows.*"

His disbelieving gaze flitted from her breasts to her face and back again.

"Which son, is how this old cow just turned you into a steer."

A pair of boots appeared beside the boy. "Any questions, Vitelli?" the boot's owner asked. Irish followed the boots to the legs, the legs to the torso, the torso to the neck, the neck to the face. It was a long way up.

It took the unfortunate Vitelli a few more heaves of his chest to find the wind to answer. "Yessir, Lieutenant Sutcliffe."

"Let's hear it."

"Only one, sir. What are the chances of this not being repeated in the mess tonight, sir?"

"Non-existent, Vitelli. You were trounced by a woman, and an untrained woman at that." His eyes took a leisurely stroll over Irish. "Although, I think that's not quite true, Miss Devereaux."

Lieutenant Sutcliffe extended his hand. She took it.

"How did you know which one I am?"

"I recognised your voice."

Irish forced herself to maintain eye contact while alarm

bells sounded code red within her. There were laugh lines around those grey eyes, but they saw too much. This man was dangerous.

"You didn't answer my question," he reminded her.

"I'm sorry?"

Abruptly he looked down. "You still here, Vitelli? Do you want Miss Devereaux here to carry you down?"

"Actually it's–" she began.

Vitelli pushed himself up. "Nossir!" With all the dignity he could muster, Private Vitelli resumed his run. He almost made it to the bend before his knees buckled.

Lieutenant Sutcliffe turned back to Irish. "Let's give Vitelli a head start before we start down. That way he won't have to limp in front of us. You were about to answer my question."

"I don't think you asked me one."

"About being untrained. I believe you said that you and your friends were untrained. By the looks of you, I'd say the opposite is true. I'd also say you have a very healthy appetite."

Irish thought about popping him one but he had dimples when he smiled. For a moment they disarmed her, as did the steady gaze from those grey eyes.

"We're physically trained. Just not in gun–" she thought better of lying to him. Something told Irish she wouldn't get away with it. "Not in battle."

"I see. That's quite a plot, for your book I mean. It's also a bit of a departure for you, isn't it?"

Irish started uncomfortably. She had lost control of the conversation almost immediately it began.

Irish ran out of explanation before they ran out of hill. He listened intently without interrupting her. When they got to the bottom, Irish turned in the direction she thought the huts would be. He corrected her with a touch.

"Short-sighted?" he asked.

Dangerous. The man was definitely dangerous. He saw way too much.

Irish could just make out the huts in the distance. She was suddenly eager to be inside.

He followed her in. The other three were unpacking her bags. Irish watched his eyes carefully as she made the introductions. He evidenced no recognition of Isabella and Teresa.

A young soldier arrived carrying bundles of wood. "Private Smith is here to light your Area 51," Sutcliffe said.

"I beg your pardon?"

"Open fireplaces aren't allowed in government buildings, so officially, they don't exist." He winked then smiled warmly. "I can trust you ladies with a secret, now can't I?"

Isabella and Teresa looked at him like sixteen-year-old girls – love struck sixteen-year-old girls.

Oh, for the love of God. "Who's for a coffee?" rather than watch their simpering, Irish went to make it.

"Not for me, thanks, Miss Devereaux."

The others tittered.

"I keep meaning to mention, that's actually my pen name. Please call me *Irish*."

"That your surname?"

Teresa mooched up to Sutcliffe. "No, it's her nickname. She won't tell anyone what her real name is. Is rude, no?"

"I see." Lieutenant Sutcliffe considered Irish in the light of this new information. All eyes turned to her.

"Maybe you can find out," Teresa said as though butter wouldn't melt in her mouth.

Irish flushed and busied herself making coffee.

"Now, I think you'll find the huts comfortable enough, ladies. Maybe they're a little spartan to look at but you'll find everything you need. There's plenty of spare blankets in the wardrobes if you need them, which you probably will, because the nights get cold here in the mountains. The sheets aren't very soft," he winked at Teresa, "but they're nice and thick. The bathrooms won't make it into *Good Housekeeping,* but they're spotlessly clean with plenty of good hot water, unless the pilot blows out in the wind, which it frequently does. If it happens and you can't manage to light them again yourselves – they can be a bit tricky – just call on Private Smith here to do it for you. He'll be coming by every evening to light your Area 51 for you anyway."

They chorused their thanks.

"I'll swing by first thing in the morning to show you around. Dinner's served in the mess between six and eight thirty. I can come back later to walk you there–"

Irish cut him off. "We can find your own way."

"Just follow the hordes of soldiers following their stomachs. Now, I'll leave you to settle in."

Irish watched Sutcliffe leave. The man could fill a doorway, no two ways about it. She handed out the coffee and braced herself.

"Hey Irish?"

And there it is.

"Yes, Teresa?"

"Lieutenant Sutcliffe seems like a very nice man, no?"

"I wouldn't know about that, Teresa."

"Nice looking.

"Didn't notice."

"No wedding ring, I see."

"Sorry, didn't notice." Irish took a swig of her coffee.

"Not a bad bulge in his pants, either."

If the coffee had been blood, the hut would have been declared a crime scene.

Chapter Thirty-Eight

They heard the *moos* long before they reached the mess.

"What's that?" asked Eve.

"I believe the cattle are lowing, my child."

Irish swung into the doorway. Planting her feet apart, she crossed her arms against her chest and swept her gaze over the mess full of soldiers.

The soldier Irish had taken on the ridge, Vitelli, was the first to get to his feet. The rest of them – at least three dozen – rose simultaneously. One of them saluted by accident, a few others at his table followed before they remembered themselves, started to laugh, remembered themselves again and stopped, at which point the first solider saluted again. One of his friends reached up and pulled his hand down.

Irish coloured, suddenly feeling very alone in the doorway. After ten seconds which felt like a lifetime, a quiet voice commanded, "At ease."

His voice, though subdued, carried clearly to every corner of the room. The soldiers resumed their seats, leaving only Lieutenant Daniel Sutcliffe standing. He met Irish's gaze, making a small bow without breaking eye contact. The other seats at his table were empty.

Irish looked behind her for the others. They hung back. "What's wrong?" Irish whispered irritably.

"Communal eating places do not equal happy memories," Isabella supplied.

"Oh. I'm sorry. You okay?"

"We'll be fine." Sophia Loren almost pushed her out of the doorway.

Lieutenant Sutcliffe was still standing. And he was still looking at Irish. They made their way to the table.

He pulled out their chairs, starting with Teresa, and ending with Irish. Sutcliffe sat her opposite him with another one of those warm-eyed, dimpled smiles.

"I've arranged for table service, in honour of your company."

"That was unnecessary," replied Irish coolly. "We'd hate you to go to any trouble."

Under the table, a toe cap glanced off her shin.

"You speak for yourself," Teresa said. "Some ladies appreciate a gentleman."

This was something to see: Teresa flirting for all she was worth, with Isabella coming a close second. Eve looked at them like they had been whacked with the crazy stick.

"Along with table service, I'm pleased to be able to offer you ladies some wine."

"Oh!"

"How nice."

Oh, good God. You'd swear they only drank wine on special occasions, instead of most days. Let's see if she couldn't throw a bucket of cold water on this.

"Wine? Oh boy, I bet that's against regulations. We'd hate

for you to get into any trouble on our account. Maybe we should pass."

This time, the toe cap dented her shin.

"Let me put it this way. We have a name for the wine which is not dissimilar to the name given to open fireplaces."

"Let me guess – Vat 51."

Lieutenant Sutcliffe's eyes lit up. He gave Irish a million dollar smile. "Why you're as smart as you are beautiful."

Isabella and Teresa made breathless little *oh's* worthy of virgins. Irish felt a sudden need to hit someone. Hard.

The drinks arrived. Irish had never been more grateful.

"Lieutenant Sutcliffe?" Eve began.

"Yes, sweetie?"

Ah shit. Hearing Eve addressed as *sweetie* was enough to cause a ripple in Irish's cast iron breast.

"Why were your men making that sound before?"

The smile Lieutenant Sutcliffe sent Irish's way was… extraordinary. She grew angrier by the second.

"I'm surprised your friend Irish didn't tell you." He gave his eye-witness version of events, in the fashion of a military report, to the delight of the giggling women. Irish looked around the mess, trying not to listen. She couldn't avoid feeling his eyes on her though.

Teresa laid her hand on Sutcliffe's arm. "Oh, it's not natural," she said. "A woman like her, running, running, running all the time. You've got to wonder, what's she running from? There are much better uses for such energy, no?"

Irish's foot landed Teresa's shin an almighty blow. The return fire was a bone breaker.

Two soldiers arrived at the table, ferrying plates.

"We weren't sure what you would like, so we've given you a little bit of everything."

"How very nice," said Teresa. "And on plates too, when everyone else has metal trays, I see. Isn't that kind of Lieutenant Sutcliffe, Irish?"

Sutcliffe gave Irish his steady grey eyes. "Daniel, please."

Irish forced the wine over her throat then gave her attention to the plate in front of her. The sooner she got the food down, the sooner they could leave. On the other side of the table, Teresa gave a running commentary.

"Mmm, some nice fresh beans, I see. Very healthy. Very good. And cooked just beautifully! Yes. And what is here? Why, some Italian meatballs!" Teresa dropped her fork to clap her hands. "Of course, these we will like very much, Daniel." Irish kept her face down and tried to tune out. "And look, some lovely pasta! Let me have a little taste."

It was the sort of silence that preceded an earthquake. "Almost al dente. I'll just go have a word with the cook."

Teresa was already half-way to the kitchen, with Eve and Isabella in hot pursuit.

"Oh shit!" Irish shot up

Lieutenant Sutcliffe got to his feet uncertainly.

The kitchen's swing door revealed the cook's startled face and Teresa's flailing hands.

"What the hell?" breathed Sutcliffe.

Irish took one look at him and was consumed by laughter. Her rear end landed back on the seat. Sutcliffe sat down.

"That has to be the best laugh I've ever heard. You

couldn't fake that laugh for a million dollars, and I'd gladly part with a million dollars just to hear it." His eyes roamed her face.

Irish stopped laughing. She felt an overwhelming need to pop him again. "What did you just say to me?"

"I said–"

"I'd better get to the kitchen."

"No, wait! Tell me what's going on?"

How to explain the glorious package that was Teresa? Irish half smiled, pushing her fingers through her hair. Sutcliffe watched her, the anticipation of a smile playing on his lips and in his eyes.

"Let's just say Teresa is an extraordinary cook with very high standards, as your poor cook is currently learning."

She got up.

"Wait." His fingers covered hers. Her smile faded. "If he's got something to learn, then let him learn it. Your friends are in there. Besides, you still haven't answered my question."

She pulled her hand out from under his. "What question?"

"About this novel you're working on."

Something clattered in the kitchen. *Thank you, Teresa.*

"Gotta go."

Irish found Teresa lifting a spoon to the cook's willing mouth. She hoped when they returned to the mess, Lieutenant Sutcliffe would be gone. He was.

"Hey, what happened to Daniel?" Teresa pouted.

A soldier stood up. "Ma'am. He was called to duties, ma'am. Lieutenant Sutcliffe sends his apologies and compliments. He hopes you will pass a comfortable night and orders me to see you to your cabins."

Irish assured him it was unnecessary.

Half-way there, Teresa spoke up.

"Irish?"

"Yes, Teresa?"

"How old would you say Daniel is?"

"Lieutenant Sutcliffe, you mean? Don't know. Didn't notice."

"If you were to think about it?"

"Younger than me." *Too young, in other words.*

"And I'd say he's older. He just looks good 'cause he doesn't have bad habits like smoking," Eve said.

They were almost at the huts. Irish wanted nothing more than to go inside and close the door.

"You notice his colouring? A lot like yours. Blonde hair, blue eyes."

"Grey eyes."

"So that you noticed. Colouring like that, goes with your colouring. Make fine looking babies."

"We're only here for a few days, Teresa."

"How long does it take to lie on your back? Like it says on the detergent bottle, one squirt is enough–"

Irish closed the door.

Chapter Thirty-Nine

Irish woke early, roused by the promise of the ridge running track, fresh air, and a country sunrise. The only thing keeping her in bed was those tree roots protruding along the track. With her eyesight, she couldn't risk them in the dark.

It was cold in the hut. The fire had made it cottage-cosy but after it went out, she had needed extra blankets.

Irish forced herself to stay in bed until the night gave way to grey light, then she bolted for the austere bathroom.

She brushed her teeth, splashed water on her face and pulled a brush through her hair. Bracing for the cold, Irish peeled off her *Sopranos* tee shirt and shimmied into clean sweats.

The huts were close together and she didn't want to wake the others. Letting herself out, Irish padded quietly down wooden steps to the narrow dirt trail leading to the hill and running track.

She had barely cleared the huts when he materialised out of nowhere.

"Good morning," Lieutenant Sutcliffe greeted Irish softly, falling in beside her.

In the early morning mist, his hair was tousled and curling. Irish would have doubted his hair was long enough to curl.

Funnily enough, she could have sworn that just yesterday he had short back and sides.

"Morning, Joe," she returned.

"Beg your pardon?"

"You know, as in G.I. Joe."

"Why would you call me that?"

"Because ... you are."

"You think so? In what way?" His direct gaze was dis concerting.

"You're a soldier"

"And that makes me a G.I. Joe?"

God you can labour a point. She smiled unwillingly.

"You had b

reakfast yet?" he asked.

"No. I didn't know when the mess would open."

"It's open now. Want to go get something to eat?"

"No thanks. Think I'll just head on up to the track."

"Good idea."

Irish expected him to shear off, but as she set foot on the hill, she couldn't help but notice Lieutenant Sutcliffe was still with her. At the top, he joined in as she began her stretches.

She must have looked surprised.

"You don't mind if I join you?" he enquired.

Oh jolly. Now she would have to make small talk.

"Of course not. I just presumed you'd already been out."

"Break my neck in the dark? Not me." He did a couple of lunges, Irish noting with a surreptitious glance that beneath his sweats he was pure muscle.

"So, what do you guys do here all day long?"

He looked into the distance. "We're not here most of the time. Most of our time is spent overseas."

Irish did a couple of twists. "Doing what?"

"Now that I can't tell you. Let's just say we're a specialised unit."

"Really?"

"You sound surprised."

"I am. Why would your P.R. Division send us to you? Surely we're a waste of your time."

"They didn't. They put word out you were looking for someone to play war games with and I volunteered."

"Why?"

"Curiosity. You still haven't told me why this book's going to be such a departure from your usual work."

"Maybe it isn't. Maybe I have more than one pen name."

"Do you?"

For some reason she couldn't bring herself to lie to him about it. "No," she admitted.

"So, tell me. I want to know how an incurable romantic makes the leap to war games."

Irish started to jog. He fell in beside her.

"I am no such thing."

"I think you are."

"You have no way of knowing that," she said coolly.

"Sure I do. I'm reading one of your books."

"Why would you do that?"

"I told you. Curiosity."

"Aren't you going to ask me which one of your books I'm reading?"

"Nope."

"How come?"

"Because it makes no difference. Whichever one it is you won't like it." Her breath plumed the air in front of her face.

"Why not?"

"Because obviously it's meant for women."

"Why?"

"Because it's a romance."

"You saying men don't enjoy romance?"

"I–" How had the conversation gotten so complicated? Irish mentally back-pedalled, trying to work out how they got here from... where?

Sutcliffe gave her an easy smile. "We were talking about you being an incurable romantic."

"Hell I am."

"That why you came up here to see the sunrise? Because you're not?"

Irish pulled ahead before he could see her smile. Sutcliffe caught her three seconds later.

"I thought mind-reading was a woman's domain," she said.

"Now, a cautious man might avoid engaging that remark like it was a surface to air missile, but being a brave man, I'll bite. So, I did read your mind then – about coming up here to see the sunrise?"

"I didn't say that. I meant that you thought you could read my mind."

"So, women only think they can read men's minds then?"

Irish laughed despite herself. "No. That's what you accuse us of."

"Well if that's inaccurate, it follows that you can actually read our minds and if you can read our minds then surely, we can read yours. Which means in all probability, you came up here to see the sunrise."

"I think my brain just fell over."

He nudged her hip playfully, or maybe it was an accident. "Come on, let's keep going until we nut it out."

Irish tried to pull away from him again, but Sutcliffe kept up.

She changed the subject. "Tell me something?"

"Shoot."

"Please tell me you don't make a habit of saying that."

"Maybe I shouldn't. What do you want to know?"

"You seem like a guy who likes to think for himself. Why would you join the army?

His laughter was loud enough to wake the dead. It bounded around the valley.

"You really think that? That soldiers are stupid?

"I didn't say that."

"As good. You said we don't think for ourselves."

"Well it's true isn't it? Isn't that why people join the military? To follow orders without thinking?"

"Irish, why would you say such a thing? Maybe it says a lot more about you than it says about us." He wasn't smiling any more. Suddenly she was uncomfortable, and all the more so for having no answer.

Irish lengthened her stride, managing to pull a good few feet away from him before he caught her.

"You and me racing?" he asked.

"No."

"Why not? After what you did to Vitelli, you afraid to take on someone your own size?"

"You're head and shoulders taller than me."

"You frightened?"

She ignored him.

"Come on, Irish, let's see what you've got." He opened up, gliding ahead of her. She stared after him.

Sutcliffe threw her a self-satisfied look over his shoulder.

And Irish saw red.

Doubling her stride, she bounded to his side.

"Knew you had it in you, Irish."

Irish lengthened her gait impossibly, smiling when his

breath came harder. They pelted along, glancing off each other's hips.

Up ahead, the track narrowed to the width of one person before disappearing into the tree tunnel. Neither one of them backed off. Neck and neck, they pounded straight for it, Irish feeling the strain, willing every sinew, fibre and muscle to lengthen.

Daniel backed off. By the time she ran through the tree tunnel, he was ten feet behind her and she was absolutely furious.

Irish came up short, her own impetus threatening to trip her up. She whirled around to face him. He was breathing easily.

"You backed off!"

"One of us had to," he replied mildly.

"The hell. I could have taken you."

"You sure about that, Irish?"

"Damned straight. Don't you ever, ever, do that again."

"I'll remember that."

"Good. While you're at it, remember something else: that business about me being an incurable romantic is bullshit and it says a lot more about you than it does about me."

"I'm all ears." He was completely at his ease. That only made her angrier.

"It's one of the many things men believe about women for no other reason than it suits them to believe it – because it's convenient to think of women that way."

"I'd like to give that some thought, Irish, but being a soldier, I'll have to ask my commanding officer to order me to believe it."

"Oh, you can believe it, Lieutenant Sutcliffe. I write romance because it sells. I do it for the money. Simple hard facts, and I'm a hard, hard woman. I need no bloody favours from you, mate."

"I'll remember that."

"Good. See that you do."

"That bastard is not to be trusted. I would not trust that man as far as I could throw him."

Irish had showered, dried her hair and dressed in pale blue jeans and a floaty white peasant blouse. Now they were in the mess eating breakfast; at least the others were eating breakfast while she glared balefully at Daniel Sutcliffe at another table.

The other three fell over themselves in their haste to disagree with her.

"Nah..."

"No, Irish, he's beautiful. A beautiful man."

"He called me *sweetie.*"

Irish lined Eve up in her sights and gave her both barrels.

"I'm telling you, he's as cunning as a fox," Irish fumed. She would have preferred to use another, much cruder saying from home to illustrate her point, but held off because of it being meal-time.

If Sutcliffe felt her baleful glares, he didn't show it. He was perfectly at his damned ease, thank you very much, and looking every inch the commanding officer of a special unit that he was. In the midst of conversation with the other behemoths at his table, he smiled easily and nodded as he listened. Irish willed him to look her way once, just once.

"Just look at them. They're probably plotting to overthrow some innocent government as we speak."

"Eh, I don't know, Irish. You think there's really such a thing as an innocent government?"

"Don't change the subject, Teresa. I'm telling you, his friendliness is an act."

"I don't think so."

"I know so. He was just trying to find out more about us the easier to defeat us."

"He only asked about you."

"Yeah and that's why. Well if he wants war games, he can have war games."

"Actually, Irish?" Eve looked at Irish like she had been whacked by the crazy stick. "We asked for the war games."

"Yeah, but they were supposed to be games. He made them serious."

"You're not making sense," said Isabella.

"I know what I mean. He's so underhanded, to make with the nice like that."

The man in question rose from his table and sauntered over. Planting his foot on the rung of a chair, he leaned on his thigh.

Locking eyes with Irish, he said, "Ladies, let's talk war games.

The valley was small and deep, the mountains surrounding it, high. Sutcliffe led them to the base of a steep hill. Behind them flowed a stream Irish hadn't noticed before. It ran through a culvert either side of the running track. In front of them, the valley floor served as a giant oval.

Lieutenant Sutcliffe nodded to the other side of the oval. "See that flagpole?"

The women sought it out while the men turned to look through courtesy or habit.

"I see it," said Isabella.

"Me too," Eve said.

"Makes three," offered Teresa.

Sutcliffe looked at Irish. "I'll take your word for it," she said.

"Okay. It's simple enough. The object – the game – is *capture the flag*. All you have to do is get it over to that flagpole to win. Simple, hey?"

There was a moment's silence. Isabella broke it. "Where do we get it from?"

"From a point to be agreed upon. Have you other ladies visited the ridge track?"

"No."

"Well then, I suppose we'll have to rely on Irish to speak for you. I'd like to nominate a starting point, if I may, Miss Irish."

"Please do."

"The tree tunnel."

The soldiers laughed softly and shifted their feet. Unflinching, Irish returned his gaze.

"You're on. So, who will we be fighting?"

"Why, all of us."

"What?" Isabella demanded. "There's three dozen of you and only four of us!"

"Yeah!" said Eve.

Sutcliffe kept his gaze trained on Irish. "Well that's the gist of this book, isn't it? A lot more of them than of you? And Irish assured me that you needed – let me see if I remember this correctly – *no bloody favours?* Is that right Irish?"

She nodded tightly.

"And that you could take us?"

Teresa stepped up. "You say that, stupid?"

"Words to that effect."

"Who died and left you in charge?"

Irish clenched her jaw and shot Teresa a look so venomous that for once she backed off. "Whoa. Somebody's time," Teresa muttered.

"What are the terms of engagement?"

Sutcliffe turned and picked up a paintball gun from where he had leaned it against a rock. He tossed it to Irish. She caught it with both hands.

"Pretty simple. Pink is for girls, blue is for boys."

"You're kidding."

"I'm not. You're blue, you're dead."

"Clarification?"

"Shoot."

Don't fucking tempt me. "What about shrapnel?"

Laughter rippled among the men.

"I'm serious. What qualifies as a hit?"

Sutcliffe thought about it. "It has to be a direct hit. Shrapnel, or in this case, paint splatter, doesn't count. Okay?"

"Okay. Something else. I say if we hit your men, they're not out of the game."

"No?" Interest warmed his eyes.

"They come to our side. Officially, they're breasts."

This was too much for some of the soldiers. They laughed while Sutcliffe, considering, eyed Irish steadily.

"Okay," he agreed, bringing forth a wave of remonstration from his men.

"Oh no, lieutenant!"

"Say it isn't so, L.T."

"Don't let them turn us into–" Sutcliffe silenced that one with a look before it could be spoken.

"Anything else?"

"I can't think of anything."

Eve clapped her hands together. "The prize! What does the winner get?"

"Ah yes. I'd forgotten about that. Any suggestions, Irish?"

"None."

"Your friends nominated the disclosure of your real name."

Oh, did they? And when did the traitors have this discussion with YOU, LIEUTENANT– Irish kept her expression neutral. "No go," she said. "You win, we'll cook for you."

"I'm not sure that's on par."

"You haven't tasted our cooking."

The other men showed obvious enthusiasm.

"Okay, agreed. And if you win, what do you want of us?"

There's not a snowflake's chance in hell of that happening and we both know it. "We'll need to think about that."

"Fine."

"I'm presuming we start at first light."

He rolled his shoulders like John Wayne. "Hell no, woman. Let's wait until after breakfast."

Every man and woman there laughed, except Irish, who gave him a cold, hard smile.

"When then?"

"Eleven-thirty. Let's be civilised and wait until after morning tea, sweetheart."

Oh, you'll pay for that. Snooky-wookums cuddle-pie.

While a smile still played on his lips, Lieutenant Sutcliffe's eyes grew grave.

"And may I suggest, ladies, that you use the rest of today to familiarise yourself with this base and its terrain, for most assuredly, you will need to be prepared."

"You're not going to show us around?"

His eyes were hungry. "Absolutely not."

"Fine. We'll do it ourselves."

"Yes, you will. But Sergeant Phillips here will show you how to sight and use your weapons."

Teresa couldn't speak up soon enough. "Oh, that we know how to do!"

Sutcliffe regarded Irish levelly. "Despite the threat of broken nails. I am impressed."

"We're completely fucked."

"You bet we are. Thanks to you we're gonna get our asses whooped clean off."

"Don't say that," Isabella said mildly. They scrambled to the top of the hill.

"Look down, Bella. What do you see?"

"A very nice view."

"Yes, a very nice open view of the valley floor we need to cross to get to the other side. There's not a hope in hell we'll make it without being bludgeoned by blue."

"So, we skirt around this ridge."

"Where they know every nook and cranny and we don't? It's hopeless. We're dead."

"No, we're not," insisted Teresa. "We have only just begun to fight." She slid her hand into her shirt, Napoleon style.

Isabella and Eve chuckled.

"Okay, wise guys. Let me show you the place we're supposed to snatch this flag from." Irish led them to the tree tunnel.

"Mm. Nice spot to grow ferns maybe," offered Teresa.

Irish could have cried.

"We are never, ever going to get the flag without being thoroughly and comprehensively bushwhacked."

The further they went, the more disheartened they grew. After a distance, the ridge track became more suited to billy goats than humans. It was rich with undergrowth, studded with rocks, and the ever present tree roots. The women scrambled, tripped and stumbled along to its conclusion at the top of a sheer bluff high above the flagpole.

Even young Eve was puffed. "Supposing we can get down here from there, there's still one hell of a distance to cover before we get to that flagpole. And all of it in the open."

"Not to mention the traps along the way. Was I the only one who thought maybe there were caves back there?"

Teresa cuffed Irish in the back of the head. "Caves? What caves? Put your glasses on woman!"

"I'm sure I saw…"

Teresa redoubled her cuffing efforts.

"Okay! Okay!" Irish might have been wrong about the caves, as she had been wrong about something else: nature did not provide the only barrier to this military base, there was indeed a fence surrounding it, and although it, like everything else on the base, was so sympathetic to its environment as to be almost invisible, in the stretches where it could be seen, Irish made two observations. Number one: she had never seen so high a fence, and number two: she had never seen so high a fence with a man-sized hole in it.

Perhaps Lieutenant Sutcliffe didn't know his men as well as he thought.

"I think it's time for plan B," said Irish.

"Didn't know we had a plan A," Eve returned.

"We didn't."

"Then what's plan B?"

"A precursor to plan C."

"Which is?"

"I suggest, ladies, that we do not fire our weapons."

"We giving peace a chance?"

"Not in this lifetime. Shit, no."

Chapter Forty

"I'm not convinced about the not firing our weapons bit," said Isabella. "Explain your logic again."

It was eleven fifteen the next morning. Earlier, as daylight broke, Eve had been despatched through the hole in the fence to run into town. She had returned a short time later with the items from Irish's shopping list. Now, Irish slipped them into their backpacks.

"We don't fire the paint guns, they don't know where we are, they don't know where we've been, they don't know where we're going. The minute we start firing they've got a trail to follow."

"Then how do we capture their men, if we're not gonna fire at them?"

"We point our guns at them and say, *Bang bang you're captured.*"

"Do we have to say that?"

"No. Feel free to author your own phrase. Listen. The other thing: we don't fire on them, they don't get pink, and their former allies don't know they've changed sides. Think of the advantage in that."

Actually, it was Lieutenant Sutcliffe who had given Irish that idea. Last night, just after Irish retired to her hut, a gentle knock sounded at her door. Sutcliffe handed her a little palette of camouflage face paint.

"You'll need that," he said.

"Thanks."

"I'd better come in and show you how to put it on."

"I think I'll manage."

"I'll show you anyway."

He shouldered his way in, tossed four sets of camouflage uniforms on her bed and led Irish to the bathroom by the hand. Tilting her chin up, he smoothed lines of rust, sand, black and olive over her face while Irish fixed her gaze over his shoulder and tried to think of something else.

"Put dark where there's light and light where there's dark. Got that?"

"Yep." He had a remarkably light touch for a big oaf. Actually, he had a remarkably light touch full stop. Had she not been so angry with him, she may have found it pleasant.

"Now I've shown you, you can help your friends do it." He finished with a playful daub on the tip of her nose. With his fingers on her chin he turned her face to the mirror. Lieutenant Sutcliffe stood beside her, watching Irish take in the sight of herself. Dimples formed in the cheeks of his mirror image. She refused to look at him.

"Thanks."

"You're welcome. How did you pass the night?"

"Just fine." She went to push past him. He stopped her with a hand on her shoulder.

"Irish." Startled, she looked up.

"I'm asking you how you slept last night." The dimple was still in his cheek, but his smile had disappeared.

"Well, thanks," she said quietly.

He kept his hand where it was. "Bed comfortable?"

"Very."

"Were you warm enough?"

"Plenty."

He held her gaze for a few moments longer.

"I brought you this." He pulled a compact clock radio out of his jacket. "I thought you might like to listen to it as you go to sleep."

"Won't you miss it?"

"I only use it when I'm shaving."

He put it on the bedside table on his way out.

Irish stared after him, colouring pink under the camouflage paint.

That was when she had thought of the advantages of not shooting his men.

"I get it," said Eve, "But I'm not sure I like it. Doesn't seem quite as satisfying unless we splatter them pink."

"Agreed," said Irish. "But maybe we can do that after it's over."

"After we've won, you mean," said Teresa.

Irish smiled lopsidedly. "Ain't gonna happen, sister. That Sutcliffe is as cunning as they come."

Right on cue there was a knock at the door. A young soldier saluted and handed Irish a slouch hat.

"With the compliments of Lieutenant Sutcliffe, ma'am."

Pinned to its side was an Australian Rising Sun badge

– perfectly new, perfectly gleaming and perfectly polished into a bright shiny target.

When they came out of the hut dressed in the camouflage uniforms and made up in the face paint, several of the assembled soldiers wolf whistled. Lieutenant Sutcliffe glanced in the soldiers' direction but did not silence them, neither did he attempt to hide the smile that went all the way up to his eyes. Sutcliffe lowered his gaze, raised it to look at the women once more then smiled all over again. He seemed to be having trouble not laughing.

Oh, you'll pay for that, you son of a bitch. It was all Irish could do not to raise her weapon and splatter him pink right there and then.

She was wearing the slouch hat.

"Ladies." Sutcliffe stepped forward. "We missed you in the mess this morning."

"We were there early," Irish said.

"So I was informed."

I'll splatter that smile so pink. Just you wait. You're mine, Sutcliffe.

Several of the men lost the battle to contain their laughter. It set Sutcliffe off. He made a show of bringing it under control, a not very convincing one.

"Hey, Daniel, you're not laughing at us, are you?" asked Teresa.

"Oh no, darling, not at all."

Laughter erupted from several lips, not least of all his. There was a hasty reshuffling of soldiers. The laughing ones moved behind while the ones at the front took their turn at trying not to laugh. They reminded Irish of Emperor penguins taking turns at buffering the Antarctic wind.

"Wish I had my period," Eve said under her breath.

"Amen to that, sister."

"Anyone wearing their Chief?"

"No."

"Well ain't that a shame."

Lieutenant Sutcliffe stepped forward, fronting up to Irish, who stood on the porch. He was still taller than her.

"Captain Irish."

Go to buggery, you patronising son of a bitch.

"Yes, Lieutenant Sutcliffe?"

"In recognition of the considerable difference in our manpower, we have decided it is only fair to give you a ten-minute head start to get into position."

"And with that beautiful ten-minute head start, what's to stop us waltzing in there and making off with your precious flag?"

While another soldier exploded and moved to the back, Teresa warned Irish of the imprudence of declining by way of a finger poking her kidneys. Repeatedly.

"I think you'll find we have that contingency covered."

"I see."

Lieutenant Sutcliffe shook each of their hands in turn. "Ladies, good luck."

They were still within earshot when the men gave into howls of laughter.

"You think they're trying to psyche us out?" whispered Eve.

"No, I think they really mean it. Their laughter is completely genuine."

The women started the climb up. One thing was certain: the only chance they had of getting the flag home was to reduce the number of soldiers who could chase them across that valley floor.

They had reconnoitred the tree tunnel yesterday with the idea of flanking it and shooting the living pink bejesus out of everything with a penis that broached it, but when they tested the theory, the women discovered that behind the trees, the ground dropped away precipitously. Teresa was reluctant to give the idea up, arguing if it was difficult for them then it would just as hard for the men – no way could they sneak up on them – until Isabella pointed out that the drop was not so much difficult as suicidal. Teresa was not to be dissuaded. They could hang there by some sort of harness, she suggested, until Irish pointed out that their gun barrels couldn't penetrate the dense shrubbery.

"We could machete it, maybe?"

"They'd see the fresh cuts. I've got a nasty feeling these guys will see lots of things we don't."

"Certainly true in your case," Teresa reminded her.

"Hey Irish, how come you don't wear your glasses?"

"Not now, Eve."

Now, they hustled to the top of the hill and ran to the tree tunnel. The flag was draped invitingly from a low branch, just begging to be plucked. "Smart-arsed bastards."

"What makes you say that?"

"Just look at the way they've put it."

"What way?"

"The way that says they're laughing at us."

"Irish, your growing paranoia is beginning to worry me," said Isabella.

"My paranoia is a product of your delusion."

"I'm not touching that."

"Come on."

Cautiously, they approached the tunnel.

"Who's got the perfume?" asked Irish.

Isabella slid the backpack from her shoulders and produced a bottle of *Rive Gauche*. Irish took off the slouch hat and gave it a generous spray, then dived into the tree tunnel, expecting at any moment to find herself suspended by the ankle in a rope trap. Making it through unstaked, unshot, unroped and unblued, Irish let out her breath.

"Hurry up!" Teresa hissed.

Irish arranged her slouch hat on a fallen tree, using a stick to prop it up. The sun broke through the clouds, hitting the shiny Rising Sun badge brilliantly.

"Come on!"

As Irish pounded back through the tunnel, the flag swirled in her draft.

"Let's beat it. The ten minutes must be up."

They ran like blazes back in the direction from which they had come.

At the first clearing, they went their separate ways, Eve and Teresa jogging a little further back while Isabella and Irish stayed on. Isabella took a run up and launched herself at the lower branches of a tree. She sat on the limb then started to climb. Irish watched her going up, springing lithely from branch to branch. When Isabella had cleared the lower branches, Irish took a run up and launched herself with arms extended. She caught the branch with a grunt, swung up and scrambled up, not nearly as agilely as Isabella.

"Oh jeez, I'm an elephant," she grunted.

"Elephants don't climb trees."

"My point precisely.

They mooched up together on a branch, looking back along the track just in time to see Eve's legs disappearing from beneath the foliage of another tree.

Movement caught Irish's eye. At first, she thought the shrub was merely moving in the breeze, until she realised there was no breeze. The only way she could tell the soldier from the shrub was that shrubs don't walk. He uncoiled himself from the ground, bringing a good deal of foliage with him as he crept into the clearing.

Irish held her breath as he crept past Eve and Teresa's post, her eyes searching the bush behind him for further signs of life.

Maybe the men had sent him ahead so the women would reveal their position. He was under their tree. *To pounce or not to pounce?*

Grimly, Irish turned to Isabella and nodded. She swung into action. In one fluid movement, Isabella threw herself backward and, hanging from the branch by her knees, put her gun to his head. "Bang, bang, you're captured," she breathed.

Irish said, "Jesus, woman, you're flexible. I bet you're a demon in the sack."

"Focus, Irish."

"Get your hands up!"

"Put your hands behind your head!"

"Excuse me, ladies, which is it?"

They glanced at each other. "Either or," said Isabella.

"I'm good with both."

Isabella swung up then dropped to the ground soundlessly. Irish, less so.

The soldier put his hands behind his head.

"Turn around," Isabella ordered, levelling her gun.

"Now, as we say at home, don't fuck about. Tell us what they're planning and do it now," said Irish.

Eve and Teresa dropped from their tree and guarded the perimeter while Isabella and Irish interrogated the enemy

"Aren't you going to shoot me?"

"No."

"Why not?"

"Because it doesn't suit us. Answer my question."

"You need to make it official, ma'am. Please shoot me."

"Look, we're not going to shoot you. Consider yourself pinked."

His face paint couldn't camouflage his misery. Irish thought she recognised the unfortunate Private Vitelli.

"That you, Vitelli?"

"Yes ma'am," he affirmed miserably.

"Okay, spill it. Everything you know, right now."

He straightened his shoulders. "No ma'am!"

"You don't have a choice."

"Begging your pardon, ma'am–"

"You lose a testicle for every time you call me that."

"Begging your pardon, Captain Irish, Lieutenant Sutcliffe

was most explicit: you may capture but not interrogate us. Those are the rules."

"He mentioned no such rule to us."

"You didn't ask."

"I see. I hoped it wouldn't come to this, but you leave us no choice. Vitelli, lie down."

When he hesitated, Isabella menaced him with the paint gun. She kept it to Vitelli's head as he lay down. Irish hefted his leg and pulled the boot from his foot, then peeled off his sock.

"Begging your pardon, ma... Captain Irish, torturing prisoners of war contravenes the Geneva Convention."

"You forget, Private Vitelli, that we are civilians and as such we are not bound by rules governing the military."

"I'm not going to allow it." He made to sit up.

Teresa bounded across the clearing. From a standing position she dropped arse-first to land on his chest. The sound of the breath exploding from his body could only be likened to a woolly mammoth stepping on a pouffe.

"Jesus, Teresa! He can't breathe!"

"What are you implying, Irish?"

"I'm not–"

"You're no lightweight yourself, Irish."

"Teresa! For fuck's sake, get off his chest!" whispered Isabella.

Teresa lifted her rear only to plonk it back down in his lap. His eyes took on a glazed look. Irish wondered at his remaining chances of fathering children.

"Vitelli, I trust now you see the imprudence of trying to get up when you've been ordered down." Irish unzipped Isabella's backpack and retrieved the feather. She dropped to her knees and tickled his naked foot with it. "Can you keep a secret? I don't believe you can..."

"Please, ma'am!" Vitelli arched his back but he couldn't throw Teresa off.

Across the clearing, Eve gestured frantically.

"Someone's coming."

Teresa launched herself off Vitelli and sprinted back to her position. She and Eve shimmied back into their tree.

"You're going to stay down here and help us capture your buddies, whether you like it or not," Isabella growled quietly at him.

He got to his feet. "Not unless you shoot me."

"Sorry Vitelli. The rules don't say we have to."

"You didn't–"

"You didn't ask."

They scurried quietly into their tree, leaving Vitelli on the ground. He stared miserably into the brush. For ten seconds, nothing happened.

"Whistle to let them know it's safe."

He hesitated.

"You're officially captured, Vitelli."

The sound was so low she almost missed it. Foliage moved at the edge of the clearing. Irish grinned. She had played a hunch and now they knew one of the soldiers' signals. Like Adam's ribs, they only needed one.

A formation of four men broke into the clearing. They came in as a tight unit, then spread apart. Keeping their backs to each other, the men faced the outside perimeters looking for any threat from the bushes.

They were just past Eve and Teresa's tree when Vitelli broke.

"Guys! Guys! They got me!"

Vitelli went down in a hail of blue, the volley of paintballs knocking him clear off his feet.

"Sergeant Atkinson!" he gasped.

"Quiet, woman!" Atkinson hissed back. "Where are they?"

Vitelli glared at him, misplaced loyalty burning indignantly in his eyes.

The men were almost beneath them. Silently, Eve and Teresa dropped from their tree to the ground and crept up behind them. With bated breath, Irish willed the men to take just one more step.

"Where the hell are–"

"Wouldn't you like to know?"

As one, the four men looked up. Before they could level their weapons, the women sprang into action. Eve and Teresa leapt forward to put their guns to two of the men's throats, Isabella did another fearless back flip to cover another man while Irish dropped to the ground aiming her gun squarely at Sergeant Atkinson's big head.

Irish grinned. "Sisters, you're pinked. Tell us everything, or we'll blow your–"

Something whirled past her ear to explode spectacularly on Atkinson's chest. Slowly, he looked down then up again.

"You beast!" Atkinson sang in a high voice. "You hit me in

my pert little breast, you big bad man!" He shoved Irish aside to return fire.

"You can't fire back, Atkinson!" yelled the assassin. "You're dead–" *Click. Click click click click click whump whump whump whump whump click whump–*

All hell broke loose. Irish dropped to the ground and crawled through Atkinson's legs. The others followed suit.

"We hiding?" demanded Teresa.

"No. We're using them as shields until this blows over."

Click click click click click whump whump whump whump whump click whump–

Irish had to shout over the noise. "We need to work out–"

The pink men started singing *Sisters Are Doin' It For Themselves.* It was too much: the women got the giggles. It started with Eve and rippled through the others. As they writhed, laughing on the ground, another troop of men broke cover. While the four pink men engaged the soldiers in the bushes behind them, others stalked from the opposite side of the clearing, guns raised. They formed a semi-circle and started closing in.

"Get up!" cried Irish.

Tears rolled down Teresa's cheeks. "I can't. Make them stop singing."

Halfway up, Irish fell down again to land on her behind. "Don't draw my attention to it!"

Isabella fell face forward and crawled around on her hands and knees, helpless with laughter. Eve kicked her heels against the ground and flailed her hands.

Teresa suddenly got control of herself, sprang to her feet

and lobbed across the clearing like a human hand grenade. Throwing herself headlong at the nearest man, she lifted her foot and delivered a cracking blow to his shin. He staggered then fell to the ground.

Irish was shocked. "Jesus, Teresa! That was low!"

"Si. I was aiming for his balls!"

"Teresa, don't!"

"But you said not to use our guns."

"Go! Open fire, go! go! go!" Irish shouted.

The clearing exploded in a flurry of blue and pink. The three soldiers still standing pointed their guns straight at Irish. She scrambled for her weapon, just as the unfortunate Vitelli chose that moment to scramble to his feet. He took the worst of it, the volley of blue fire knocking him flat.

Isabella took out two of the men *click whump click whump.* They hit the ground as the first felled soldier lurched to his feet and another aimed at Irish, squeezing one off a millisecond before she did. The paintballs collided mid-air and exploded. It rained purple over a ten-foot radius.

Irish rolled away. Eve got hit by purple shrapnel while Teresa wrestled the sore-shinned soldier back to the ground. Another soldier lobbed a shot at Isabella that she escaped with a minor gymnastic miracle.

Absolute demon in the sack, Irish thought again.

While Irish lay on the ground trying to recover her breath, several bushes uprooted themselves and stalked into the clearing. There were eight of them.

"Ladies, incoming!" Irish bellowed. Roaring, the pink men whirled around and opened fire.

"Oh screw this." Irish lurched to her feet.

A soldier dived in front of her, determined to cut her off at the pass.

Saltwater crocodiles.

Irish lowered her chin and charged him. Either Sutcliffe's men were less gentlemanly or were not as easily surprised as Dominic Albrici's. The man didn't budge. Rather, he grinned. *Bad move, sport, you just showed me your funny bone.*

Irish roared, "VIVA LA REVOLUTIONNNNN!" Felled by laughter, the soldier dropped to his knees, blocking the path. She couldn't stop. The whites of his eyes grew large. Irish launched herself into a jump. Wisely, he flattened himself on the ground to give her clearance. A second later Irish heard a familiar *oomph* and looked back. Teresa was on top of him.

Irish took off for the tree tunnel, belting along for all she was worth. The flag was still there. Every instinct in her clamoured *trap!* but Irish threw herself headlong into the tunnel.

Full pelt she reached for the flag; her fingers glanced its silk as a bayonet pierced the tunnel – *why didn't we think of that!* – followed by a barrel which fired a bright blue explosion into the semi-darkness. Irish tried for one of Isabella's spectacular gymnastic moves but only succeeded in falling clumsily. Immediately she rolled, her spinning eyes checking her torso. *Shrapnel – keep going!* Irish burst from the tunnel in time to see a solider balanced on one foot, leaning over the log to lift the rim of her hat with the tip of his gun. She pinked him in the back of the head, leapt over the log, scooped up her hat, rammed it on her head and spun on her heel to run back the way she came.

The sniper on the tunnel roof was on the way down, dangling

from the tree tunnel by his fingertips. His shirt had pulled from his waistband, exposing the small of his back and a goodly part of his – *hmm* – rump. Irish took aim at the right cheek and scored a direct hit, relishing his high little cry. Twisting and ducking, she whizzed around him and through the tunnel, flag in hand and hat on head.

Irish opened up her run then forced it open further. She braced herself for the clearing, arms pumping. She would hear nothing, stop for no-one.

The battlefield was in chaos. Soldiers were arguing about who was alive or dead, pink or blue. Eve and Isabella had gone stark raving, tommy-gun mad and were raining pink on anything that moved while Teresa appeared to be mud wrestling with at least two soldiers and – *what a mess if anyone thinks we're cleaning that up they're mistaken* – battle lust thundered through Irish's veins. Instead of taking advantage of their distraction to slip through unnoticed, Irish held the flag aloft and yelled, "America! I've got your nose!"

She tore through the clearing – *out, clear!* – smiling madly – *made it!* And then the ground thundered with the sound of twenty-one pairs of boots.

Her battle lust cooling, Irish understood her mistake: she hailed from a country whose people considered it their God-given right not to take themselves seriously. This was a right her compatriots frequently asserted by liberating the nation's flag from flagpoles in the wee small hours and replacing it with monuments of empty beer cans. It was almost a national pastime. The average Australian thought it hilarious that no one, other than politicians, knew the words to the national anthem.

But she wasn't in Australia.

Americans took their flag seriously.

Irish was afraid to turn around. The noise grew louder. Frowning, she chanced a glance over her shoulder.

Suddenly Irish didn't have a friend in the world. The men and women had joined forces. One united front of angry Americans was coming after her.

And they were gaining.

Irish threw herself down the hill, skidding down the last third, her tush bouncing painfully on rocks studding the track. At the bottom, Irish hurled into the culvert under the hill, plunging her legs into the icy stream. Her heart hammered, demanding that she suck in oxygen. Irish forced her mouth to stay closed.

The stamping feet grew louder, louder still, LOUDER, LOUDER, passing, subsiding, fading into the distance.

Cautiously, Irish stuck her head out of the culvert.

The paint splattered band of irate Americans were running flat out across the valley floor toward the flagpole. Not a man or woman had noticed they weren't chasing Irish anymore. Isabella was in front and everyone else was following Isabella.

Irish fell over laughing. *Too good.* She couldn't resist.

Irish waded out of the icy water. Maybe, just maybe in the heat of the moment, the confusion and battle lust – *just maybe* – Irish could sneak up behind them and slip past to victory.

Discarding her weapon, Irish tied the flag like a beauty-pageant sash over her shoulder. Nobody would get it off her without wrestling her to the ground.

Grinning fit to burst, she sprinted across the valley floor, cruising up behind the stampeding horde.

Irish was halfway to catching them when the earth rumbled.

The smile on her face died a violent death.

She swallowed. Hard.

Either elephants had come to North America, or Lieutenant Sutcliffe and his merry band of behemoths had just broken cover. She glanced over her shoulder: they were coming from the direction of the bluff.

And gaining fast.

Irish lowered her chin and pumped her arms, pushing herself beyond endurance. She would not give them the satisfaction of turning around. She would *not* give them the satisfaction of turning around.

She turned around.

Oh, Jesus.

Had they looked grim, determined, or angry, they would have been less frightening, but they looked perfectly calm. Running like machines, evidencing no sign of effort, they almost seemed to be flying.

Irish had nothing more to push herself with. She found a little more.

In no time, they were upon her, flanking Irish left and right in a swiftly closing vee formation.

Irish feinted left. A man closed in her. She feinted left again, then right. A soldier broke from the formation, drawing level with her. Irish didn't need to look to know who it was.

"Good afternoon, Captain Irish."

She kept running. "I was wondering where you were, Lieutenant Sutcliffe."

"Well here I am," he said conversationally.

"Here you are," she agreed.

"Shall we?"

"Shall we what?"

Irish shrieked as she was plucked from the ground mid-stride, tossed through the air and swung against his back. Daniel drew her legs around his waist, held onto her thighs and took off. Bounding to catch up to the frontrunners, he sprinted through and past them.

As Teresa had pointed out, Irish was no lightweight.

"You'll kill yourself," Irish said.

"We'll see," he returned mildly.

Irish tightened her arms around his chest.

A cheer went up as Lieutenant Sutcliffe charged the flagpole. With Irish still on his back, he turned around and jogged back.

"Sergeant Phillips, if you could be so good as to relieve Captain Irish of our flag and hoist it."

"My pleasure, Lieutenant."

Irish began to slide down his back, but Daniel tightened his grip on her thighs.

The men cheered again as the flag went up.

Sutcliffe inspected Sergeant Atkinson's outfit, splattered entirely blue, without a drop of pink in sight.

"I can't help but notice you sustained a lot of friendly fire, Sergeant."

"L.T., you wouldn't believe it if I told you."

Daniel laughed, his chest shaking beneath her spread fingers.

With falling faces, Isabella, Teresa and Eve joined them.

"We got done, girls," said Irish, a little sadly.

Daniel raised his voice. "The ladies have admitted defeat. Who would care to tell them the base rules for vanquished combatants?"

"Into the drink!"

"Hope you like ice water, girls!"

Channelling Sophia, Teresa rounded on Sergeant Atkinson's pinked outfit. "You gonna get into a wet tee-shirt competition with us, you flat-chested women?"

Atkinson splashed water from his canteen over his chest.

"Yes ma'am," he said solemnly. "Your turn."

The soldiers didn't make good on their threat to throw them in the river. Instead, they carried the women home. Daniel didn't try to let Irish down, so she didn't try to get down. Three soldiers stepped up to hoist Isabella, Eve and Teresa onto their backs.

Nobody said *no.*

They left the flag flying on the pole and trekked toward the huts.

"You got wet diving into that culvert," Daniel remarked.

Binoculars. Why didn't we think of binoculars?

"I did," Irish agreed.

"You also got bumped about coming down that hill on your…"

Her eyebrows raised a fraction. "So I did," she agreed again.

Daniel swung Irish off his back to land feet first on her patio. Teresa, Eve and Isabella were deposited beside her.

"If you're tired, we could put dinner off."

"No way."

"Uh-uh."

"We'll be there with bells on."

"You won fair and square."

Sutcliffe trained his grey eyes on Irish. "If you're sure you're up to it."

"We are."

"Well, get out of those wet clothes and have a hot shower and a rest first."

"Will do."

"Good afternoon, ladies."

Lieutenant Sutcliffe and his men moved away in the direction of the barracks. The four women watched them go, for a long time saying nothing.

Teresa broke the silence. "I've never been so horny in my life," she said.

Eve fell off the edge of the porch.

Irish stared after Daniel with a sad half-smile, then turned around and went inside.

Chapter Forty-One

"Hey, you wearing make-up?"

"Certainly not," replied Irish.

"Looks like," insisted Teresa.

"My cleanser couldn't handle the camo face paint. Some of it stayed on."

"Only around the eyes. Nice blouse too."

It was a satin trimmed, soft dress number with frills that drew attention to Irish's ample bust. "It's the only clean one I have left," she mumbled.

"Too good for cooking in. I'll get you one of mine."

Isabella elbowed Teresa in the ribs. Irish gave them her back and went to work at the other bench.

It was late afternoon. They had showered and rested as Daniel suggested. Lying on the bed listening to Daniel's radio, Irish drifted to sleep. She couldn't remember the last time she had an afternoon nap. Then again, Irish couldn't remember the last time she felt this relaxed. Now they were in a safe place, she realised just how draining the last months had been – the constant worry, the fear every time they set foot outdoors. It was so... *nice* to be here.

When Irish woke, her Area 51 was lit, she was covered cosily in blankets and the radio was turned off.

The others had gone into town for supplies and were in the mess kitchen when she arrived.

"What are we cooking?"

With more than three dozen men to feed, only four cooks, *and* only a few hours to manage it, their choices were limited. While Isabella worked on a suite of chargrilled vegetables to be dressed in a peppery-sweet sauce of lemon, olive oil and basil, Teresa and Eve worked on great trays of lasagne, the unfortunate Vitelli seconded to kitchen-aide as punishment for refusing to follow orders.

"I wish we could do more," Irish said.

"I know, Irish, but it's the best we can do for today."

There would have been more options had Eve and Teresa been staying, but as hoped, Eve changed her mind about looking for her cousin. After they helped with preparation, she and Teresa would take the car and drive sixty miles to the next town, find a place to stay overnight, then search out Eve's cousin in the morning. They intended to spend the day visiting then return to the base tomorrow evening. All of them would go back to Jersey early the next the morning.

Irish mooched around the kitchen, imagining how Daniel might enjoy their incredible minestrone and wishing for more time to cook.

Teresa gave her attention to assembling the lasagne, nodding as she worked. Isabella smoothed another layer of béchamel down which Eve followed with lasagne sheets.

Advance preparation didn't suit Irish's mood. She wanted to shake sauté pans about and swing and sing and dance the food at the last minute before serving.

As though she had read her mind, Isabella said, "Forget it, Irish. Can't be done. There's three dozen of them. They've already beaten us once today, remember?"

Teresa said, "How about ..."

"Mmm?" Dreamily, Irish bounced her hip off a bench.

"... those beautiful egg and bacon pinwheels of yours?"

"No good without organic free-range eggs."

Three sets of high-minded eyebrows raised themselves. Three sets of hands reached under work tops to produce several dozen eggs of the variety in question.

Irish's smile was deeply felt. "Oh, how I do love you three."

Irish rolled up her sleeves while Private Vitelli turned up the radio and began washing dishes.

They worked without speaking, each of them content to think their own thoughts.

Two hours later, they were ready for action. Eve and Teresa set off to visit Eve's cousin.

They never made it.

Chapter Forty-Two

At seven fifteen, every man on the base presented – shaved, showered and in dress uniform – to the mess.

Isabella and Irish peered through the window in the swing doors.

"Will you stop worrying!" Isabella reached up and ruffled Irish's hair. "Come on. Let's get going."

Irish lingered another moment at the door. Daniel was nowhere to be seen.

Teresa had left a gift for Irish on the bench top: a bottle of dishwashing detergent with its *one squirt is enough* motto highlighted in fluorescent pink. Irish pushed it aside and got to work.

They put the trays of lasagne in first. The pinwheels would only take ten minutes. Isabella and Irish were arguing the logistics of serving when word came that Daniel had arrived.

"Lieutenant Sutcliffe sends his compliments to the ladies, requests to know if they have all they need, and begs the ladies to know how much he looks forward to dinner," reported Private Vitelli.

"We'll probably need some help getting the food to the tables."

When he went to report, Irish took another look through

the swing door window. Daniel's back was to her. She lingered until Isabella tugged on her shirt. "Come on, honey, we need to feed them."

One tray at a time, they lifted the egg and bacon pinwheels from the oven and plated them carefully on platters which Lieutenant Vitelli conveyed to the mess.

"Okay, that went well."

"Trickier with dinner."

Private Vitelli returned. "Begging your pardon, ma– Captain Irish. Sergeant Atkinson says if there are no more of those egg and bacon things, it will truly break his delicate feminine heart. He might have to shoot something, or someone, he said."

Isabella and Irish grinned at each other and pulled the next round of pinwheels from the oven. As Vitelli disappeared through the swing door, a cheer went up in the mess.

"Well, we got that much right."

Private Vitelli reappeared. "Sergeant Atkinson–"

"Is out of luck. And no, he's not getting my recipe. We need two volunteers from each table to help serve mains, Private."

When Vitelli went back into the mess, there was a low boo followed by a series of *Ooh me, me, me, pick me!*

Isabella and Irish began plating the vegetables and lining up plates in rows on the stainless steel benches.

"So far, so good," said Isabella.

Sex On Fire came on the radio. Vitelli turned it up. Plating the food, Irish and Isabella fell into the rhythm. Irish threw her head back and belted out the chorus, startling them all. While Isabella laughed, Vitelli threw an amused glance over his shoulder.

"What's wrong, Private? Surprised an old cow like me would know a song like this?"

"Frankly ma'am, yes."

Irish seized a fork from the bench top. Isabella slapped it from her hand. When the chorus came around again, they all joined in, wailing for all they were worth, Vitelli doing a heartfelt rock star impersonation that nearly brought Irish to her knees.

Isabella checked the lasagne. "It's ready."

Irish drew a breath. "Here we go."

They each took an end and hefted the tray to the bench while Vitelli went out to retrieve two volunteers from the first table.

It went like clockwork, the kitchen door swinging open again almost soon as it had closed. Irish felt like she could have kept going all night. She looked up as the burly Sergeant Atkinson came through the swing door.

"Good evening, Sergeant."

"Good evening, sister. I've been meaning to ask you which moisturiser you use."

Isabella chuckled and handed him two plates.

"And whose table are you on, Sergeant?" Irish asked.

"Lieutenant Sutcliffe's."

Irish coloured. "I'll take his plate out to him," she said, not looking at anyone.

She arranged a plate, her presentation restaurant standard. Balancing it on her fingertips, Irish followed Sergeant Atkinson through the swing door.

Daniel watched her come. In dress uniform, Irish thought

him a little intimidating. Shyly, she laid the plate before him. "To the victor goes the spoils."

Daniel got to his feet and gave her a small, formal bow. "I look forward to it very much and on behalf of the United States Army express my hope that your time on our base has been fruitful."

Her smile faded. The heat of the kitchen was in her cheeks. Daniel bowed stiffly again and sat down.

Isabella glanced up as Irish pushed through the swing doors. "Hey, what's wrong?"

"Nothing… I just… suddenly I've got absolutely nothing left."

"You sick?"

"No, just bone tired, that's all."

"Well I'm not surprised. All that running around. How about you have something to eat then head to your hut?"

"I'm not leaving you to clean up on your own."

"Yes, you are. Have something to eat before you go."

"For once I'm not hungry."

"You sure you're not sick? I'll walk you back."

"No need. The fresh air will revive me. I think I'm just too hot."

After the heat of the kitchen, the night air was like a slap in the face. Her burning cheeks and smarting eyes owed nothing to the cold night air – not that wild horses would have dragged the admission from Irish – least of all, to her herself.

"How come you don't have a cell phone? Young people always have cell phones."

"Because I've been in prison for the past year and a half, Teresa. How come you don't have a cell phone?"

"What for? Who would ring me on it?"

"Other people with cell phones. And you could ring them. Like now."

The car had broken down ten miles short of their destination. Now the sun was setting as they walked along a lonely country road.

"Hey, here's a fence. We follow it, maybe it goes to a farmhouse."

If the fence belonged to a farm, it was a big one. Twenty minutes later they were still walking, the forest around them growing denser.

Eve started to get jittery. "Maybe we should go back. It's getting spooky in here."

"What good will that do us? No cars coming along that road. We'll go a little farther."

The trees gave way to a clearing that suggested a farm. "See? It's all working out."

In the clearing, a group of cowboys on horseback looked to be having a meeting. Seeing Teresa and Eve they cantered over.

"Mm, Marlboro men," murmured Teresa.

"What's a Marlboro man?"

"A smoking corpse on horseback."

"Sorry?"

"Never mind."

"Good afternoon ladies," said a cowboy.

"Good afternoon, sir," Teresa addressed him in her best Italian. "We are very sorry to be of trouble to you–"

"No trouble. We don't get many ladies here. You got car trouble?"

"Ah! You read minds."

The other two cowboys arrived. "You want to jump up on the back here?"

Teresa giggled. "Oh no. It's a long way up. I'd never get up there."

"Well sure you can! Just stick your foot in this stirrup–"

She was up there so fast that Eve stood blinking at the place where Teresa had been.

"Whoa, that's a good grip, you got there. You frightened of falling off?"

"Sorry. Don't know my own strength."

"Nothing wrong with a strong woman. Nothing wrong at all."

Eve refused her invitation to get on board. She jumped back, shaking her head vehemently.

"I go near it, that horse gonna eat me alive."

"No problem, little sugar. Hal will walk with you while we ride."

The cowboy called Hal dismounted, tipped his hat to Eve and walked beside her while the others rode up ahead, Teresa giggling and holding on to her cowboy nice and tight.

At the car, they dismounted.

"Now, Teresa, what seems to be the problem?"

Teresa stopped giggling. Her cuffing hand itched. "The car no go. Is simple, hey?"

Dennis and Frank laughed good-naturedly. "Maybe you can turn her over for us to have a listen to."

She tried. Nothing happened.

"This car been sittin' idle for a long time, Teresa?"

Teresa clapped her hands. "Why, yes, Dennis! How do you know this?"

He leaned in and whispered confidentially. "I think, Teresa, that old battery just had enough charge in her to get you where you were going, but maybe it was too old to hold the recharge from the trip."

"Ah," Teresa nodded. "That makes sense. You maybe got some jumper leads, Dennis?"

"You gonna hitch them up to my horse?"

"Aaah no! You a very funny man, Dennis! Very funny."

"Darlin' I'm sorry to say that jump leads won't be no help to you. You're gonna need a new battery."

Teresa nodded. "Maybe there's a garage around here?"

"Afraid not. The nearest garage is fifty miles back the way, near the army base."

"Ah fucking shit."

Dennis blinked rapidly. Frank's head almost spun one eighty degrees before his body remembered it had to keep up or die.

"Why, Teresa, I do like a woman who speaks her mind."

Sophia was in the house. She rolled her shoulders elegantly. "Thank you, Dennis. Maybe we could trouble you to use your phone?"

"No trouble at all, Teresa. I'll call Joe at the garage myself, tell him what the problem is. He can come up with his tow truck and take your car back, keep it safe from the road. Only thing is, it might take him a day or two to get the new battery in. We're a little isolated here."

"Thank you, Dennis. Would you mind please taking us to the hotel in town?"

"Oh no, you don't want to go there," warned Frank.

"Why not?"

Dennis looked around and lowered his voice to a confidential level. "It's frequented by people who pay by the hour, if you know what I mean, Teresa."

She recoiled. "Ladies of the night?"

The men nodded solemnly.

"Oh, how terrible!" cried Teresa.

"Tell you what, I've got a better idea," Dennis told her. "How about we put you and Eve up here? We've got some nice cabins. If maybe they're a little primitive, then what they lack in facilities they make up for in charm."

"Yes, they do," agreed Frank.

"They've got nice open fireplaces for these chilly mountain nights, and high old antique beds the likes of which you probably haven't seen since you was a little girl." His smile cut deep grooves in his dusty cheeks. "Just yesterday," he added.

Teresa was growing taller by the second. "If you're sure it's no trouble…"

"We'd be grateful for your company." He tipped his hat. "After dinner, the boys and I will put on a barn dance for you."

"I'm not sure I know how to barn dance, Dennis."

"That's okay, sweetie-pie, we can teach you."

Like Irish, Isabella could have cooked all night, but shortly after dinner, some soldiers all but evicted her from the kitchen, insisting they would clean up.

Isabella knew how to take a hint. Maybe things got a little rowdy in the mess on a Saturday night.

She exited via the mess. Lieutenant Sutcliffe rose as she passed. "Miss Irish not with you?"

"Miss Irish has retired."

Isabella hoped Irish may have stayed out of bed long enough to have a drink, but when Isabella got there, she heard the shower running in Irish's cabin.

Isabella was too hyped for bed. It was a moonlit night; she would take a stroll. Earlier she had noticed a quaint little hut set back from the flagpole.

Isabella sauntered across the moonlit valley floor, enjoying the frosty night air and the scent of pine needles crushed underfoot.

At the flagpole, she hesitated. A large tree overhung the hut. It was dark and spooky back there.

Curiosity got the better of her. Isabella walked on.

Eyes closed, Irish ducked her head out of the deluge to grab a breath of fresh air. The bathroom may have been sparsely appointed, but it sported a gloriously old-fashioned shower rose, the sort you could actually get wet under. Irish couldn't remember when last a shower had showed her such a good time.

She turned the water off, in no hurry for her solitary bed,

and grabbed a towel. Tousling her wet hair, Irish rubbed her skin dry then wrapped the towel around her, fastening it at her breast. She would dry her hair by the open fire.

Irish opened the bathroom door. The smell of pine filled the air.

Her eyes locked on the fireplace. A fresh pine cone rolled in the flames, caught fire, then dropped behind the burning logs. Her heart climbing all the way into her throat, Irish stepped forward.

A swirl of cold air drifted from the direction of the hut's closed door, strafing goose bumps across her naked skin.

Someone had been in her hut.

The radio station changed.

And they were still here.

A familiar figure stepped from the darkness into the moonlight.

Isabella looked straight into the eyes of Dante Alessandri.

She had her Chief levelled at him in two seconds flat, but he was faster. When Isabella looked for Dante's chest in her gun sight, she found his gun barrel instead.

Her arm unwavering, Isabella steeled her grip.

The cowboys cooked Teresa and Eve a barbecue dinner then retired to bathe in preparation for the barn dance.

As Teresa and Eve meandered from their cabins to join the men in the barn, Eve grumbled without let up.

"Don't see why we have to dance with cowboys."

"Because, Eve," Teresa explained patiently, "They have shown us their hospitality. They are very nice men to do these things for us. Now you be nice back like a good girl, eh?"

Through the open barn door, music played while prisms of circling light spilled into the darkness.

"Look at the trouble they go to for us!"

"Mirror ball not so special," Eve muttered, throwing in another *goddamn cowboys* for good measure as she dragged her heels.

Teresa and Eve stepped into the doorway. A dozen figures peeled themselves from the walls. Like a herd of bulls, the cowboys corralled themselves in the centre of the room for their inspection.

Twelve men stood before them, every one of them tall, every one of them broad, all with shining, clean-shaven faces and washed hair, every one bulging muscles from their t-shirts and straining their jeans in all the right places.

"Yee-*hah!*" whispered Eve. "Oh, yee fucking hah hah hah."

Little by infinitesimal little, Dante pointed his gun at the night sky and held up his hands. His eyebrows rose a fraction. Whatever the question was, Isabella only had one answer for him. She spread her feet and disengaged the safety.

"Today's the day you die, Dante."

Slowly, Dante lowered his hands and drew the gun behind his back. Holstering his weapon, he held his empty palms up for her to see.

The gun shook in Isabella's hand, if only by a fraction and just for a fraction of a second, but it was all he needed. Like lightning, Dante was upon her, knocking the Chief from Isabella's grasp. Twisting her arm behind her back, Dante clapped a hand over Isabella's mouth to stifle her screams and forced her into the hut.

The radio hissed static then settled on a station. *Slave to Love* drifted silkily through the room.

Irish went for her Chief, hit towel instead and came back empty.

Silently, Irish edged back. She stumbled, throwing up her arms to keep her balance. Her shadow gyrated merrily across the room.

Ah shit! Holding her breath, Irish eased back another step.

Lieutenant Daniel Sutcliffe stepped around the corner.

"Good evening, Captain Irish."

Irish closed her eyes and let out her breath.

"I didn't frighten you, did I?" He held up a little amber bottle. "I brought you this."

"What is it?"

If Daniel had noticed Irish was naked but for a towel, it didn't show. His eyes rested on hers levelly. Instinctively, Irish covered the towel knot at her breast with her hand.

"Massage oil. It should help your aches and pains, your bruises too."

Daniel leaned forward to put the bottle on the bedside table. Irish had to lean back so their bodies didn't connect.

Irish stared up into his grey eyes. She needed to find something to say.

"You completely trounced us today."

"Oh, I don't know. I'd say you put up a pretty good fight."

Daniel brushed her hand away, slipped the knot and pulled the towel from her body. Lowering his head, he kissed Irish softly and pushed her onto the bed.

Dante pushed Isabella face first onto a soft bale. The pain from her twisted arm was brutal. She bit his hand.

"Stop it, Bella!" he whispered urgently. "Stop fighting me!"

Isabella bit him again and kicked out backwards.

Dante lay on top of her. She could barely breathe. Isabella moaned angrily and bucked beneath him.

"Stop it!"

Something brushed against her face. Isabella flinched, her eyes widening. Dante reached into the bag he had dropped by her wide, terrified eyes then held his scooped fingers to the window. In the moonlight, something glittered weakly.

Isabella stopped breathing.

Dante held the diamonds long enough for Isabella to see them, then one by one, he let them drop back into the velvet bag.

His hand over her mouth, Dante turned Isabella over. Raising his eyebrows, he nodded encouragement. "Yes?" he asked softly.

Dumbly, Isabella nodded.

Slowly, Dante took his hand away, letting it hover above Isabella's face in case it was needed. When she didn't scream, he stroked the hair from her forehead and kissed her lavishly. Dante kissed his way down Isabella's body, undressing her as he went, and once again had to cover Isabella's mouth to stifle her screams.

Fifty miles away, Eve and Teresa were riding rodeo like seasoned cowgirls, while at the army base, Irish was being reminded that men were good for something other than target practise.

When she woke in the morning, the little bottle of massage oil stood untouched on the bedside table, and Irish couldn't tell which bruises belonged to rocks and which were owed to Daniel's fingertips.

Chapter Forty-Three

Irish lay on the bed, staring at the ceiling.

When she woke in the morning, Daniel was gone. He hadn't been in the mess at lunch, nor at dinner. Several hours had passed since then. He hadn't come to her hut.

The day felt sad, like the last day of a summer holiday. Teresa and Eve had left a message explaining the problems with the car. It had been fixed and delivered to the base in the afternoon. The sentry who took their call had asked whether Teresa and Eve would like a car sent to collect them. He told Irish and Isabella that they had been most insistent on staying where they were. They left directions to the ranch where they could be collected in the morning.

Now the morning was fast approaching.

Isabella tapped on the open door. "What'cha doing?"

"Cleaning the ceiling."

Irish mooched over, making room for Isabella on the narrow bed. Isabella linked her hands behind her head and joined Irish in contemplating the timber ceiling. "I see what you mean."

They were silent for a while.

"Bella?"

"Mm?"

"You think Teresa's okay? I think her nightmares might be getting worse. Sometimes I hear her crying in the night."

"Me too."

Irish turned her head. "What do we do about it, Bella?"

"I don't know, Irish. People like us, we don't just waltz into a psychiatrist's office and spill our guts. Know what I'm saying?"

"I do."

"Maybe once this is all over... maybe that will make her better."

They fell silent again. In the distance, the lights-out siren sounded. *Daniel isn't coming.*

"Irish?"

"Mm?"

"What do you suppose will happen to Lieutenant Daniel if his higher ups ever find out he helped to train us?"

"It's not as if we're terrorists, Bella."

"It's not as if we're innocents, either. What do you suppose would happen to him?"

"I don't know, Bella," she whispered.

Chapter Forty-Four

It was still dark. "You sure about this?" Isabella asked Irish.

"They knew we were leaving today. What difference does it make if we leave early or later?"

"After Lieutenant Daniel made as so welcome, it seems a shame to leave without saying goodbye." From the patio of Teresa's hut, Isabella tossed Irish a bag.

Irish caught it. "I've written a nice goodbye letter thanking them all. We'll leave it with the sentry at the gate." Irish caught another bag and loaded it into the trunk. "Besides, goodbyes are a woman's thing. We'd only be embarrassing them and they'd only be humouring us."

"I'm not sure that's true." Daniel's boots appeared beside the car tyre.

Irish felt people move out of the darkness behind her.

"Sisters! Oh sisters, you aren't leaving without saying goodbye!" That unmistakable falsetto belonged to Sergeant Atkinson. Irish would be very surprised if the man didn't have testicles the size of baseballs.

Isabella disappeared behind Sergeant Atkinson's immense, camouflage swathed back. Refusing to meet Daniel's eye, Irish scooped up bag after bag from the pool at his feet and hastily stuffed them into the trunk.

"I'm sorry I missed seeing you yesterday," Daniel said quietly. "I was off base at a meeting with Army Intelligence."

Ah. And there it was. The army version of something came up at the office.

Daniel's feet shifted. "We've been on a training exercise this morning. Have you ladies had breakfast?"

Isabella's head shot around Atkinson's body. "No! And I'm hungry."

"We'll get something on the road. Get a move on, now Bella. We have to go."

Daniel's feet echoed Irish's every movement. "Will you at least have a cup of coffee before you go?"

"I don't drink coffee in the morning." Irish realised the stack of bags was too high for the trunk to close. She levelled the pile with a sweep of her arm then slammed the lid down. The rear suspension rocked but the lock didn't catch. Irish lifted the lid, beat the bags into submission then tried again.

"Maybe we could rustle you up a cup of tea?"

"It's time we got out of your hair, Lieutenant Sutcliffe." Irish almost flinched. She had been wrong about the length of Daniel's hair: it wasn't short as she thought. In fact, it was long enough to curl fingers into. And it was as soft as the rest of him was hard. "Thank you for having us, Lieutenant."

"It was my pleasure, Irish."

Now she did flinch.

"Bella! Get a move on. We've got to go!"

Daniel's feet moved in the dirt as Irish began to walk around him. Then she remembered that was the wrong side of the car and doubled back. Irish leapt into the driver's seat and turned the ignition key. The engine purred into life. On the patio, Isabella shook hands with Sergeant Atkinson, exchanged a kiss, then with a little jolt dived back inside the hut.

Irish revved the motor. A large figure appeared at the driver's window. Irish dared not look up. A paw-like hand entered the car. One glance told Irish it wasn't Daniel's: after watching his hand at work last night, the sight was indelibly burned into her memory. Irish swept her gaze up as Sergeant Atkinson embraced her fingers in his warm and incongruously gentle paw.

"Sister," he said.

"Sister," she replied.

"Maybe next time you'll tell me how to get into my panties."

Her laugh was too loud. The door of the hut slammed shut. Isabella dived into the passenger's seat, tossing the slouch hat with the Rising Sun badge into Irish's lap. Irish picked it up like it was a serpent, thrusting it through the open window.

"Here's your hat back."

The camo figure behind the camo figure at the window said, "You keep it."

Irish tossed it into the back seat.

The tyres threw up dirt as they pulled away. Irish fished around the console for her glasses and slid them onto her face.

In the passenger seat Isabella said, "Irish, maybe I should–"

"No, Isabella. Today I drive."

A figure moved into the rear vision mirror as they pulled away. Irish didn't look to see who it was.

Isabella and Irish arrived at the ranch as the sun was coming up. A cowboy riding off to check the fences gave them directions to the cabins. He tipped his hat to them then led his horse across the frosted grass.

At the cabins there was no sign of life, so Isabella and Irish parked and got out of the car to watch the chill sunrise. Leaning against the side of the car, Irish put a cigarette between her lips and lit it. When she looked up, the cabin doors stood open.

Taking a drag, Irish tilted her head. Her limited vision seemed to be informing her that a dead cowboy lay in the doorway of the first hut. From the second hut, a slight ebony figure emerged, followed by another cowboy who seemed to be having difficulty walking. The cowboy behind Eve threw his arms in the air then dropped to the ground beside his fallen comrade. Had Irish been closer, she would have heard this:

"Dennis! Dennis! What did she do to you, man?"

An F.B.I. voice expert could not have sworn under oath that the next voice had not come from Sophia Loren. "Hey, if he stops working, you just put the jump leads to his chest. Worked for me." Teresa stepped over the cowboy and walked on without a backward glance.

As Teresa and Eve came down the hill, Isabella and Irish walked up to meet them.

"You smoking, Irish?" Teresa enquired breezily.

"Looks like I'm not the only one. What did you do to that cowboy, Teresa?"

"What do you think I did to him, Irish?"

"I think that whatever it was, you did it a lot."

"Hey, they ride the horses all day, the horses no complain. Maybe these cowboys can dish it out but not take it so good."

"Come on, let's go home."

The four women joined arms and walked into the rising sun.

Irish took them back by the scenic route, swinging the car through the bends.

"Whoa!" Isabella cried.

"Sorry," Irish murmured. "A bad habit from my misspent youth."

Eve leaned forward in the back seat. "In Australia."

"Yes, in Australia."

Teresa leaned forward too. "Even though you're called *Irish.*"

Irish glanced in the rear vision and smiled. "Okay. You want to hear it, I'll tell you."

"Hooray!"

"At last!"

Irish glanced in the rear view again. Eve was wearing her slouch hat. "Don't get too excited. I warned you: this is not a pretty story."

Eve and Teresa leaned forward as far as the inertia reels would allow.

"On the day I was born – that would be Saint Patrick's Day–" *Ahh,* came the communal response, "…my father got well and truly pissed."

Isabella frowned. "He got angry because you were born?"

"No. He got pissed because I was born. In Australia, pissed means drunk."

"Ah. Why'd he get pissed?"

Irish looked at Teresa in the mirror like she was a complete idiot. "He was Australian, Teresa."

Teresa looked none the wiser.

The road straightened out. Drawing to a stop at the t-intersection, Irish flicked on the indicator to take to the main drag. Irish checked her right, remembered herself, checked her left then took to the highway.

"So, here's my father, pissed as a newt on Saint Patrick's Day. He staggers from the pub to the hospital where his baby girl has newly been born to his long-suffering wife, following a three day labour."

"Three days! No way!"

"Things were different in those days, Eve. So, with a wealth of good feeling for Saint Patrick who has blessed him with a reason for becoming profoundly mellow–"

"Pissed."

"That's right – pissed, – daddy dearest staggers from the hospital to the registry office in our little country town, entrusted with the simple task of naming his baby girl, *Jane.*"

"Eh. It's a good name."

"A little plain, maybe."

"Hah hah, Isabella."

Eve looked perplexed. "What'd I miss?"

"Plain Jane was married to Gary Cooper."

Eve's brow creased. "That guy again? Old Brad Pitt's great grand-daddy?"

"The same."

Isabella slapped Irish on the thigh. "No tormenting the little league."

"You want to hear this or not?"

"Shit, yes."

"Really, Teresa? You gonna tell me how they get the orange in the cannoli in exchange?"

"Shit, no."

"Language, ladies, for Chrissake's!" Eve clipped Teresa in the back of the head. Teresa's head turned ninety degrees, sheer adoration flooding her eyes.

"Oh, you very good girl. I love you so much."

The wheel turned to the wrong side of the road. Irish brought it back and decided not to look in the rear vision mirror again.

"You wanted to hear it, but now I'm trying to tell you–"

"Go on!" three voices chorused.

"So daddy dearest, in a flood of good feeling for Saint Patrick who has blessed him with mellowness this day by way of an amber bottle, goes to the registry office to name his infant child, *Jane,* but there encounters a kindred spirit: an Irishman also pissed as a newt."

"Uh oh."

"Yes indeedy," said Irish.

"How bad is it?"

"Fionnghuala."

Their loyalty could not be doubted. They steadied their expressions and lifted their chins.

"Is not so bad. Just a little difficult to pronounce, maybe."

"It's poetic."

"Could be a black name."

"Oh, but wait, ladies. We're only warming up here." The tyres hummed the passing miles through the chassis. "This Irishman – this kindred pissed spirit, – in a wealth of good reciprocal feeling for daddy's pissed-up appreciation of Saint Patrick, hands my daddy a list of possible second names, and my daddy takes them all." Irish drew a breath and steeled herself for the delivery.

"My name is, Fionnghuala Bairrfhionn Aoibhegréine Bláthnaid Neamhain."

There was a sudden need in the car to sit back and admire the scenery.

After a few moments, Teresa shrugged and backhanded the air eloquently. "Least your surname is easy to pronounce."

"Neamhain isn't my surname, it's my last middle name."

They considered this silently for a little while. One of them had to ask. It may as well have been Eve.

"What's your surname, then Irish?"

Irish hesitated. "Smith."

They settled their shoulders into their seats, then they settled their shoulders into the seats all over again. The scenery required their undivided attention.

"So, your name is …"

"Fionnghuala Bairrfhionn Aoibhegréine Bláthnaid Neamhain … Smith."

They howled. They absolutely howled.

Chapter Forty-Five

Most of the trip home passed in silence. Irish had tried to get them talking about the lessons learned from the war games, but no one seemed particularly interested.

They unloaded the car and trudged up the stairs.

Irish pushed up the living room window and scrambled around in her bag for the packet of cigarettes. She sat on the sill, inhaling deeply then blowing the smoke out the window. Sounds from the street drifted into the room.

"You thinking about making that a habit again, Irish?" The other three had gathered around.

She sighed. "I wasn't intending to."

Isabella moved closer. "Something troubling you?"

Irish took another puff. She had no idea she was going to say it until she had already blurted it out. "I don't want to do this any more!" Her voice caught, she started to shake.

"What, honey?"

Irish tossed the cigarette out the window and stood up. "The Whack Club. I can't go through with it!" Nothing could have prepared Irish for what she heard next.

"Me neither."

That quiet voice had belonged to Eve.

Now they sat around the living room table, Irish alternately putting her head in her hands and running her fingers through her hair.

"You first, Irish," said Eve softly.

Irish reached for the packet and started to shake out another cigarette. Isabella's hand covered hers. Irish left the cigarette where it was. "I can't bear the thought of letting any of you down."

Isabella took hold of her hand. "You must curse the day you laid eyes on me."

Irish could barely trust herself to speak. "Nothing could be further from the truth. You're the first real friends I've ever had."

Teresa slipped her hand into Irish's and held it.

"Let me be clear about this. I want to support you."

"Maybe not."

"Isabella, don't leave me out. I couldn't stand thinking about you and worrying about you."

"We're all in this together. I know that now."

"I will help you. I will stand by you and back you up. It's just I can't…"

"Participate," offered Teresa.

Irish looked into Teresa's face. The world was in her eyes.

Isabella tossed a velvet jeweller's sack onto the table. "Maybe Domenic doesn't seem worth the stain on my soul anymore." She dipped her fingers into the bag. When Isabella held her hand up, it was filled with diamonds.

"Jesus Christ. Where did they come from?"

"Dante Alessandri."

"Okay, so him we spare," Teresa said.

Isabella told them everything Dante had told her. Phillips, the prison governor was in Domenic's pocket.

"Eh, no surprises there."

Dante had paid off half of Jersey to get the diamonds out of the evidence locker, and then he had tipped off the news before anyone had the chance to cover it up. He had sunk his life savings into bribes, but it hadn't been enough: Dante had to steal from Domenic.

"Oh fuck."

"Yes, oh fuck."

With so many people involved, it was only a matter of time before Domenic found out. Dante had taken off for Italy. He wanted Isabella to join him.

"Why did Dante wait until now to tell you all of this?"

"He could never get me alone. And he thinks Domenic is watching him."

Irish was certain her heart would break. She had prayed for this moment, when they would see sense and call off the whacks, but now she was going to lose them.

"What do you have to say, Eve?"

"I keep thinking about my daddy, what he'd want me to do. Part of me thinks calling it off is like saying he didn't matter. But I've got friends, a future. Maybe I'd honour him more by living the life he gave me."

Suddenly Teresa looked a hundred years old. She thrust her hands over her face.

"God himself wouldn't blame you for going ahead, Teresa," Irish said.

"Maybe once I didn't care about dragging you into this, Irish, but now I think you're more Italian than Australian."

Irish regarded Teresa through eyes that swam. "That mean you're going to tell me how they get the orange in the cannoli?"

"Not in this lifetime, Irish."

"Didn't think so."

Isabella contemplated her lap. "I was so certain whacking them was the right thing to do. Now I'm wondering if I wasn't trying to salve my own conscience."

Teresa looked at Eve. "But I think about the innocent people they hurt. It isn't right to let it go on."

"I've got a life now, Teresa. We all do. I don't see why we should risk what we've made, not for them. They're not worth it."

"Others would step up to take their place," Isabella said quietly. "Whacking them will achieve nothing."

Looking at the tired faces around her, Irish tried for a weak joke. "I suppose the alternative is joining the witness protection program."

Isabella gave her a lopsided smile. "Doesn't exist. That's just a bogey man we invented to frighten our children with."

"And let's not forget Lance fucking Jameson," said Teresa. We'd be dead before the ink dried on our confession."

The conversation ran out. They contemplated the table for a while.

Irish didn't want to be the one who said it. "Where does this leave us?"

"It leaves us with something to think about for a few days," said Teresa. "We go back to our lives, to our cooking and our writing, and maybe in between the bad things we think about the nice things too, like all the fun we had with Lieutenant Sutcliffe and his men."

Teresa smiled at Eve. It was a smile so brilliant they could be forgiven for not realising that Teresa Benedetti had just lost her last reason for living.

The others went and unpacked then headed straight to the kitchen. The last thing in the world Irish wanted to do was think, much less about nice times with Lieutenant Sutcliffe. She turned on the television in time to catch the beginning of the evening news.

The screen came to life on a beautiful blue bay. *Italy. The Bay of Naples.* Something that sounded like *andri* followed by the unmistakable *Albrici* and a word that may have been *associate.*

Irish sat forward, trying to see.

A burnt out car. The camera closed in on the blackened chassis. Irish kept hitting the volume button on the remote, straining to hear above the noise in the kitchen.

Firebombing. Victim burned beyond recognition. The car was registered to Dante Alessandri.

Chapter Forty-Six

Teresa told no-one about her dreams. They were her burden to bear and hers alone.

Her nightly visions often recalled scenes from Gabriel's childhood, Teresa's favourite, a sunny winter's day when he rode around their courtyard on his tricycle, wheels squeaking with every turn, observed at a distance by a wary cat.

As she recollected the days when life had just begun and was certain to be kind, always, Teresa's heart swelled with joy, undiminished by the passage of time.

Countless nights, Teresa dreamed that her son was living again. In the way of dreams, her sleeping mind conjured a seemingly plausible explanation as to how it could be so.

In the loneliest hours of the night, as Isabella slept on, Teresa woke to the excruciating truth. With tears rolling over her cheeks, she questioned how her dreams tricked her every time, why, no matter how often she had them, Teresa could not recognise the cruel deception until she woke.

That night, Teresa dreamed differently: Gabriel could live again, if only his mother did one thing.

Teresa watched her bare feet step into a puddle, the water's surface reflecting flashing lights. Her feet were cold; stones dug into her soles. Beside her, car tyres drove into the puddle, splashing her ankles and the hem of Teresa's nightdress with muddy water.

Teresa levelled a gun at Carlo Scatera.

In this soundless place, Teresa couldn't hear Scatera shouting, but discerned the knowledge from his contorted face.

Turning the gun sideways, Teresa studied it curiously as sound returned. A man grunted rhythmically, a woman screamed and another moaned. Pain seized Teresa's stomach in time with the grunts. She lay on the ground, staring at the car tyre in front of her face while the pain repeated itself and a woman screamed *You stop kicking her motherfucker! I've called the cops! They're on their way!* and then there was an empty place where the tyre had been.

A woman's crying voice called for an ambulance. Teresa tried to get up, but instead she floated.

In the still of that sorrowful night, Teresa Benedetti made it home, flying above the city streets, through the door hanging from the hinges of her firebombed house, where among glass shards, lay a framed photograph of an angelic boy.

Chapter Forty-Seven

"Did she have a bad night?" Irish asked quietly.

"I didn't hear her at all. When I woke up this morning, she was gone."

Still in their pyjamas, the three women stared at each other.

"What do you suppose the chances are she just went for a run by herself?"

"Not great," Isabella replied flatly.

"Let's see if her sweats are here," said Irish. "You two check the bedroom. I'll look in the laundry."

Ten seconds later Irish joined them in the bedroom. "No sweats in the wash."

"They're all here in the wardrobe."

"Irish, she's taken her Chief."

"I can't think," said Irish. She rested her forehead against the window pane while Eve and Isabella debated.

"You think she's gone to clip Scatera?"

"We have to go after her."

"Bust in on Scatera with guns blazing, say, *Is Teresa here? No? Sorry, we thought she might have come to kill you,* then mosey on out?"

Irish watched a police car pull up outside the building. The lights were out, the sirens silent.

"Maybe we should give her some time, see if she comes back."

Irish smiled as the first heavy tear slid down her cheek.

"What if it's like what happened in prison? You said it yourself, Isabella. The only thing keeping Teresa going was the whack plan."

A police officer climbed out of the car. Another slow tear coursed over Irish's face. It splashed onto her chest.

"What if we're wrong? What if she has gone to do Scatera?"

Irish didn't kid herself that the police might be going to another apartment. Entwining her fingers in prayer, she pressed them to her lips.

The knock on her door came anyway.

A sledgehammer hit her heart. Her legs were jackhammers.

Isabella screamed and something in Irish died.

Irish slid to the floor. On hands and knees, she crawled off to rail and moan with the others.

Chapter Forty-Eight

Sometimes friendship is measured by space: room left for one who lingers no more. Sometimes loss is heard: a silence where once a voice rang out. Sometimes grief is seen: a shadow where once was sunshine.

Where once were four, were four no longer.

Irish, Eve and Isabella barely spoke and didn't leave the apartment for days. The first time they went out, it was to make arrangements for Teresa's funeral.

No priest prepared to bury Teresa in consecrated ground could be found.

Isabella Albrici, the once regal mafia queen, was not too proud to beg.

The same church, the same priests, who hearing Isabella's confessions had counselled devotion to husband and family – knowing full well the nature of her husband and his family, they who declared it would be a sin for Isabella to leave her husband, no matter how egregious his sins – refused to bury a woman whose only crimes were unendurable grief and the desire to redeem herself.

Isabella kept trying until no priest in the parish would see her.

Mister Alfonso and Mister Cicero suddenly lost their reluctance to be seen in the company of the Don's estranged wife. They came to the apartment door in their best suits, hats in hand.

Mister Cicero would bring his family bible, he said. Their prayers would be better than the prayers of a thousand priests. God, looking into the hearts of those who loved her best, would understand that Teresa Benedetti belonged in his Heaven.

Their sad little procession entered the prettiest cemetery in New Jersey, on an afternoon when the blinding sunshine made no sense in a world now so terribly and irrevocably darkened.

Mister Cicero went first, arm in arm with Isabella, carrying a little potted rose in his free hand.

Irish stared at the urn that was all that remained of Teresa. *How could so much – that wondrous tangle of humanity that was Teresa Benedetti – be reduced to so little?*

Mister Cicero led them up a hill to the Catholic corner of the graveyard where there was a rose garden shaded by tall old trees. He read from his bible, the others making the appropriate responses that Irish wept too desolately to hear.

Isabella reached for the top of the urn.

"Don't!" cried Irish.

Isabella stayed her hand.

Irish had those jackhammer legs again. She swiped at her cheeks with the heel of her hand. "Not in the shadows. Put her in the sun where she belongs."

Isabella's hand rested on top of the urn. "I can't do this."

Eve stepped forward. "I will."

"She'd be proud of you honey, but that's not what I meant. I say if the church doesn't want her, it doesn't deserve her."

They regarded each other tearfully.

"I won't leave her where she's not welcome," said Isabella.

So they took their friend home, where she was welcome and loved. In the garden outside Irish's apartment, Mister Cicero knelt on the ground and transplanted the little potted rose into a sunny spot with his bare hands, then they went upstairs and held a wake.

As on their very first evening together, they ate savoury pastries and sandwiches from Cicero's, and, drinking a glass or two of wine, listened, sometimes sadly and sometimes joyously, to stories about Teresa.

That night, Isabella lay in bed with the light on, hearing her girlhood friend saying, *Eh, Bella, what do you suppose this is?* while Eve wept in the dark for the first real mother she had ever known, and Irish, longing to be held as she grieved the friend she found too late and lost too soon, wished Daniel had liked her well enough to see her again.

Chapter Forty-Nine

The ashes haunted Irish.

How could the glorious, soaring spirit that was Teresa Benedetti be reduced to so little?

Isabella and Irish toyed with their food. Eve stared into the empty place at the table where Teresa should have been.

"It's my fault. I shouldn't have told her that Scatera killed her son."

"She had the right to know," Irish replied. "And you had the right to say it."

Besides, you didn't give her a gun like I did. You didn't put a gun in her hand then take away the only reason she had for not using it on herself.

The envelope had arrived that afternoon. Irish slid out the portraits of the Hell's Belles taken on their night out, all frocked up and gloriously red.

There were four copies and one less of them than there should have been to put hers in a frame. Irish carried the portrait to Teresa's bedroom and, burying her face in Teresa's favourite sweater, caressed its softness with her wet cheeks while drinking in Teresa's scent: a modest amount of good perfume and a lavish expanse of home-baking.

Dry-eyed, Irish returned to the living room with Teresa's sweater in one hand and her Chief in the other.

"I say we do Scatera first."

Part Three

HELL'S BELLES

Chapter Fifty

"How do I look?"

"Like a complete slut."

"Thanks, Irish."

The women Teresa had once referred to as *reformed characters* took a leaf from the New Jersey Mob Manual – a leaf indexed under:

Bribe

Cops: Venal

Irish's fortune burnt a hole in her pocket, but bent cops turned out to be as cheap as they were mean – a virtue not shared by the hooker who had called the ambulance, whom they traced through the cops. She was neither cheap nor mean. In fact, she wouldn't take a dime for telling them what Scatera had done to Teresa, and a whole lot more besides.

Now they knew that Carlo Scatera liked his women young, black and paid for. Lucky for the Whack Club, they had one of those handy.

Wig-less, sans glasses, just daring the bastard to see them, they followed Scatera for weeks. Now they sat in the dark parking lot behind his favourite club.

"Ready?" Irish asked Eve.

Eve leaned forward, resting her hands on top of their seats.

Irish's hand flew up to cover Eve's. She squeezed it fiercely. In the passenger seat, Isabella did the same. Eve nodded and turned to the door.

"Fuck it up, we'll cut off your cake allowance," Irish said.

"Try it, bitch."

Cold air swamped the car. The overhead light came on. Irish reached up and switched it off.

They watched Eve stride on five-inch heels through the parking lot and disappear into the club. The bar lights flashed; music thumped into the night.

Isabella and Irish stared at the club door, their eyes never leaving it for a second.

"Here they come," Isabella said.

Isabella and Irish ducked sideways, out of sight. Waiting until they heard car doors slam, they popped up, peering over the dashboard.

Eve leaned in the gap between the passenger and driver's seats, her hand on Scatera's head. She stroked his hair.

Scatera reached for his zipper. "Do me."

Say it one more time.

"Take me somewhere I can get turned on."

"Who gives a shit about you? Just blow me."

"I got something better in mind."

Eve whispered in his ear. Scatera burnt rubber peeling out of the parking lot.

"Well, that went splendidly." Irish started the engine. "Seems Eve made him an offer he couldn't refuse."

"You're a real comedian, Irish."

"Thanks, Isabella."

"I was being sarcastic."

"Oh."

They followed them to the alley between the warehouses where Cino Malatesta had jumped Irish. The Hell's Belles were in a mood for sending messages – the sort that came with Molotov cocktails.

Scatera's car slid into the alley. Irish and Isabella waited for the headlights to go out, then got out of their car.

Eve rubbed Scatera's crotch with one hand and ran the other down his leg. "Oooh, what's this?" she giggled, taking the snub nose from his ankle holster.

Scatera opened his eyes. "Hey, don't play with that!"

Dropping the snub to the floor, Eve rubbed his groin. "What, this?"

Moaning, Scatera's head fell back as his eyes fell closed again. Eve resisted the overwhelming urge to snatch up the snub and ram it into his open mouth. Rubbing him harder, she reached around and took the gun from his strong side holster, dropping it to the floor beside the snub.

"I'm ready," Scatera said. "Get in the back."

"Give me a minute to get ready for you."

Eve skirted around the car and jumped in behind the driver's seat. She rammed her gun through the headrest into Scatera's neck.

Scatera froze. "What the fuck is this?"

"The antidote to Viagra, limp dick."

Two figures emerged from the darkness to stand either side

of the car. They folded their hands in front of them in a familiar, funereal stance.

"Do you know who I am?" hissed Scatera.

"I know who you were."

And then Eve sent him to where he was going.

Chapter Fifty-One

When Scatera's hit was reported on the news, the women opened a bottle of good champagne.

Standing before the framed portrait of the Hell's Belles, which rested on the mantelpiece beside the A3 study in fat bastard portraiture, Isabella, Eve and Irish slung their arms around each other and toasted the quartet that once was.

Having enacted the Whack Club's charter, they began to plot the best ways of furthering the war.

They couldn't know the war was about to come to them.

They grieved in their own quiet and sometimes not so quiet ways. Painful though it was, daily life had to go on – to create covers and alibis if for no other reason – and because they had commitments, Irish not least of all.

A few days after they hit Scatera, Irish returned from a lunch meeting with her agent and publisher, feeling pleasantly melancholy. Lingering outside, she sat on the garden wall contemplating the transplanted rose which had perked up in a way that said its little feet had found a home. Its face was wide open to the sun.

With a last look at Teresa's rose, Irish took her wistful self into the building and up the stairs.

Isabella gave her the news.

"They've got Eve."

Chapter Fifty-Two

Irish pressed her trigger finger to her lips and swallowed hard.

Isabella's chest was heaving. "Domenic called. He said they've got Eve and... *Oh God, Irish...* they've hurt her!"

Irish flew to her. They clasped each other's forearms.

"How bad?"

"I don't know. Domenic got her away from them. He's looking after her until I can get there."

"I'm coming with you."

"You can't. He said if I don't come alone, it'd be more dangerous for Eve."

Something tugged at Irish's brain. "Wait, Isabella! We need a plan—"

"There isn't time! Eve's hurt and she needs help!" Isabella tried to tug her arms away. Irish was too strong for her.

"Show me your Chief."

"I don't have it."

"Then go get it."

"I won't need it—"

Irish tightened her grip and raised her voice. "*Isabella!* You're not going anywhere without your fucking gun, so the quickest way for you to get out of here is to *go get it!*"

Irish let her go. Isabella flew to the bedroom with Irish hard on her heels.

"He's taken Eve to the house?"

"No." Isabella strapped her holster on. Irish snatched a jacket from the wardrobe and held it up for her. "Domenic took her somewhere safe, where they couldn't find her."

"Where?"

Isabella holstered her Chief then shrugged into the jacket. "Some warehouse. I wrote the address down. The note's on the coffee table."

Irish sprinted into the living room. There were two pieces of paper on the coffee table. Irish snatched up the one in Isabella's handwriting and read the address aloud.

"Got it! I'm gone!" Isabella only had eyes for the door. Irish tossed her the car keys.

"Bella, for the love of God, be careful!"

Isabella spun around to face her. They looked at each other for a heartbeat longer, then Isabella whirled and was gone, leaving Irish staring at the open door.

Chapter Fifty-Three

Isabella blinked at the sudden darkness. The door swung back on creaking hinges, closing behind her. Something scurried in a distant corner and she shivered.

Isabella took in the warehouse. It was filthy. Domenic must have been desperate to bring Eve here.

"Domenic!

No answer.

"Domenic!"

On the mezzanine floor a door slammed. Isabella took the stairs three at a time. At the rear stood a small office. She pushed the door open.

Domenic's familiar figure was outlined against the broken window. Blinded by the light, Isabella could barely see him.

"Domenic! Where's Eve?"

Her eyes adjusted. Domenic smiled.

Isabella's blood ran cold.

"Bella, I believe you have something that belongs to me."

Irish wrapped her arms over her chest and hugged herself. When today was over, once they got Eve back and fixed up, that was it.

If the three of them were still alive at the end of this day, there would be no more hits. They would leave New Jersey, never to return.

The door opened.

Irish leapt to her feet.

Eve walked into the living room.

Isabella cast an involuntarily glance over her shoulder.

"We're quite alone, Isabella."

"So I see, Domenic. I can't help but wondering why that is."

"I didn't want to talk to you with your dyke friend around."

Isabella smiled, thinking if Irish were here, Domenic would be less one testicle right now.

"That what you think, Domenic? That any woman who doesn't spread her legs to you has to be a lesbian?"

"This is a private matter between a husband and his wife."

"We were never that, Domenic. In name only."

"That why you fucked Dante Alessandri behind my back, Isabella?"

"He never touched me."

"I don't believe you."

"That why you had him capped, Domenic?"

"I know nothing of that."

Isabella smiled coldly. "I'm sure you don't."

Irish's legs wouldn't hold her up. "Please tell me Isabella is with you."

"Isabella? No, why would she be?"

Irish could barely speak. "Where have you been, Eve?"

Eve held up the paper sack in her arms. "Where does it look like? Shopping. Didn't you get my note?" She nodded toward the coffee table.

When Irish's feet hit the ground, they were already running.

"Did you really think I wouldn't find out the truth about you and Dante?"

"If you had, then you'd know nothing happened."

"A man doesn't steal diamonds for a woman unless he got laid for his trouble. That is not the nature of men."

"You should know, Domenic."

"You've really got quite the mouth on you these days, Bella."

"All the better to say *fuck you* with."

"Domenic's got Isabella!"

Irish vaulted down the stairs, bouncing painfully off the walls in her haste to take the landings. She had run three blocks before Eve caught up with her. Side by side, arms pumping furiously, their gait impossibly long, they tore up the streets.

"Where?" Eve demanded.

"Warehouse."

They kept their breath for the run.

"I want my diamonds, Isabella."

"You swore in a court of law they weren't yours, Domenic. You swore they belonged to me."

"We're not in court now, Bella."

"The hell we aren't. Who ordered the hit on Gabriel Benedetti?"

"You know better than to ask such things."

"When you killed her son, you killed my best friend along with him."

Isabella drew the Chief and levelled it at her husband.

A movie started playing in Irish's head.

With every pounding footstep, with every rise and fall of her chest, with every rasp of her breath, pictures played. Isabella, the first time Irish saw her outside Cicero's. Isabella on the lawn with the bread knife in her hand. Teresa in the hospital, her neck bruised, and Eve's gentle, comforting hand. Three women who had been in prison so long they couldn't remember how to eat cake. The scars on Isabella's hands. The scars on Eve's heart. Teresa's soulful brown eyes when she interrogated Irish about her ideal man, wishing for Irish the greatest joy of her own life: a child. Their first tentative smiles. Eve giving Irish the prettiest scarf and kissing her cheek. Teresa in the kitchen, singing. Teresa in the night, screaming. Teresa bathing Eve and Eve's childish love of sweets. The wine. The food. The running, the singing. The night of the Hell's Belles. Isabella and Eve gone stark raving, tommy-gun mad shooting everything *pink pink pink,* the howls of laughter and the cuffs to the back of the head *never more, never more* someone whimpered and sweat poured into Irish's eyes; Teresa's smile passed forever from this earth *never more.* Irish pounded on, her poor heart breaking with every desperate stride.

"You going to shoot your husband, Isabella?"

"Better you than me."

Isabella lined him up in the sight.

Over Domenic's head, a ray of sun broke through the window, dust motes dancing in its beam. Isabella's mind began replaying memories: stained glass windows, altar, votive candles, their flames flickering, piano organ, confessional boxes, water tinkling from a baby's head into the baptismal font, the stations of the cross: Jesus, condemned to death, Jesus, given his cross, Jesus falling, once, twice, thrice; Isabella's first communion dress, the nativity scene at Christmas – Isabella saw them all and smelled incense and the smoke of extinguished candles. It all happened in a second but it was enough time for Domenic to draw.

Isabella squeezed the trigger. The futile *click* echoed Irish's warning loudly in Isabella's ears: *a semi-auto malfunctions, no two ways about it, you're on your own. By the time you get it cleared, bang, bang, you're dead, baby.*

Domenic fired. Isabella fell to the floor.

And Domenic Albrici looked straight into the red-hot eyes of Irish Fionnghuala Bairrfhionn Aoibhegréine Bláthnaid Neamhain Smith for a half second before her muzzle flash blinded him.

Domenic stared at his chest then lowered his gaze to his groin.

A slender black arm thrust under Irish's arm. Eve took the shot. Domenic's head jerked back; his gun clattered to the floor.

Irish fell to her knees beside Isabella's body.

"God help me, what have I done?" she whispered.

Chapter Fifty-Four

It was not possible that one slight woman's body should have held so much blood.

Irish kicked open the door to the emergency room.

"Gunshot!" she bellowed. "Gunshot here! Help her *please God* help her!"

When they tried to take Isabella, Irish couldn't let go. Two orderlies prised Isabella away while a nurse ushered she and Eve out through the swing doors.

Eve threw herself into Irish's arms, holding Irish like she was life itself.

"Does your friend have insurance?" the nurse asked.

"She has all the money in the world to pay for her own treatment."

The nurse's dark eyes glistened. "I'm sorry, but I'm going to have to ask you for proof of that."

"I'll run home and get my last bank statement."

"Something else: gunshot wounds have to be reported to the police. When you get back, I expect they'll be here, wanting to know what happened, if they haven't already learned it from your friend here."

Irish rounded on her. "She doesn't know anything. She wasn't there. They're going to have to talk to me."

Eve jogged with her to the door. "Not a word, honey, not a word," Irish cautioned. "You weren't there. You came in afterwards. They talk to me."

Eve nodded. Irish threw herself at a taxi.

When Irish flung open the apartment door, their smell – the combined scents of Teresa, Isabella, Eve and Irish that made home smell like home – hit her like a freight train. Sobbing, Irish ran for her study where she tipped the organiser upside down. Several hundred pieces of paper fell to the floor.

Why not just look under 'b' for bank statement, stupid? Why wasn't Teresa here to call her stupid?

Irish beat on the papers with her fist, pulled herself together, then located her bank statements.

The taxi waited in the street below. Irish was at the apartment door when a thought hit her – a thought that stilled the tears on her cheeks and froze her heart. She retrieved another item from her study and several clean handkerchiefs. She and Eve were going to need them.

Please God, don't let that be all that's left of us.

Eve jumped up the moment Irish was through the hospital door.

"Any news?"

Eve shook her head as Irish slid the bank statement over the reception desk. Five minutes later, they were informed Isabella had been taken to surgery.

"Your friend got any next of kin?" asked the nurse.

Tears streaming, Irish shook her head. "Just us."

"Don't know why you're crying, girl. Seems to me, that's all she needs."

Irish and Eve took a seat in the waiting room. When a suit showed his badge at the desk, the nurse nodded in their direction.

"You come in with the gunshot wound?"

"The gunshot wound has a name, and it's Isabella."

"So I'm told." He flashed his I.D. "Lance Jameson of the Federal Bureau of Investigation."

"No shit. Lance middle name *fucking* Jameson, in the flesh."

Irish and Eve got to their feet. If looks could have killed, they had just fitted him with concrete shoes.

"I beg your pardon?"

"I *said*, Lance fucking Jameson." Irish raised her voice. "Domenic Albrici's pet F.B.I. agent."

"I'd caution you against repeating that."

Irish smiled and reached into her pocket to retrieve a fresh handkerchief, which she handed to Eve.

"And I'd caution you against cautioning me, sunshine. Some men can't handle their curling irons."

His expression darkened. "I think you'd better explain that, ma'am."

"I mean, Lance *fucking* Jameson, that before he squealed from this earth, young Paolo Discenza blurted his life philosophy into a handy little tape recorder. Specifically, of the lessons he learned in his short and imminently *eminently* painful life, most of all he regretted assisting in the framing of one Isabella Albrici by her husband Domenic Albrici – aided, abetted and facilitated by none other than the good Don's pet F.B.I. agent, Lance *fucking* Jameson."

"More than one way to do time, sugar," chimed Eve. "All

time is hard, but some time is harder than others – real hard. Ass like yours, pretty boy, you'll soon be having plenty of soapy sex with a nice man called *Horse* in the prison shower."

"You'll add new meaning to the term, *blue eyed soul singer,* Lance."

"Mmm. Just *think* of all that soapy sex, sugar. Won't it make your brown eye blue?"

"You're in the wind, my friend."

"I want that tape," he said.

Irish dealt him a backhander. The tiny little thing that was Eve grabbed Jameson by the lapels. "Lady talking to you, fucker."

"Here's what you *get*, corrupt agent, Lance *fucking* Jameson. You get to walk away from this hospital alive and you get to run interference for as long as we tell you to, for as long as it takes Isabella, formerly Missus Albrici, to recover here in this hospital, and in that time, we will not be troubled by reporters–"

"I can't–"

"Buy a motivational tape, Lance. We will not be troubled by reporters and we will not be troubled by law enforcement agencies, or members of the New Jersey family – or their distant cousins. Clear?"

Jameson paled. "Then I get the tape?"

"No. Then you get to keep breathing. Now fuck off."

Irish reached into her pocket, withdrew the Pearlcorder and hit *Off.*

"You're a genius, Irish."

You're a comedian, Irish.

Thanks, Isabella.

I was being sarcastic.

Oh.

Irish covered her face with her hands.

No major organs, significant blood loss. She'll pull through.

Eve was nestled in Irish's arms when they got the news. Gazing into her upturned face, Irish kissed Eve on the forehead and held her tight.

The kind nurse waited until the doctor had gone for the night, her eyes following him past the desk and out the door, before she motioned them over. She wheeled an empty gurney into Isabella's room. "Don't have two to spare," she said.

They pushed the gurney flush with the side of Isabella's bed and climbed on. Irish got on behind Eve and spooned her back.

When Isabella woke to the news of her husband's death, Eve held her hand.

Isabella wanted to know who pulled the trigger.

"We all did," said Irish.

Chapter Fifty-Five

During the days of Isabella's recovery, Irish and Eve took turns sleeping and standing guard.

While Domenic's death didn't make the news, they had no way of knowing whether the news had made it to the family.

After Isabella's release from hospital, the women spent one night at the apartment, solemnly packing the little they would take with them. The Hell's Belles portrait went into every suitcase.

They wandered from room to room to check on the others' progress, or to silently touch hands. Each of them wore a scarf from Irish's first gifts. Eve wore two, and Irish, the prettiest.

Glancing at her half-empty suitcase, Irish made another sweep of the apartment, finding it difficult to believe she wished to take so little. What she least wished to leave behind could not be packed into a suitcase.

Irish went and sat on the edge of the bath so the others wouldn't catch her crying.

Zips quietly closed in another room.

Remembering the coffee mug, the one from her twenty first birthday that said, *Behind Every Successful Woman, There's A Man Who's Surprised,* Irish retrieved it from the kitchen and returned to her bedroom.

One of her runners lay on its side. Irish picked it up, its florescent eye vomit smeared now with camouflage paint. She ran her fingers over the stripes, trying not to think of Daniel.

Then she ran her fingers over the stripes, thinking of Daniel.

Good enough. You deserve to come. Irish nestled the runners in the corner of her suitcase beside the coffee mug, then slid the slouch hat, replete with Rising Sun badge, from a shelf.

Placing the hat on her head, she went into Teresa's room and picked up her favourite sweater. And that was all Irish wanted. The rest would be packed for goodwill after they had gone.

Eve and Isabella sat on the living room floor, an open bottle of wine before them.

Irish lowered herself to Isabella's side. Without making a toast, they touched glasses and drank.

Irish removed her watch and strapped it to Eve's wrist.

Wordlessly, Isabella unclasped her necklace and refastened it around Eve's neck.

Eve said, "I have nothing to give you two."

Irish croaked, "You've already given it, but I'll take a lock of your hair as well."

They left her with bangs.

Irish heard Teresa in her head. *Ah, that's pretty! You a very pretty girl! So beautiful!*

Holding up the sack of diamonds, Isabella tossed them to Eve.

Eve's voice shook. "You sure about that, Isabella?"

"Never surer."

Irish slipped the lock of Eve's hair into an envelope, put it in her suitcase and closed the zip.

Mister Cicero helped them carry their suitcases to his delivery van, waiting in the alley to carry them to the airport.

Eve was already downstairs.

Irish hesitated at her apartment door.

"Don't look back," Isabella urged.

"No, never look back," Irish agreed quietly. Then she looked back and closed the door on the best time of her life.

As Irish and Isabella climbed into the rear of the van, Eve reached for Isabella's hand.

Mister Cicero slammed the door then reappeared in front of the wire mesh separating the driver's cabin from the back. Starting the engine, he pulled from the alley into the traffic.

Soon, too soon, jet engines roared overhead. Isabella, Eve and Irish exchanged urgent, frightened glances, regarding the van door as though it were a guillotine.

At the airport, embracing them in turn, Mister Cicero promised to tend Teresa's rose. Irish figured it was the least he could do. One way or the other, his cannoli had a lot to answer for.

Too quickly, they found the departures lounge.

Slinging their arms around one another, the women rested their foreheads together and let their tears mingle.

"Good luck in Italy, Bella."

"Good luck in France, darling Eve."

"Good luck at home, Irish."

Irish blinked. Without them, she had no home.

"Think we'll ever see each other again?" This, from Eve.

"I hope so, honey. Maybe one day we'll find a way, but right now, it's too dangerous."

Irish whispered, "Isabella, do you think we got away with it?"

"I don't know. But I do know if they hit one of us, there's another two standing–"

"To whack 'em right back!" They laughed through their tears.

When Isabella's flight was announced, Eve flew into her arms. Taking Eve's face between her hands, Isabella kissed her once then reached for Irish. Irish gave her a fierce hug then pulled away.

At the gate, Isabella turned around. They exchanged nods, then Isabella disappeared from sight.

A man regarded Isabella over the top of his newspaper. His hair had been coloured but Isabella recognised him in an instant. Her heart hammered; her ears roared. Slowly, Dante Alessandri got to his feet, his hand reaching inside his jacket.

When Irish's flight was called, she clung to Eve.

"I can't let you go," Irish wept.

Eve swallowed hard. "You go, girl. Go on, now. We'll see each other again, one way or the other, this world or the next."

Every step hurting, Irish broke for the gate, while in the departure lounge next door, Dante pulled from a flower from his pocket.

"From Italia," he said, his voice as soft as his eyes, and his eyes as soft as his kiss.

Dante threaded the flower in Isabella's hair then drew her to his side. Together, they walked to the plane, while Eve made for the observation deck, and Irish headed for a departure gate about to get million miles away from her.

On the edge of her vision, a newspaper went down. In this place, camo didn't blend in so well.

Rising from his seat like a mobile skyscraper, he fell in beside her.

"Lieutenant Sutcliffe. This is a surprise."

He matched her step, his hip glancing off hers as it had the first time they ran against each other.

"Miss Smith."

Hope crashed and died in her chest. Irish kept walking anyway.

"Did you really think that U.S. Army Intelligence would let you and a couple of mob wives onto a military base for war games without questioning why you wanted to play soldiers?"

Facing forward, Irish kept walking. "I'm merely a romance novelist about to board a plane."

The hand that stopped her was a gentle brick wall.

"I'm afraid I can't allow that, Irish."

Sutcliffe took the slouch hat, with its shiny Rising Sun badge, from her head. "I'll carry that for you."

"Don't want any witnesses remembering me, Lieutenant Sutcliffe?"

His grey eyes sombre, Daniel made no reply.

They returned the way she had come, Irish calculating escape routes and odds of success. She already knew the man could outrun her. Certainly, she had no hope of bringing him down.

Irish was grateful there was no sign of Eve on the main concourse: she need never know Irish hadn't made it.

Daniel guided Irish to his side with a warm hand that reminded her of a hot night in a cold bed.

"Where are we going?"

"To a private part of the airport. You should have been more careful, Irish."

"I saw no reason for you to be curious."

"A safer bet if you'd fallen in with a standard army unit."

"But not yours."

"We handle the sort of extraditions that don't make it to the six o'clock news."

"I see."

"No need for me to spell it out then."

Several large, heavy-booted men fell in behind, marching in sync.

"More of you, Lieutenant Sutcliffe? How many did you think you'd need to take me?"

"About as many as I needed to take you before."

Irish flinched. "Low blow."

"You tell the beast, sister."

"Sergeant Atkinson," said Irish. "I'm surprised at you, sister."

"Don't be, sister. I'm under orders to kidnap you, if necessary. All we girls are."

Passing a sign with RESTRICTED writ large, Sutcliffe and his soldiers marched Irish through a cavernous hangar. A plane waited on the tarmac.

"Where are you taking me?" she asked again.

"Someplace that doesn't have an extradition treaty with the U.S."

Irish stumbled. Daniel's smile pushed a dimple into his cheeks.

"Australia's no good for you, Irish. We'll take you where you can't be found, at least not by someone other than us."

The soldiers skirted around them and headed to the plane, leaving Irish and Daniel alone.

"You don't know what I've done."

"Maybe not, but I'm a soldier, and I know what I've done. Come on, let's get you on that plane. More than one agency is interested in you, Miss Smith, and I can't guarantee that none of them is here."

"What'll happen to you when you get back?"

"Darling, what makes you think I'm coming back?"

Her knees buckled. Daniel's arm captured Irish's waist. Her heels dragged along the ground.

"Daniel?"

"Mm?"

"Won't the rest of your men come after us?"

"Not in this lifetime. Though they'll visit, if you'd like, for a game of paintball. Would you like that, sweetie?"

Irish was suddenly shy. "Yeah," she admitted playfully.

Daniel gave her a gentle shimmy. "All those big guys to pink?"

"Yeah!"

"Irish?"

"Yes, Daniel?"

"Now I know your real name, you mind if I keep calling you *Irish*?"

"No, Daniel."

"I mean, for ever more, all the time. Not even on special occasions will you expect me to pronounce one of those other names."

"I see."

"I mean it, Irish. I will have no tears in the middle of the night because I called you *Irish* during sex rather than one of those other names."

"Daniel, get on the plane before I drop you, mate."

"Irish?"

"Mm?"

"You are rich, aren't you, sweetheart?"

Irish swung a punch and went for her Chief. Her right hand came up empty. Daniel caught her left hand and held it to his chest.

"Interesting manoeuvre, Captain Irish. I can't wait for you to repeat it in bed. Get on the plane, woman. Right now."

"You thinking about relieving me of my panties on that plane, Daniel?"

"I am, Irish. I really, really am."

"You got a bed in there?"

"No, just a nice soft coat to put under your back for the next eight hours or so."

Swinging Irish onto his back, Daniel carried her across the tarmac.

The engines were already going.

Irish shouted above the noise. "Won't the army miss their plane?"

"Nah. I filled out the paperwork. Give the army the right form, they don't care what you put on the damned thing."

As the plane cruised along the runway, Eve, on the observation deck, watched a flight to Italy take off, then another to Australia. She admired the sunset for a little while then headed for the exit, leaving her checked luggage to take the flight to Paris alone.

It seemed wasteful to part with those fine clothes, but Eve knew Irish would understand that on her person, and in her shoulder bag, Eve carried all she needed: two pretty scarves, a watch from Irish, a necklace from Isabella, a heart full of Teresa and a framed portrait of the Hell's Belles.

Opening the sack, Eve let the diamonds catch the setting sun.

Maybe Domenic Albrici's men would come after her.

And maybe she'd be ready for them when they came.

Acknowledgements

Terrie O'Connor of Terrie O'Connor Realtors in New Jersey was kind enough to answer a question from an unknown writer on the other side of the world. Completely without his knowledge, Lee Laster, via Expert Village, afforded me the benefit of his weapons expertise. Jill Dupleix is owed recognition for the fennel sausage/lemon cream pasta dish. The egg and bacon pinwheel recipe is my own, and no, you're not getting the recipe. Tony Starr advised on matters Catholic and kept me in pilfered chips and chocolate during the final week of writing *The Whack Club*, then known as *Grace*.

About the Author

In her first job, Susan Bennett sold large knives, replica pistols and handcuffs to complete strangers. Many years later, it occurred to her that some of those nice strangers may not have been purchasing these items for joke gifts as they claimed. Maybe they weren't even nice.

Her writing prizes include first place in the EJ Brady Award (twice), the Sydney Writers' Room Short Story Competition, The New England Thunderbolt Prize for crime writing, the Joseph Furphy Prize and Field of Words Short Story Competition, second place in the ESU Roly Sussex Awards (twice) and the Grace Marion Prize. Her stories have also enjoyed high commendations or shortlisting in the Scarlet Stiletto Awards for crime writing, the Albury City Short Story Awards (twice) Ink Tears, the Los Gatos Writers' Festival, The Big Issue and in the Southern Cross Literary Competition. Her work has been published by The Fish Anthology, The Moth, Etchings, The Australian Broadcasting Commission and the Shepparton News, among others.

Made in the USA
Columbia, SC
28 May 2023

17443690R00205